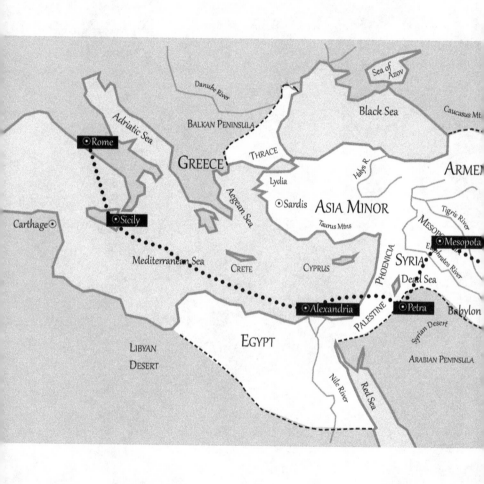

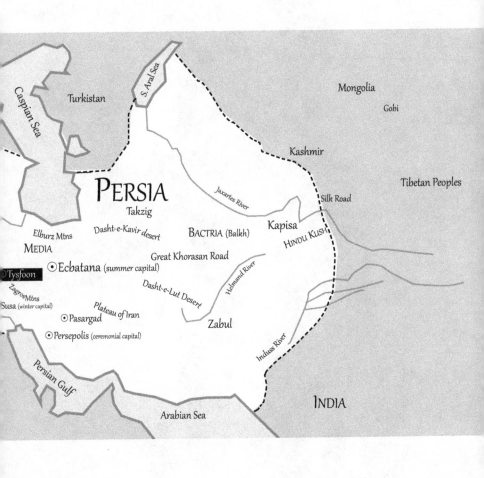

WE are tiny pieces of light, love, and history.
We are stars interconnected by
magic, music, and words.

Also by Dr. Nooshie Motaref

Bird of Passage
Tapestries of the Heart (second edition)
Land of Roses and Nightingales

The Girl Raised in Bull Blood

Thea, bold as a bull,

but soft as a morning breeze

Dr. Nooshie Motaref

A3D Impressions

Tucson | Minneapolis

A3D Impressions

First A3D Impressions Edition February 2024

Publisher's Cataloging-in-Publication data

Names: Motaref, Nooshie, author.
Title: The girl raised in bull blood : Thea , bold as a bull , but soft as a morning breeze / Dr. Nooshie Motaref.
Description: Includes bibliographical references. | Tucson, AZ; Minneapolis, MN: A3D Impressions, 2023.
Identifiers: LCCN: 2023917336 | ISBN: 978-1-7371922-4-4 (hardcover) | 979-8-9864049-5-0 (paperback) | 979-8-9890817-1-4 (ebook)
Subjects: Slaves--Rome--Fiction. | Iran--History--To 640--Fiction. | Women—History--Fiction. | Historical fiction. | BISAC FICTION / Own Voices | FICTION / Women | FICTION / Historical/Ancient
Classification: LCC PS2613 .O83 G57 2023 | DDC 813.6--dc23

Cover and book design: Donn Poll

Come!... Come!
Dream with me!

CHAPTER 1

Rome

20 BCE

"CATCH HER!"

"CATCH THAT FERAL BOAR!"

Once again, a couple of palace guards ran after me, a fifteen-year-old girl, Thea. Since seven, I could identify a dark seed growing within me. My rowdiness grew roots in not knowing my father. Each time, after grabbing me, they dragged my body like a rag to the same dungeon underneath the palace. Their masculine fingers always left some marks on my thin, bony torso, invisible to others. It was my punishment for losing my temper and making the Empress, princesses, and concubines horrified. However, the maids, servants, and enslaved persons cheered me mutely, and none chased me. Finally, the guards had to be called.

I even increased my speed when my mother, Tamra, screamed, "Stop, Thea! Stop! You're embarrassing me!"

1

Her words made me forget where I was or what I was doing. Instead, I kept hearing my inner voice: *Run, Thea! Escape the walls around you, Thea!*

My disobedience started when my mother turned a deaf ear to me and refused to talk about my father. I had yet to learn whose name 'Mousa' was that I had to use as my last name. It was not even hers. She never disclosed anything about him. After asking her repeatedly, her drooping upper eyelids and pulled-down lip corners were my only answers. If you looked at her, you could never guess she was the one who gave birth to me. Her squat, ungainly body was so unlike mine. My father had to be lean and tall, just like me. Each time she combed my hair, Mama repeated, "Thea, I don't know how you got your chestnut hair. Mine, like most people, is almost black."

I shrugged. "Don't I have the same hair as my father?"

She turned a deaf ear and continued, "Your green eyes are very unusual, too."

In an eager voice, I exclaimed, "Must be like my father's!"

My long legs, and slim figure like a gazelle, the best gifts from the gods, helped me sprint.

While running away, I snatched and threw anything I could pick off tables—a few silver goblets, plates, bowls, or heavy sets of candlesticks to slow down the guards. When they were getting close to catching up with me, I knocked down even a table or two. And sometimes, as they were gaining on me, I picked up a chair or stool, hurling them toward the pursuers' horrified faces. It baffled me where my strength came from!

Like an arrow released from the bow, the guards chased me through several courtrooms, halls, and corridors in their hefty armor as if ready to kill their worst enemy. I slowed down only as I smelled the fresh air of the lush garden. The scent of sweet jasmine at this time of the year urged me to stop and smell it. However, enjoying the park was forbidden for a slave girl. So my desire to get to the hiding place, far from the disgusting palace and its wealthy people, was my ultimate wish.

Finally slowing down, I could envision their triumphant smiles. And at last, the guards caught up, clenching onto me, and with some pushing and shoving, led me to the usual underground cell. However, they only dropped me on the festering floor this time without chaining me. *Very unusual!*

In the dungeon, Tamra's withered face came to me. She and I were slaves, but no one called us that. We lived in the palace's outskirts, home to Octavius or Emperor Augustus. My mother worked for the Empress and never complained. But not me! I despised all the beautiful princesses to whom I had to bow and take orders. Preparing their bathwater, washing their dirty clothes, or sweeping the floor occasionally churned my stomach. The worst punishment was to bend and clean their shoes when they were ready to go out; then, they complained about them not being shiny enough.

Most days, they received massages enhanced with olive oil. Beautifying their eyes and eyebrows like Cleopatra was another way to spend their idle time. I'd also covered their soft and shiny skin with colorful silk dresses interwoven with gold and silver. While walking, the scent of lavender and gardenia filled the air. All that preparation was for attending the nightly orgies to make the royal men fight over each one of them.

All alone, I welcomed my cell's foul smell and found happiness by ceasing the growth of the dark seed.

Tamra's whispering startled me when the first sun ray crept through the trapdoor. "Thea, I'm here to set you free."

To my shock, she was alone—no guard, not even a nightwatchman. The heavy iron door screeched in my ear. One of the princesses had summoned me and ordered Tamra to run to the rescue.

I pushed the hatch from within, and her from outside. After sliding it aside, she grabbed my hand with surprising strength and pulled me out.

While wiping her wet eyes with her long black sleeves, Tamra's sad face bewildered me. She hugged me while trying to hide her trembling. "Dear Thea," she murmured, "I must let you go."

"Why, Mama?" I swallowed hard to rid the knot in my throat.

"Please, don't look at me with your wide unfamiliar eyes." She lowered her head and uttered, "The Empress commanded you never return to the palace."

In my utmost misery, I exclaimed, "Never, Mama?"

"Never, ever, my dear Thea!" She reached out and hugged me again.

"Where do I go?" I looked left and right in confusion.

Tamra gestured to the faraway horizon. "Go east. Walk toward the sun, my child."

I pointed far out to the backbone of Rome, the Apennines. "Toward the mountains, Mama?" I could barely get any words out. "I ... never climbed any of them. And never ... been away from you! And now you are sending me toward that unmovable creature?"

Tamra did not budge. "You'll find your way." After clasping me to her bosom and swallowing her tears, she suddenly pushed me away and started running back to the palace. Her discarding me like a rotten apple broke my heart.

I could only watch until she disappeared out of my sight. With no other choice, I walked in the opposite direction. As for now, I had only me, no one else to rely on. No princesses to make the dark seed grow. Or for me to obey their condescending orders.

CHAPTER 2

S trolling through the heart of Rome, not far from the palace, I reached our majestic Senate, with high marble columns as if touching Zeus's territory. I wished I could step up and see the inside. But, this building was not for us, the enslaved men and women. It was only for a handful of influential men. Long ago, the senators elected Julius Caesar to be our Emperor. But, after a few years, he did not follow their directions. So they attacked and killed him in the *House of Justice* with their bare hands. He was the uncle of our present Emperor. Could senators be murderers? *Ney!*

Some steps away, the smell of filth and a poverty-stricken city appeared. At least I faced the grubby dungeon in the palace only occasionally. But these unfortunate folks were born and died here. The stench of decayed streams had me holding my nose in some places. I wandered along the rocky roads and alleys, with clay huts and shacks more similar to wild animals' lairs—the commoners' dwellings. People in tattered clothes strolled the only city road separating the town's farmers market. My black washed-out coarse cloth wrapped around me was a shining star compared to the patchy holes of theirs. These impoverished people had no way of washing or cleaning themselves regularly. Most of the treasury's gold and coins were spent on the troops' expenses to make them superior to the mighty Persian forces. They were the only ones with the strength to battle us, the Westerners. Our armies had already conquered Greece and Egypt, which previously belonged to them.

However, our forces recently suffered a considerable loss from being unable to take over Armenia, a Persian estate. Emperor Augustus was amassing all the country's resources to ensure Rome would crush the Persian Empire in future battles.

If anything was left in the treasurer's chest, it went to the Emperor and his family's upkeeping. The rest of the people had to furnish the Chief Commander with their sons, some of whom would never return home. Ignoring the mothers' outcries in the street was impossible, but no emperors or kings seemed to hear them. The rulers did not even try to muffle any mother's wailings. They acted like hungry *mantichora* devouring the young men with unlimited gratification. It did not matter how fast the commoners fed their boys to them; they always came back for more.

To see these unfortunate commoners suffering was so hurtful that I sped up while wiping my forehead with my hand. I could not get away fast enough to distance myself from the thick layers of Rome.

As I was getting closer to the countryside, I felt the invisible rope around my neck connecting me to the palace starting to unravel. The dark seed within me became smaller and smaller.

"Here, I am free! Free at last!" I shouted.

In this peaceful arena, I could cry, scream, or laugh

without fear of punishment. The scent of trees and bushes in the fresh air brought me delight. While passing several farms, I could see a few industrious farmers cutting golden wheat with their sickles. Each one had to be the most even-tempered human on earth. They spent their days in the wide open, plowing the fields, planting the seeds, watching them grow, and grinding them to feed us. None of them were unhappy, even with the dirt covering their clothes and faces. I yearned to have a farmer's hut and call it "home." *Wishful thinking... maybe one day!*

My happiness did not last for long. Soon, thick, dark clouds covered the calm blue sky. I waited to see the moon and stars but to no avail. When the rain began to fall, the smell was delicious. I soon found myself in the woods. However, a needle or stick poked my face, arms, or legs with every step, keeping me on guard. A little later, my shoe soles melted in creeks as if they were made out of papyrus. The straps around my legs stayed in their place. The deep darkness of the woods made me welcome the howling of animals—my only companions.

Searching for shelter became my urgent desire when the rain strengthened. Suddenly, without warning, a strong wind twirled me so that the ground underneath gave way, and I rolled down onto a flat floor. As soon as I could get up, a sharp pain in my right leg took me back down.

Heavy rain mixed with hail and muddy water lashed at me as if the bottom of the sky had opened. I could see nothing except Deimos, the god of terror, with his horrifying eyes and massive beard ready to devour me at any moment. Then Medusa, with bloodshot eyes and wiggling snakes as her hair, appeared on top of every tree, laughing as if my misery was an enjoyable time for her. I closed my eyes.

In the middle of the darkness, I heard the breathing of some creatures nearby. In horror, I opened my eyes and could see only the light of a few stars. But when shadows moved closer, I had to rub my eyes with a fluttering heart—a pack of wolves was approaching me. The god of horror, Phrike, ran his fingers from my head along the length of my spine. A chill took over me.

The creatures were multiplying, and I was losing control. I took a deep breath and contemplated my situation. These wolves were not more dangerous than the lions the gladiators fought to entertain the Emperor in the Coliseum. I was no gladiator—a woman alone with one injured leg; all I could do was glare back at them. They reminded me of the hefty stray dogs I fed and sang to at home. They would sit beside me and listen to my songs as a token of appreciation. As soon as the wolves heard my melodic voice, they, too, rested on the ground and closed their eyes. However, to my relief, they all ran upon hearing their leader's call to locate another prey. I was alone again.

The rising sun kept me waiting while the thunder and lightning kicked up again in full force. The heavy clouds buried me with pouring rain and threw more rocks and mud from the top of the mountains.

Here, I'm a sitting duck. I must search for a safe spot. To make a fire the way our forebears did was impossible. I tore the bottom of my garment and wrapped it around my swollen foot with the leftover straps of my shoes, then started limping. Finally, I found a stick that helped me to climb. The uphill path was more challenging with every step. At one point, I started crawling while pulling the injured leg behind me.

The higher I climbed, it became a tremendous effort to take a breath. For sure, I would collapse at any moment. But remembering I never had to live in the despicable palace or the dungeon again gave me the strength to keep going.

I concentrated on finding shelter, and after a while, a massive hole in the belly of a birch tree caught my attention. I crept in and fitted myself as small as a fetus. Closing my eyes was the only escape from Deimos, Medusa, and the world's dark forces.

The rhythm of trickling rain forced me to open my eyes. In the distance, some trees coming together near a colossal rock ignited my enthusiasm. The faster I hobbled toward it, the faster it went farther and farther away. It had to be a mirage. Finally, I trusted my eyes no more and gave up on seeing the sun, moon, and stars again. Their brightness was running away from me.

To prevent myself from falling, I grabbed a rock before darkness blanketed my eyes, and my triumphant scream was the last sound in my ears. I had to reach the Apennines Mountains—a desire for every Roman man.

CHAPTER 3

N o idea how long it took until I could open my eyes. Where was I? *No clue!* In disbelief, I looked around. *This can't be the underworld!* The room was filled with the meadowsweet scent, and the sun on my bed warmed my entire body. I tried to get up, but severe leg pain forced me down. The pounding in my head made me aware that Haydes had not taken me yet.

The sound of a heavy wooden door, until then invisible, creaked open. A silvery creature slid in. Her hair, as long as her washed-up cloak, ran to her ankles. Like two dots under her protruding forehead, her eyes were barely visible in a wrinkled face. It appeared as if someone had shoveled her crinkled lips inside her mouth. *She must be an avatar.*

"Well done, Thea!" Her lips moved, and like in a dream, I understood her. "You found your way to me." She smiled. Her blackened teeth made me shiver.

I swallowed hard, trying to hide my fear. "Where am I? How do you know my ..."

She did not let me finish. "Shush!" She put her finger with a dagger-size nail on my lips. "You need to save your energy. Don't be scared. I'm Cordelia, Master of all the sorceresses. Nothing is hidden from me—past, present, and future." Her eyes twinkled. "Now, rest! It's time ..."

I did not hear the rest; a deep sleep overtook me.

Cordelia's gentle shaking awakened me when she shoved a clay bowl into my face without a word. She pushed it to my locked teeth so hard I had no choice but to open my mouth. Then, she poured a gooey, tasteless porridge into my mouth. "The faster you swallow this, the sooner you'll heal." She rushed some more into my mouth and continued, "We'll start your first lesson once you're done with this."

"Lesson?" I gasped between gulps. "What lesson?"

"There is a reason for you to be here. I'm your Guiding Light—until it's time for you to leave."

Cordelia pressed the bowl to my mouth each time I tried to speak another word. Once the bowl was empty, she put it aside, grabbed my arms, and pulled me upward with a strength I didn't think she had in her.

I leaned on her and hobbled until we reached a vast room. After she freed me from my old torn robe stuck to my weak body, she signaled me to sit in the middle of a pool empty of water. She left me sitting in dismay and went outside. With my body trembling, I dared to look up. I was horrified to see a thick iron plate with several large holes somehow attached to the ceiling.

Moments later, Cordelia entered, leading a bull by a rope up some stairs to the roof. The sight of a dagger in her other hand petrified me. Once at the top, she positioned the bull on the wobbly plate. When she slit his throat swiftly, blood poured all over my head. Shortly after, the bull collapsed, and his heavy body covered the holes. The thought of the roof caving in on me urged me to run out. But my broken leg kept me in the blood pool. With trembling hands and disgust, I rushed to wipe my eyes. In no time, the clotting blood came up to my neck. I yearned to jump out. But my broken bone gave me no chance of running away. With my eyes closed, my breathing became shallow. When I felt Cordelia's grip on my broken leg, it raised a little hope of being rescued. To my surprise, no severe pain, only a mild ache. It was a miracle!

Cordelia guided me to the next pool filled with lukewarm water. After rinsing the blood, she dried me off and put a new earth-colored garment on me.

"Now that you survived the bull blood ritual and have most of your strength," she announced as if highly entertained, "we go to my workroom."

I mumbled, "What ritual?"

Without answering, her slight push on my back made me obey. Walking through a long corridor with no light, I whispered, "Where are you taking me?"

"By this time, most apprentices would have panicked and ran away instead of agreeing to bathe in the bull's blood."

If only it weren't for my broken leg.

The workspace had no windows, except a few rays of light penetrated through small holes in the roof. *A cave?* Some colorful glass bottles sitting on shelves caught my attention. Against the wall, there were also a few tin containers. Cordelia gestured for me to sit on the ground when she approached them. She removed the top of one and stepped toward me. Inside, wilted leaves in various shapes looked unfamiliar. Before I could open my mouth, she whispered, "What do you smell?"

I breathed in, "Hmmm! Sweet and delicious!"

Cordelia moved her head in agreement and approached me with another box.

The new scent caused my eyebrows to pull down; I responded with my nose wrinkled and my upper lip curled. "Foul scent!" I pushed the box away and held my nose tight.

"See," Cordelia gave a crooked smile, "there are all kinds of scents between aromatic and vile."

"Do scents like colors have different shades from black to white?"

She nodded. "I'll teach you all. Trust me."

I pointed to the vast array on her shelves. "It looks like you have remedies for everything."

"I have remedies for everything except one," she said ominously.

I couldn't hide my smirk. "And what is that?"

"Death! My child!" She tittered, clearly amused with herself.

I was delighted to hear Cordelia talking, especially in a friendly tone. I continued with another question, "After my training, do I become like you and know the world's secrets?"

Cordelia heaved out, "An extraordinary task is waiting for you."

"What is that?"

"Don't rush destiny." She pointed to me. "You'll know when it's time."

When my eyes adjusted to the dim light better, I noticed a big table in the corner. Several piles of papyrus letters and many tablets were covered in dust and spider webs. Without any hesitation, I started brushing them with my hands.

Cordelia asked me, "Would you like to learn how to read?"

"Reading and writing are *not* for a slave girl," I repeated what the princesses had told me.

"Don't worry. Time changes everything."

Her words sounded like a breeze; not wanting to stop it, I asked, "Would it be possible one day I'll be like you?"

She stared at me. "Perhaps one day ... You're more like me than not."

"Really? How then?"

"All you need is to open your eyes and ears."

"How?"

"Come."

She led me outside. The majestic dark sky looked as if it was hiding thick secrets. But the stars were attempting to face it off. "What do you see?" She pointed to the full moon.

Looking at the stars always made me dream. "I'm mesmerized by the shiniest dot closest to the moon."

"Yes, it's the Eastern Star. Some call it Vega."

I was bewildered. "Was I supposed to reach the Eastern Star when my mother wanted me to go to the East?"

"No, dear!" She grinned. "Tamra meant for you to go to the east side of the world."

In delight, I said, "To the Persian Empire!"

"For now, go to bed," Cordelia gave a soft order and led me to the same room I was in before. "Just listen and watch with your total being."

She then pulled a cover as soft as a feather over me.

CHAPTER 4

I closed my eyes. But, instead of falling asleep, I saw myself rising through a long, dark tunnel into a brilliant light as if it was my first encounter with light. My mother's wailing, a sign of the tremendous pain and discomfort, shook the walls. But then, a man's kind voice enveloped my heart: "Amaya. Ahura Mazda blessed us with a girl. She's the light of our lives." Before picking me up, he wiped her blood off me and put a warm blanket around me. While holding me in his arms, he whispered, "You're Mithra."

Amaya gave him the shade of a smile and responded, "Yes, indeed, Ormazd! She's our light."

The husband, in a cheery voice, declared, "Look outside. The first rays of the sun also shine at the top of the Zagros Mountains and start to brighten our entire city, Susa."

The cozy room with the holy fire in an adobe house felt like heaven. Each time my mother embraced me in her bosom to feed and cradle me, I wished I could stay there forever.

Suddenly, I had a glimpse of this other self at age seven. My parents and I sat by the holy fire in my birth room. My father uttered, "Mithra, what are the three pillars of our faith?" He had already removed his sacred white robe, belt, and hat. I was mesmerized by his cap decorated with the emblem of an angel with two wings, evidence of him being a wise man to the king.

Confidently, I strolled to one of the three columns. After hugging one, I said with a proud voice, *"This column stands for Good Thoughts."* I proceeded to the second and third: *"Good words and Good Deeds."*

"Bravo, Mithra." He gave me a warm smile. "It shows you've been mindfully practicing all these three pillars of our religion daily."

"Thanks to Mother." I pointed to Amaya with pride. "She teaches me by imagining these three columns. No way for me to forget them."

"Dear Mithra," my mother said, "why is it imperative for us to learn these three?"

I shrugged. Ormazd's kind voice then filled the room. "To repeat these three axioms, the love of Ahura Mazda occupies our bodies and souls. No room for Ahriman to grow within us."

"Then, we successfully harmonize our souls and bodies," Amaya smiled.

Ormazd turned to me with delight when I murmured, "Father, I'm confused!" But then, I swallowed hard. "I know what a body is ... what's a soul?"

"Don't worry," his words soothed me, "once you practice it repeatedly, you'll see the 'light' within you."

"That's your soul, my dear Mithra," Amaya said.

At this time, I felt my parents' immense affection toward me. So, to stretch my time with them, I came up with a new question. "Why do we have our fire lit all the time?"

While Ormazd was rubbing his long beard, Amaya voiced, "Fire or light protects us from darkness and Ahriman."

"Your mother is right." He reached and held my hand. His warm hand blanketed me in Love. "Fire, water, and earth are the basis for our existence, created by Ahura Mazda."

"Does this mean," I chuckled, "like a ray of light, *I* also protect you two?"

Their nods were accompanied by huge smiles when like a kitten, I asked again, "How did we come to exist?"

In his shiny black eyes, Ormazd responded, "According to our holy scripture, we exist because of a celestial event ..."

"Created by Ahura Mazda." Amaya's eager voice completed his statement.

It became clear to me. My family's faith was different from most people's. I jumped in with no hesitation, "Some of my friends' parents pray to idols. They sacrifice animals in their temples and eat their meat. How come?"

"In our holy book, *Avesta*," Ormazd said, "our prophet, Zoroaster, abhors killing even animals."

I enjoyed being the center of my parent's attention, and I kept up with my questions. "Father. Must we pray to Ahura Mazda?"

"No, my child. We're *free* to choose between Ahura Mazda or Ahriman. But we're responsible for our choices—to get rewarded or punished."

"The reason is," Amaya allayed my confusion,

"Ahura Mazda is our *Anchor of Love*."

That night when he tucked me in bed, he whispered in my ear, "Love, Love, Love, my daughter. Fill your heart only with Love."

≽ ☘ ≼

I opened my eyes, aware of a seed of Love in my heart, wishing I could find Amaya and Ormazd by my side instead of Cordelia. The reality hit me hard. Then, as if she could read my mind, her lips moved. "You had a lovely dream last night, didn't you?"

Cordelia's relaxed demeanor gave me some time to sort out the confusion in my mind. After a deep breath, I beseeched her, "Dear Cordelia, I don't know what to make of my dream." I swallowed. "I was born to a family with utmost Love toward me. It was so real."

"Yes, last night, you journeyed to *your* past ..."

I gasped. "My past? No! No! Tamra wasn't my mother?"

She nodded. "Don't look at me with your horrified eyes. If you don't know something, that doesn't mean you have to be scared of it."

"I learned we, humans, like everything in nature, are born one day, and we must take a trip with Hades another day. And the past is only my life here and now."

Cordelia shook her head. "Your dream shows that you were born as a Persian girl long ago." She grinned.

"Really! Can we do that?"

She rubbed her forehead. "Perhaps sometime around six hundred years ago."

Amazingly, I cheered, "And my name was not Thea. I was Mithra!"

Cordelia moved her peculiar head. "Very likely, you had dark eyes and hair."

"True! True! I felt right at home. No sign of my chestnut hair or green eyes."

"Now, in this life, you are a Roman girl."

"Are you telling me that I had other lives before today?"

"It's what I'm saying," Cordelia affirmed. "You're the reincarnation of Mithra." She brought pants and a shirt for me to wear. "You have a gift to dip into your past."

"How come? I know you can put my confusion at rest."

She turned a deaf ear, and while stepping away, Cordelia murmured, "Our physical world is full of mysteries. You wouldn't be so confused if you believed in your soul and its ability."

CHAPTER 5

Rome

19 BCE

E very day, as soon as I climbed into my seat next to Cordelia, the whip cracked the air, and the two horses began panting while taking gentle strides. Their legs trod the ground gingerly—we were in Cordelia's command. In the beginning, the ride in the wooden *clickety-clank* wagon with the two-adult Yakut, more similar to ponies in shaggy fur, transporting me through the damp, dark jungle scared me to death. Cordelia's ears were deaf to my imploring to stop. I had no choice but to beseech the god of horror, Deimos, to escape me. Not that it did any good!

One time, she turned to me, and her lips moved after reading the horror in my eyes. "Don't be afraid of the jungle's darkness, Thea. When you come out of it, you'll be braver and wiser than before."

I couldn't care less. Through my teeth, while

trembling within, I replied, "I'm not used to going through the darkness!"

"Did you like your life in the Emperor Palace?" Cordelia challenged me.

I shook my head in dissatisfaction.

Her soft words became clear to me, "Well, the gods answered your prayers and brought you to me."

To uncover my confused heart, I mumbled, "I don't know what I want."

Cordelia snapped, "It's time for you to concentrate on *NOW*."

As a habit, Cordelia stopped the wagon at a prominent spot, not cramped by trees, and gestured for me to get out. We walked a long way to the forest's heart, where several giant trees had brought their heads and branches together, blocking the sun's light. Like a willow tree caught in the storm, ending my wobbling was impossible.

For the first few days, she stepped ahead, picked up a handful of withered leaves, and after crushing them, wanted me to smell them. Then, with head or hand movement, she showed me whether to put each in the sack or discard it. Sometimes, digging a massive root of a dried tree took me all day. Understanding the collected leaves' usefulness based on their shapes and scents was yet another learning ladder for me.

A few weeks later, I had to collect any animal or bones I came upon. When Cordelia saw my head askew, she commanded, "Pick up any dead ones."

"Like what?"

"Hum ... waterfowl, sparrows, geese, hare, bats, and shrews' bones."

One day, while getting close to a wild dog's body and examining it to see if it was dead, a lynx jumped out, hissed, and grabbed the dead animal with his padded furry claws.

Startled, I screamed and ran as if my body was on fire.

Cordelia appeared before me, blocking me. "Stop, Thea!"

I wailed, "The dangerous beast was about to attack and send me to Hades!"

"The jungle is his home," Cordelia said calmly, "we're infringing on his territory."

Her coolness, not caring about me, made me sweat. I exclaimed, "Are you saying I should've waited until the wild cat came after me?"

With my heart thumping, Cordelia was still cool as a cucumber. "Why didn't you just leave or step away quietly? He didn't attack *you*, did he?"

"No! But ..."

This time, she interrupted me, "You could've stayed and unleashed your love toward him."

"I've no love in me." I shrugged. "I've known only my dark seed." Without giving her a chance to respond, I continued, "With an empty hand, how do you want me to stand up against a wild animal?"

She took out a dagger from her sack. "Defend yourself with this only when your life is in danger." She showed me how to use it with simple movements and concluded, "Usually, they turn around and leave—unless they're starving."

I held the dagger close to my chest. "Is this mine now?"

"Remember! The human laws won't work in the jungle."

I put the dagger in my bag. *So an enslaved girl is now armed. How unbelievable!* "Is that why you never wanted me to separate a branch or a leaf from a tree?"

"Yes. They're alive, as you are. How would you like me to cut off one or two fingers of yours?" The wrinkles on her face became more profound.

After that day, I left any bones with flesh without touching them and quietly walked away.

"It's some other creature's food." Cordelia's voice stayed in my head. She also repeated that if a human touched a dead animal, no other creature would be interested in devouring it.

To disturb the balance of the jungle or its inhabitants was not allowed. She, however, came to help carry the intact skeleton to the wagon, especially one as big as a wolf, brown bear, or red deer.

Today, for the first time in front of me, she dug into the ground with her nails to find some human bones.

In my fear, I asked, "Why don't you use a dagger?"

"I have none."

"Use mine."

She shook her head in disagreement and moved on.

The most horrifying time of the day was when she trusted me with some human bones or skulls. My duty was to pick up and carry them in my apron pockets. However, I could never miss her angry words each time one of them slid out of my hand to the ground. They were the most fragile and precious items in nature. But my churning stomach, like a stormy sea, took away my concentration during the first few days.

One day, to escape her baffling practice, I walked away from her sight, sat, and leaned against a tree trunk. While gnawing on some dry roots and leaves, I wished to escape to my previous life as Mithra. So far, I have preferred my past life over my present.

≳ ✤ ≲

Instantly, I heard Ormazd's voice calling out, "Amaya! Mithra! Come to my room. There is something to discuss."

As Amaya and Ormuz's daughter, at this time, I saw myself in the body of a woman with full breasts despite my thin and tall stature.

"Even before dinner?" Mother Amaya's soothing voice came to me.

"Yes! Yes!"

I entered my father's room before she did. He had already removed his white robe, belt, and cap with the unique emblem of an angel in opened wings.

Amaya and I sat before Ormazd as he gave me a fatherly look. His kind voice sat on my ear. "As you all know, the Median King's entourage is finalizing the negotiation of his daughter, Princess Mandana's wedding, to our Prince, Combys."

"Interesting." Amaya sounded confused. "Astyages would like to add the Persian estates to his."

Ormazd pivoted to me and claimed, "Certainly, he'd prefer to have the Persian King as his friend rather than a foe."

Amaya nodded. "Especially now that the Persian King has recently earned some power by defeating some of the Median's friends."

In awe over the tying knot of two wholehearted enemies, I was baffled when Amaya broke my thoughts. "What does it have to do with us?" She turned to Ormazd.

"The Median Chief Commander, Harpagus," my father said tentatively, "has heard of our daughter, Mithra, and asked me for her hand in marriage."

Wow! Now it'll be my wedding too!

"Does that mean," a confused blanket covered Amaya's face, "he'd take our Mithra away from us?"

"Yes, very likely." Ormazd swallowed hard.

"It's all right, Mama." I put my hand on her lap. Bolstering with courage, I said, "Here, in Persia, women travel alone. I'll visit you and Dad often if the nuptial occurs."

"Mithra, the choice is yours, not mine." Ormazd's voice cheered me immensely.

I asked, "Is it possible for me to meet him?"

"Of course, my child," Ormazd affirmed. "It's all your decision."

"Despite him not practicing our faith?" Impatient, Amaya did not wait for an answer, and as a distraught mother, she raised her voice even higher, "But, he'll take our *Light* away from us."

"It's wonderful for her," Ormazd sounded, "to light up other parts of the world, too."

Amaya mumbled while making a knot from the corner of her skirt, "Is Harpagus coming here to meet her?"

He shook his head. "The King has invited the three of us tomorrow night for a party at the palace."

I kept hearing Cordelia's voice interfering with my thoughts. She was summoning me to keep helping her pick up the bones. In abhorrence, I ignored her and climbed the enormous tree. I sat between the two huge branches hoping the numerous leaves would block me from her sight. The desire to know what happened between Harpagus and Mithra in my past stayed with me for a long time.

Amaya and I were crushing wheat germs to squeeze oil drops to smooth my coarse hair. Finally, after the day ended, we had enough to wash my hair. She brushed and braided part of it in the back and decorated it with a band of fresh white rose blossoms. When I wore an ankle-length blue sleeveless dress outlining my curves, I felt like a bride and was joyful to have a mother who cared for me.

That night, the alluring flute music drew us to the rotunda. The walls' decorations, with arrays of white and purple lilacs, trumpeted a festive atmosphere. When the sound of drums, tars, horns, and harps enveloped the palace, Ormazd gestured and announced, "Look, Harpagus is coming to us."

As soon as I laid eyes on him, it felt like my cheeks were on fire.

He bowed to my parents and extended his hand, inviting me to dance. Even though I could speak Median, I only praised him with my eyes. His bronze armor covering his broad shoulders and his alluring neatly-groomed crimson beard made me aware of the butterflies in my stomach. Each time his sharp hazel eyes locked with mine, they evoked a passionate feeling in my heart. Despite the ongoing music, he and I stood by each other's side. I could detect his warm affection toward me without any words.

On our way home, it was impossible to erase his stunning face from my mind. Harpagus had conquered my heart. At home, I confessed the invisible thread knotting my life to his.

I spent several days wondering whether Harpagus liked me or not. On the seventh day, my father announced to Amaya and me, "Now, Harpagus' task at the court is done."

My heart was thumping so hard that I thought it would jump out of my chest at any moment.

"Tomorrow," Ormazd turned to me and looked squarely into my eyes. "Harpagus comes here to talk with you ..."

Amaya interrupted, "Didn't he ask you for her hand first?"

Ormazd nodded.

When Harpagus sat before me, looked into my eyes, and asked me to marry him, my immediate response was, "Yes!"

Ormazd married me to Harpagus in a heartwarming ceremony before the holy fire. I thought I was a dove soaring into the sky.

"Hurray!" with the sound of my voice, I opened my eyes and found myself dancing in the dark woods—no idea how I came down from the tree.

"Thea, here you are!" Cordelia called out. "This is not a time to dance."

I said, undaunted, "I'm ready now to look for more bones."

"You have to be exhausted," she observed. "Let's go home now."

CHAPTER 6

A fter several months, I did not quiver at the sight of any animal or human cartilage. And I ventured into the darkest part of the forest without any hesitation. So, Cordelia decided I was ready for my next lesson. She guided me to dig in the ground to find some human bones without using my dagger. After a while, I hated to look at my nails. They never grew as long as hers. They were broken, chipped, or split. But after a while, ignoring the hurt also became a habit of mine.

More often than not, the fog moved in, and finding bones was more tricky. But as if Cordelia's eyes could penetrate deep into the underground, she would locate most of them. As a result, we usually returned home with full sacks.

One day, after reading the exhaustion on my face, Cordelia suggested, "Thea, why don't you go to the wagon and rest your eyes? Then, when you're ready, come back to me."

I followed her suggestion, stretched out my body in the wagon, and closed my eyes to escape my horrible life with her.

The sound of galloping hooves resonated in my ear. Harpagus and I were on the way to King Astyagus' castle. Harpagus went to murmur to His Majesty's ear about the future Persian Prince and Median Princess's wedding. The King's sour face and deep wrinkles gradually smoothed out. However, the pounding feet of two guards entering the hall diverted everyone's attention.

After throwing an older man as if handling a rag before the King, the guards bowed; and one declared, "Your Highness! This man refuses to sacrifice the ox gifted to the royal temple in honor of Your Majesty!"

"A subject of ours?" The King caressed his long white beard, and the line between his eyebrows became more renounced. He decried, "How does he dare?" He turned to his three Wisemen sitting to his right and asked, "What should be his punishment?"

"Death, Your Majesty!" All of them agreed in one roar.

I, however, could not stay quiet. I approached the King and bowed. "Your Majesty, by ordering to kill this innocent man, you are ripping off the cloth of his body from his soul. A benevolent king never would steep so low as to make a man's soul naked." I lowered my head in deference; the corner of my eye caught the King's admiration as his voice came into focus.

"Lady Mithra, you speak brilliantly. Would you like to join our court and be part of our Wisemen?"

"I'm honored, Your Majesty!" I replied and bent my head again, respectfully.

When I sat beside Harpagus, he kissed my hand and whispered, "Mithra, you've made me proud before the King and all these noblemen." His eyes were filled with love for me.

➣ ✹ ➢

I knew my wiggling did not cause me to open my eyes, but the smell of smoke did. In the distance, a massive fire and dark smog reaching the sky caught my attention. I started running. When I got closer, I saw Cordelia standing in the middle of a bonfire. Her lips were moving as if she was talking with someone. My eyes could see no one. While sprinting faster, I screamed, "Cordelia! Cordelia!"

She was oblivious to my presence. I rushed to her and tried to grab her from behind to pull her out of the fire. However, like a tree trunk, she was rooted to the ground. Her bulging red eyes frightened me when she turned, and her dry, bloodcurdling laugh made my body hair stand on end. I took long steps backward. Then, to my shock, there was no fire anymore. As if Cordelia turned to be her old self again, she walked to me and held my hand. Without any words, I followed her like a faithful dog toward the wagon.

"Thea, I admire your selflessness." While on the way, she turned her head to me and continued, "You acted like a 'hero,' putting yourself in danger to rescue me without thinking of harming yourself." She touched my shoulder.

"Then, why did you scream at me with your angry eyes?" I pouted.

"You were taking me away from what I love to do," she explained. "Your interference destroyed my happy time."

I turned a deaf ear to her remark. At that moment, I felt proud and tasted immense joy.

"But," I said, "what about the dark seed in me?"

"The dark and bright seeds always exist in you and everyone else. When you act like a hero, the bright seed grows. And when you act maliciously, you allow the dark seed to grow."

I asked in bewilderment, "Can sometimes the dark seed grow like a sturdy tree and take over?"

Her eyes narrowed. "Of course. You've noticed only the dark seed and ignored your bright seed."

"My anger was the growth of my dark seed," I challenged her. "I've never had any reason to be happy until now." I gave Cordelia no chance to speak. "What does an enslaved girl have to be happy about?"

"Did you ever learn something new in addition to your chores?"

I shook my head. "I was busy obeying orders, nothing else."

"Have you ever sat and let the rising sun mesmerize you?"

"What about it?"

"The BEAUTY of it, my child!" Cordelia exclaimed.

In the present, my mind flew to Mithra in Persia and brought a wide grin to my face.

While riding in the wagon, I noticed Cordelia's hands showed no sign of the burning. In shock, I asked, "Cordelia, weren't you in the middle of a fire?"

After a pause, she opened the curtain of secrecy to

me. Her beloved older brother died when she was a little girl. So once in a while, she conjured him, and they had a visit. "You didn't see him, did you?"

"I saw no one." I was so scared that I held my hands together, preventing them from shaking. "Who were you talking to?"

I stared at her neck and clothes—no burned flesh or burn anywhere. In shock, I continued, "It's amazing that you were in the middle of the fire without burning!"

"Not a real fire!" she yelped. "Your eyes told you it was a fire. Did you burn your hands when you tried to grab me?"

I looked at them. "No." I swallowed hard. "To think of it, I didn't feel the heat either. But why was there a thick smoke if there was no fire?"

"To create a world of illusion."

"World of illusion? What's that?" I was baffled.

Cordelia smirked. "Not to see the reality. The smoke made you believe it was a real fire. So, without any fear, you rushed in to save me."

"But its smell woke me up from the delicious dream of my past life as Mithra."

"Nay. You grew up connecting the smoke with fire."

At this point, I was almost losing my patience, ready to scream. Instead, in a firm voice, I said, "Then, did even my eyes deceive me?"

She shrugged. "Very much so."

"At least tell me how you created the fake fire with smell and smoke?" I demanded.

"There are many mysteries in the world, and one person can't crack them all." She turned and uttered, "Enjoy the ride."

CHAPTER 7

By sunset, we reached the dwelling. I was responsible for pounding the collected bones in the stone mortar and pestle in the vast backyard. The crushing bones hurt my ears. I had to crumble and batter them until they became fine powder. At first, distinguishing between animal bones from humans' was impossible, but not for Cordelia. She also guided me through how to determine between pulverized bones. Within a few days, my eyes could see the different shades of white.

Her task started when I finished grinding the collected bones, leaves, and roots. Cordelia then meticulously combined one of two, three, or four to create a new ointment or scent with a distinct smell. She also explained how some herbs had the miracle of healing or a malice effect. Beaming, she said, "The best way to know is by sharpening your nose. It's one of the best armors to keep you out of danger."

"And how do I do that?"

"Practice! Practice! Practice!"

Usually, while she was making her potions, I pored over the books about Persia in the corner. I searched every papyrus paper to find anything about my life as

Mithra. But to no avail. Succumbing to tiredness, I put my head on the documents and closed my eyes.

➢ ✲ ➣

I felt a sparkle of new love while breastfeeding my baby boy, Bardia. After his birth, despite still being a Wisewoman at King Astyages' court, I had a good excuse to only sometimes be at His Majesty's disposal. The Median way of thinking put me in complete discord. They were nonbelievers of souls and only dealt with the worldly sphere. However, I ran to her side whenever Princess Mandana asked me to assist her with the wedding to Prince Combys. To see her happy face, and witness her enthusiasm for going to Persia, made me joyful too.

Today, she even showed interest in learning about the Prince's Land. With a doe-eyed expression, she uttered as if she was releasing one word at a time, "Mithra. Tell me. What does Persia look like?"

Excitedly, I replied, "Your Majesty, you'll love your new homeland." Proud of my birth country, I expressed, "It is a beautiful land with a few high ranges of mountains, clear rivers, and fabulous rose gardens full of nightingales."

"Sometimes, I hear you murmur something soothingly," she noted. "What is it?"

"Your Highness, they're some hymns from *Avesta* to keep my mind away from the darkness of Ahriman."

"Dear, would you repeat some for us?" She clapped and gathered all of her maidens-in-waiting. "Come! Come! Mithra will recite some rhythmic prayers."

I sang:

> *To what Land shall I go to flee,*
> *whither to escape?*
> *They sever me from nobles and my peers,*
> *nor are the people pleased with me...*

"Charming!" The Princess called out. "You have a lovely voice. Go ahead!"
Her smile was my permission.

> *Nor the Liar rulers of the Land.*
> *How am I to please thee, Mazda Ahura?*

≳ ✿ ≲

In Cordelia's workroom, I repeated the memory in my mind. At least, in my past life, I, as Mithra, knew, I moved from Susa, Persia, to Babylon, Media —unlike me as Thea ... from Rome to find Cordelia. Or did she find me? Where am I? *No idea! My present life, however, is enveloped in mystery.*
To think of it, Cordelia's house looked empty of any servants or maids. But everything was done and ready for me whenever I opened my eyes. There were likely many *avatars* beside her. I could feel them but never met or saw any of them.
She repeated the ritual of killing a bull every month as if the feeling of sorrow in me washed away by taking a bath in its blood. Instead, I felt the happiness of being as strong as he was and accepted the part of me similar to the wild animals living in jungles—kill, not to be killed.

37

Cordelia's words sat in my ear: "To kill is the lesson we learn early on from our rulers."

≥ ✲ ≤

Banging on Mithra and Harpagus's gate sounded in my head, and someone called out, "His Majesty summons Chief Commander Harpagus and Lady Mithra at once!"

Harpagus put on his armor in a rush. Opposite the other Wisemen, who covered themselves in black robes, I wore my white robe, just like my father, Ormazd. Except my head wore no cap with the Persian royal emblem. I combed my shoulder-length hair hurriedly, and we rushed to the court.

Before we could pay our respects, King Astyages shouted with slanted eyes, "Earlier tonight, I had a horrifying nightmare."

No one spoke. The King took a deep breath and continued, "A vine grew, grew, and grew out of Princess Mandan's pelvis, so large that it covered the entire world."

I pressed my lips not to say a word along with the rest of the Wisemen. I listened as Harpagus said, "Your Majesty, an unusual dream."

King Astyages' voice trumpeted anger, "These Wisemen believe our beloved Princess will give birth to a son. He will not only conquer many countries," he swallowed a knot in his throat, "but my life will be in his hands too." The King could no longer calm his anger. He stood up and screamed, "It's ridiculous! How is it possible? My grandson gets more powerful than me and uproots everything I have! Why are you all quiet? Answer me at once."

He directed his eyes squarely into mine and addressed me, "Tell me, Lady Mithra! Do you agree with them?"

I did not let the King's fiery red eyes and gritted teeth like a wolf scare me. "Your Majesty," I hesitated while only thinking about the truth, not necessarily playing the King, "I concur with them."

"Harpagus!" The King's piercing cry from the bottom of his lungs shook the palace's walls. "Right NOW! Leave for Susa!" In exasperation, he ordered, "Return our daughter to us. It has been only a few months passed since their wedding." His face looked like a tethered beast, straining to be released.

I hugged my husband to say goodbye, wishing to go with him, but I had to stay behind in case the King summoned me again.

Although it was months, it seemed like the blink of an eye when I saw through the window that they had returned to the palace. I rushed barefoot to Harpagus and bowed to the Princess.

But, with her teary eyes, she didn't even notice me. Instead, she ran to the King, and after prostrating to him, she exclaimed, "Father! Why did you separate me from my beloved husband and the country I've come to love?"

The King sighed in relief and said, "The Wisemen advised us that getting pregnant is dangerous for you."

The blood drained from her face. "But, Father, I'm already with child."

"What?" King Astyages howled. "How is it possible?"

Then, with a hand gesture, he dismissed her, and with fury, he yelled, "Do not come to my presence any longer!"

Princess Mandana was crying so hard that her shoulders were heaving. I held onto her arm, and both of us left the palace.

Soon, the King sent for me. "Lady Mithra. Go and stay with my daughter for days and nights." At this moment, the King's fury had subsided, and calmly, he said, "As soon as she delivers, bring the infant to us, only if it's a boy. And tell her he was born dead."

"Your Majesty," I exclaimed in shock, "I can't rip any infant from his mother's arms." I paused to catch my breath. "You're commanding me to shake hands with Ahriman. I'm afraid I won't be able to do so."

A grin spread across his face. "You'll be rewarded handsomely." He signaled the guard to give him a sack full of gold coins. "You can have this one now. And after you bring the baby to us, you'll have ten more of these."

"Your Majesty!" I countered his offer with a firm voice, "I'm afraid no treasury in the world can buy me to do this devilish task."

The King's kind demeanor abruptly disappeared. He cried, "Are you disobeying *Your* King's order?"

I remained silent and bowed. The impatient King dismissed me with a swift hand. "If you weren't a Persian woman, you would be punished harshly."

Wow! Bravo, Mithra! If I were so brave a long time ago, how come, as Thea, I'm so fearful and cowardly? First, obeying the princesses, and now Cordelia.

Today, Cordelia broke into my thoughts after washing my hair with mysterious herbs. She gave me an object bright on one side and said, "Look!"

"What's this?"

"A mirror, silly," she chuckled. "Haven't you ever seen one?" I remembered that the Empress and Princesses used one after dressing up. The commoners had no access to it. And it was forbidden fruit for an enslaved person. This Chinese ingenuity came to us via Persia. I stared at the strange girl peering back at me with red hair, wide green eyes, and a pale face like those skeletons. "Who is she?"

"YOU!" Cordelia shrieked. "Your curly hair is the same color as wine—unique." She threw an admiring look my way. "No one can resist you now!"

"Who cares? A slave is not supposed to be even thinking of wooing anyone." As I was about to put the mirror face down, Mithra's countenance appeared before me with long, shiny black hair and dark almond-shaped eyes. *I wished I had Mitra's look, not Thea's.*

CHAPTER 8

E ach night, if I had no other chores, I spent most of my time learning to read by candlelight or moonlight—not an easy task. Nevertheless, I was eager to learn about the Persian Empire, especially the women. Once, out of frustration, I wanted to rush out and forget about it all. But Cordelia blocked my exit. "Be patient, Thea. Now you know you were a Persian girl in the past. What was her name?"

"Mithra," I murmured.

"The more you learn about her, the better you can tame the dark seed within you."

"But these are written in Greek and Persian," I argued. "So difficult, and it takes so long to understand!"

She moved her head in agreement. "Open your eyes and heart wide. Then the etched words won't appear so hard and long."

"Sometimes, I see myself as Mithra. Was she a ruler like a king?"

"No, she was only a reverend to keep her ancestors' religion alive," Cordelia explained. "Mitra finds a way to rescue King Cyrus's life when he was a boy."

"King Cyrus, who is he?" I raised my head and saw

Cordelia's sad eyes when I heard no reply.

At last, she murmured, "So sorry for the Roman women." She walked away and left me with heaps of documents.

Cordelia created a new enthusiasm in me. Reading stories about Persian women enthralled me to no end. So one day, I asked, "If you can conjure the dead people, can you also journey to the past, present, and future?"

She lowered and raised her head briefly.

"Why don't you transport me to the Persian Empire?" I eyed her warily. "The same way you move between the worlds."

She gazed at me. "In dreams, there are no boundaries. You have the same capability as I do."

"I do?"

"Haven't you seen yourself as Mithra in Persia?"

I agreed when Cordelia's soft voice resonated in my ear. "Watch me." She sat in the corner of the room with her legs crossed and rested her hands on her lap. After closing her eyes, she did not move for some time. When she finally opened them, her lips moved. "This is the moment of silence. It's very much like dreaming. Let yourself go, and with practice, witness how far your soul takes you."

"Cordelia, you sound very weird." Confused, I held out my hands. "Don't we go underground when we die?"

"In the cosmos, nothing goes away." She stood up. "Our flesh and bones get annihilated and become dust, but a part of us always remains alive."

I scratched my head with squinting eyes. "Not the way I've understood."

"My child," she started dancing, swinging her hands and torso like tree branches in the breeze while smiling. "Easterners believe in the soul, but not Westerners."

"Dear Cordelia, I hate to break into your joy dance. I still don't get it."

She paused. "In Persia, the part that survives after our death is called the 'soul.'"

I smacked my head. "Now I get it. We, Romans, do not believe anything stays alive after our bodies ..."

"Except the gods," Cordelia affirmed. "They live forever outside of us. But in the East, one person has one soul, travels throughout time and places, and sometimes occupies a body."

"Like me," I said, starting to get it. "Thea in the present time, and Mithra in the past. I lived many years ago as an Easterner. But now, I'm a Westerner."

Cordelia only smiled.

That night, she and I stepped outside under the dark sky and twinkling stars. I followed her and sat on the bone-dry ground like the lotus flower. I closed my eyes and was instantly transported.

> ⇒ ✼ ⇐

Upon entering Astyagus' court, the scene before the King shook me to the core. First, my beloved Harpagus stood with a pale face as if his blood had been sucked out. Next to him was an older man, stooping down in ripped clothes with several wounds on his face, trembling like a twig caught in a storm. A few steps closer to the King, a boy, around ten, stood erect in washed-out but clean clothes. He looked like he was proud of being in a king's presence.

The King beckoned to me with a stern face and a foam of anger at his mouth. "Lady Mithra! Listen to this boy's outrageous deed!"

The loud thumping of my heart felt like it reverberated throughout the entire chamber. I enveloped it in my soft words, "Yes, Your Majesty."

The King's wrinkles deepened as he shouted with wide-open, glaring eyes. "The shepherd's son dared to slap one of our royal boys. SO UNTHINKABLE!"

I could barely breathe while trying to vocalize some remarks.

Suddenly, the boy fearlessly rushed to correct the King, "Your Majesty, *I* did not slap him."

Full of wrath, the King asked, "Then who did?"

"A few of my friends from the royal families." The boy's unyielding voice sounded like a mature man. "They chose me as their king. Later, one of them refused to obey my order. So, I ruled the others to punish him—just as any king would."

The entire court dipped into a deep silence. King Astyages cried at the top of his lungs, "How is it possible? A shepherd's boy dared to play the role of a king and command a punishment on a royal chap!"

The shepherd, who seemed to be breathing his last breath, wailed, "Your Majesty ... the boy isn't ... my son."

"Whose is he?" The King hollered and jumped up, "Tell me, or I'll have you all put to death."

An ear-splitting silence enveloped the hall again. I could not wait any longer. "Your Majesty ..."

The shepherd interrupted me, "My wife gave birth to a dead boy." He took a breath and pointed at

Harpagus. "This man offered me gold coins to exchange the alive infant in a blanket with the royal emblem with my ..."

"Your Majesty," I rushed in forcefully, "it was my idea." I took a breath. "To take the life of an innocent infant is siding with Ahriman," I pleaded. "The day my husband came to me with your grandson, I suggested he make the exchange." To calm the fire within me, I bowed.

I was, however, ready for any punishment as severe as possible, even death. Yet, amazingly, not being afraid of losing my life, a blanket of serenity covered me. I had saved the life of a Persian Prince.

"We know," King's loud voice encompassed the entire palace when his index finger pointed at me, "Lady Mithra! You practice a different religion. Be silent! Your faith does not matter in my court."

King Astyages' silence kept everyone in suspense, waiting on his ruling. Finally, the enraged King realized his plot had not succeeded. He ordered the shepherd beheaded for complying with Harpagus's plan. The King also stripped Harpagus of his rank. In addition, his and my punishment was to be under house arrest with two guards standing by the door, day and night, to prevent us from communicating with the outside world. The King also commanded two royal guards to take the boy to the Persian Monarch. In Persia, King Cyrus, the boy's grandfather, called him Cyrus.

During my conversation with Harpagus on our way home, under guard, I whispered, "King Astyages shakes hands with Ahriman."

Harpagus turned to me, and in his cloudy eyes, he said, "What are you talking about?"

"I swear to Ahura Mazda that I shall never return to the court or abide by this dark-hearted King. They can only carry my body without my soul ..."

≫ ✤ ≪

"Thea, why are you shouting?" Cordelia was touching my shoulder when I opened my eyes.

"Oh, I can't believe how horrible a ruler could be!" I shuddered.

She mumbled, "Wait until you witness the ruler's devilish acts."

"Can a human in the highest rank of society be crueler than King Astyages?"

"Well, you haven't seen how a dark seed grows in a ruler."

She left me in a confused state, as usual.

CHAPTER 9

I could never forget how Mithra felt about rescuing the Persian boy. But I was determined to know more. When Cordelia and I arrived home, I insisted on meditating with her every night. But, of course, her response was, "Not tonight. You collected many roots and dried leaves. Go to work."

At last, one night, when I finished grinding everything, Cordelia called me out, "Thea, come and sit in the backyard."

The light of the full moon blanketed the shining stars. I sat beside her. Cordelia closed her eyes, and so did I.

≽ ✼ ≼

Drum music jarred my ears as if I had traveled through a fog. All the royal family and friends looked immensely happy for King Astyages' at this festive celebration—but I had no happiness. Next to me, Harpagus had his muscular hand grasping my knee, preventing me from leaving. While munching on some grapes and sipping wine, he whispered, "My Mithra, I'm thankful you accepted the King's invitation and came with me."

I shrugged and went to get up. Harpagus again pushed my knee down with more force. "Darling, we can't leave until the King arrives."

"I have no interest in sitting at the treacherous King's table."

"Please," Harpagus pleaded, "by giving this elaborate celebration in our honor and choosing to reinstate me, it shows His Majesty is sorry for what he did."

Upon trumpeting the King's arrival, Harpagus had to take my arm and pull me up to stand like everyone else.

Soon the main course was served. I noticed the meat on his and my plate looked different from everyone else's. Some ground meat mixed with many spices. And it was difficult to tell whether it was lamb or deer. I elbowed him and whispered, "Our food doesn't appear to be the same as the rest of the attendees."

He emptied the wine goblet, swallowed a mouthful, and mumbled, "It's delicious."

I have yet to reach to touch mine. To see Harpagus devouring all of his and consume mine with more wine shocked me to no end. Afterward, he suggested, "Would you like to dance?"

I shook my head in disagreement and started to get up when I felt his hands on my shoulders pushing me down. "Dear, it's disrespectful of us to leave before the King."

Without any reply, I turned my body away from him.

After the sound of a trumpet, our attention went to the four servants carrying a large tray, stepping inside the middle of the courtroom. When they came closer, I took a double look at the scene unfolding before my eyes. In an instant, I recognized my slaughtered son ... Bardia's head. To my horror, I understood. His arms and legs were grounded into his flesh for serving Harpagus and me. I started screaming from the bottom of my heart, and my husband began vomiting, to the absolute delight of the King, who was laughing uproariously about what he'd pulled off.

I must have fainted. When I opened my eyes, I was in my house. I wished to be struck dead by lighting so my soul could be with Bardia. But instead, a dark veil covered my eyes again.

$$\geqslant \text{❉} \leqslant$$

Confused about where I was, I wiped away my tears and opened my eyes. Cordelia was standing before me. "Oh, dear Thea, now you know how ruthless a ruler can be."

"How could King Astyages feed them their son's flesh and bone?" Without waiting for a reply, I reconciled, "But, the good news is that King Astyages lived in the past. Our Emperor can't be that barbaric."

"Well," she scratched her head, "we, the common folks, can't see or understand what a ruler might do. Did you even think Astyages could feed the boy's flesh to his parents?"

After a short silence, I uttered, "Of course, it's easy for a ruler to carry out his ungodly deeds."

"Naturally," a smirk crossed Cordelia's face, "a ruler has enough of the 'yes-men' around him to carry out his orders. He doesn't even have to get his own hands dirty."

I looked at her in amazement. "Cordelia, how could you know what my dream was about?"

With a serious face, she said, "It's time for Thea to get away from the past and concentrate on NOW!"

With delight, I boasted, "Today, I feel the light of love in me." Knowing she had my best interests in her heart, I rushed to hug her. But, instead of her body, my two hands came together. Then, in awe, I stepped back. In reality, I was holding nothing except my own hands. Perplexed, I mumbled, "Cordelia, how come I can feel my own hands today but not that day of trying to rescue you from the fire?"

"Well, now, you are not hesitant. But that day, you were mixed up between your hands and my body out of confusion."

She signaled me to follow her. Instead of riding the wagon to the wilderness, she drove to the Apennines Mountains and stopped at a cave. The space was filled with at least a hundred filthy slave men, each covered in a one-piece rag tied around his waist. Every torso was coated with sweat and dirt. The quiet crying shook my heart. About half of them sat on little stools; before them, a small, tallow-burning lamp kept the water boiling. Many cocoons in the pot were jumping up and down to escape. But none were successful. When each opened up, another man standing pulled it out skillfully with a thin stick.

Amazingly, as soon as the larva hit the air, it became solid and formed threads. He collected all the lines in a straw bowl until it was packed. Then, another enslaved man picked it up and took the bowl to where another group wove them into the silk fabric.

Surprised, I asked, "Is it true?" I continued when Cordelia turned to me, "The Chinese gather cocoons from the special trees?"

She shook her head and grinned. "Silkworms make cocoons in China."

"SILKWORMS!" I screamed. "We're suffocating them before they can become beautiful butterflies!" Frustratedly, I said, "Must the Emperor and his family have silk robes?"

"These cocoons produce the best silk in the world by eating special mulberry leaves which only grow in China."

"Of course," I said with realization, "the rulers and their families *deserve* the best and softest fabric in the world. They're the only ones who can afford it."

Cordelia's sad eyes, full of tears, were my response. While walking ahead, I followed her to the back door, where the fabric sheets were packaged in colored-coded papyrus with the country's flag. Some were headed to the Roman Palace. Several huge loads were marked for the Persian royals, and some enormous piles went to the Chinese palace.

When Cordelia saw my mouth wide open, she whispered, "The production never sleeps."

"So, never a break for these enslaved men?"

"When this group goes, then another group comes and works."

I could not believe my eyes. "I had no idea the world is so full of slaves."

Her murmuring words touched my heart. "Did you

think you were the only slave in the world?"

"Yes." I breathed out.

"You should know most people are slaves under different names."

I became joyful whenever Cordelia and I conversed. So, I listened delightfully. "When one drops to the ground, the head of the production replaces him with a younger one."

"How do they transfer these packages between East and West?"

"Through the Silk Route. Since the Parthian Dynasty came to power in Persia over two hundred years ago, they have restricted any Chinese merchants from entering their land."

It became evident that Roman merchants bought these cocoons from the Persian merchants. Then, after making them into silk fabric, they sold them back to the Persians. In return, they traded this precious fabric back to the Chinese. *The way of trade in my time!*

"So," I concluded, "the Chinese produce the cocoons, we do the work, and in the middle, the Persians, without harsh labor, only collect their money."

"It's profitable for us, too," Cordelia explained. "It costs us practically nothing to produce it." She paused to draw me a map on the floor with a stick. The Persian land served as a bridge between Rome and China, putting the East and West together. They had the best roads in the world. We would never have today's speedy trade without the Persian King, Darius I. With admiration, Cordelia went on. "It takes only six months, a one-way trip, from their border to Anatolia, Egypt, or even the Mediterranean Sea."

I asked, "Are the merchants safe on those roads?"

"They're safe traveling on the Persian Royal Roads, but not when they get to the other countries."

"How come?"

As usual, my question disappeared into the air like smoke. I also had to promise Cordelia to keep the secret of cocoons becoming silk fabric in my blossoming bosom and never divulge it to anyone, not even in the future. *But, of course, I know no one. Why is she worried I'd tell someone?* And she only revealed to me what she wanted me to know, nothing more.

When she started to leave, I followed her like an obedient dog. After a short corridor, we stepped into a reasonably small room. Heaps of rainbow-colored silk and many silver and gold threads were scattered everywhere. Cordelia opened a small velvet sack and pulled out a handful of teardrop rubies, round opals, turquoise, emeralds, topaz, and garnet gems. Their light practically hurt my eyes.

"Make a robe or two using all these silk fabrics," she commanded.

"Me?" I pointed to my chest. "I've never done any needlework."

"Concentrate, my child." She gave me a sharp look. "Focus your attention on the task presented to you."

I asked in a suspicious voice, "But how?"

She gave me a glaring look. "You must use all the materials here. Then, the room will be orderly instead of being a mess." And she left me in wonder.

CHAPTER 10

For a while, I sat mute among the heaps of silk fabrics, silver, and gold threads, needles from small to large, and a pair of shears. The pile looked higher than the Apennines Mountains. *What am I supposed to do?* Misery filled my body. I had to cut and sew to create one or two outfits. In addition, I had no one to make a robe for, and no princesses needed a priceless robe. I was in a fog worse than when I was born as Mithra in Persia.

The thought of leaving Cordelia knocked on my head. However, like a tree rooted in the ground, my legs did not move. *What is it that keeps me here to obey Cordelia's orders? Maybe the dark seed ... or ... the light of love?*

Her spell had to prevent me from even getting away from the task. My mind, however, freely flew me to Persia.

≥ ✤ ≤

I was a twenty-year-old Mithra, daughter of Harpagus and Mother Mithra. She took me as an infant away from my Median father, Harpagus, the

Chief Commander, to her hometown, Susa. Today, I was galloping down the mountains from Susa toward the plateau of Pasargad, the new capital of Persia.

My mind took me to a month ago. The house where she and I lived was filled with neighbors and friends. They all loved my mother and came to console me in her death. I felt a well-dressed stranger staring at me among all these familiar faces. After a while, he approached me and whispered, "Lady Mithra, I have a message for you from King Cyrus II. Please walk with me to the backyard."

In the garden, the sweet scent of red roses reminded me of my mother. I sighed when the man said kindly, "I am Marzban, one of King Cyrus's advisors."

"It's nice to meet you, and thank you for attending my mother's funeral."

"His Majesty sent you his condolences…"

Wow! Even the young King heard of my mother's passing.

"How would you like to be the governess to our seven-year-old Princess Atossa?"

I could barely open my mouth. "How did the King know about my mother and me?"

A wide smile enwrapped his face. "His Majesty is very familiar with your mother, the only woman among the Wisemen at King Astyages's court."

Today, I found myself traveling alone. In those days, it was common for a woman to ride a long distance without a chaperone. I followed the road eastwardly and stopped at the stations when the sun was almost in the middle of the sky. I ate some flatbread and goat cheese from my sack, changed the tired horse to a fresh one, and kept going. I was excited, so I only stayed one night at a station and cut my trip from three days and two nights to a day and a half.

After I reached the Palace and rested, in the morning, I changed into my white robe and belt—as the only child, I took my mother's role as our religious leader after her death. When I entered the little Princess's chamber, I bowed and addressed her: "Princess Atossa."

"Do not call me 'Princess'!" She extended her hand to me. "I'm simply Atossa. And you are Lady Mithra, my mentor to light up my life with your wisdom."

"A sharp young lady!" I said with a grin.

She immediately asked, "Lady Mithra, how come your hair and eyes are not jet black like the rest of us?"

"Dear, I got my red hair and hazel eyes from my Median father."

There was no end to Atossa's curiosity. "Babylon is far away. Is it hard for you to leave your father and come here?"

After a pause, I uttered, "Harpagus still lives there. It's his hometown."

"Oh," she looked surprised, "where tyrant ruler, King Astyages, lives?"

Later that day, she and I witnessed Queen Cassandance presiding as a judge over the court's councilmen and women. She conducted the country's business affairs independently from her husband, King Cyrus.

On the wooden bench, sitting motionless beside me, little Atossa was enthralled by the goings on in the court as if etching every event in her head.

"What is the first dispute, Ashkan?" the Queen inquired.

Her simple wardrobe and absence of jewelry were notable despite her father's untold wealth and her husband, King Cyrus, a prince from both sides of his parents.

The young, handsome Ashkan, one of the Queen's assistants, replied, "Your Majesty," while signaling the two guards to enter.

They marched in, escorting a woman in a grubby robe, holding an infant to her bosom.

He continued, "This woman is from …"

Raising her right hand, the Queen interrupted him softly, "Let her tell us who she is and how she has found her way to us."

The woman rubbed away the dirt and sweat from her face. "I'm Areva, Your Majesty. And my daughter is Anahid." She swallowed hard. "I escaped the slavery of my master." Areva was trembling like a willow tree caught in a strong wind.

The Queen whispered to one of the ladies-in-waiting, "Go and hold the baby. The mother does not look very stable." She gestured to another one and said, "Cover her shoulders with a shawl. She must be freezing."

Once the baby was secured and her shivering quelled, the Queen addressed Areva, "Go ahead, sit down first before telling us what brought you here."

"Your Majesty," her voice was barely audible, "I come from the North, where masters do not pay us for our work."

The Queen's voice, with an underlying admiration

for Areva, was distinctive, "You must be a brave woman."

"Your Majesty, my master came to my room every night and forced himself on me." Areva's eyebrows knitted, and her wailing filled the entire Palace. She continued through tears, "When I gave birth to a girl, he threw my baby and me out of his mansion."

"How horrible for you." The Queen listened attentively when Areva continued, "The King and Your Highness' generosity are well-known all over my home country." She dried her eyes.

Atossa, clapping, turned to me. "She means my father, the King!"

"Yes," I whispered, "your father, our King, is truly a liberator, not an oppressor."

≥ ✲ ≤

While reflecting on my past life as the brave Lady Mithra, the present challenge of making robes appeared easy. The silk fabric, the same color as the sun, took my attention and warmed up my heart. My hands landed on the soft piece and pulled it up against my body from my neck to the ankles. It was too long for my height. So I had to cut the extra part. After stretching the measured silk on the table, I took the colossal shears and put the minor side under the fabric. To my amazement, the material slid from the edge as if the worms were alive. The only remedy was to hold it with one hand and not let it escape from the edge. I pushed the other side of the shears on it and moved it throughout the length. While gnawing under the shears,

I had to listen to the silkworms screaming in my head. *Gretch! ... Gretch!*

I did not remember what had happened in my head and kept working days and nights to free myself from the underground. Most of the time, I needed to remember to eat the food left behind the door. But, the dream of Persia, the Magical Land, carried me on. For sure, Mother Mithra and her daughter guided me through the process with no doubts.

However, I wouldn't say I liked cutting the measured piece into three pieces—two sleeves and one to cover my front and back. Each time I pressed the two parts of the shears together to cut, I wept inside. Still, to make myself beautiful and presentable to a possible lover, perhaps the King of Persia, enticed me. So I had to complete the process of separation one piece at a time.

While uniting the pieces together, piercing and putting silk and gold threads through their bodies, a soothing blanket enveloped me. To create a prairie with stones in the shapes of apples, pomegranates, and flowers like jasmine, gardenia, and white moon satisfied me to no end. Then, one more cutting for the top, large enough for my head with its long curly red hair to go through it. Finally, adding some rubies and jades around the neckline gave it even more of a royal look. It became a perfect cover for my bone-tired body.

A large part of the fabric in royal blue was still left when I looked around with weary eyes. In despair, I called on Daughter Mithra.

I saw myself sitting with Princess Atossa when one of the royal messengers entered and extended an invitation from the Queen for their family dinner on the same night. The opportunity to meet King Cyrus elated me.

When the King entered the room, I had difficulty controlling the loud thumping of my heart. *Incredible!* His sculpted muscles made him physically appealing. His entire chest had swelled outward—and there was a wily attractiveness about him. His jet-black mid-sized beard and mustache outlined his kind face. The sun had created a few wrinkles around his eyes, giving His Majesty, around thirty, a mature look needed for a leader.

His sharp eyes conveyed that he was a defender of Ahura Mazda, regardless of him not practicing my faith. He looked strong as a lion and gentle as a lamb. I bowed to him. "Your Majesty!"

His kind voice surprised me. "Do not bow to me. You are one of my family members. We are grateful to your parents. We are sorry for your mother's passing."

I bent my head slightly. "Your Majesty."

"Your father is still alive. We've learned through our undercover agents that Harpagus tries to smooth our path to Babylon."

While waiting for dinner to be served, the King put Princess Atossa on his knee. His callous knuckles shocked me. *The King's hands are like enslaved people... so unthinkable!*

My staring at his hands did not pass his eyes. He declared, "I still love farming, and during the harvesting, I help out some farmers. After all, I spent my first ten years running after goats and sheep." He smiled. When he turned to the Queen and whispered in her ear, the love he showed her melted my heart.

Soon the smell of lamb kabob and saffron filled the quaint room when we gathered at a round table. His Majesty turned to me. "Lady Mithra, since you've been here, Princess Atossa's behavior has changed for the better. So, how would you like to be the leader of Ahura Mazda in our court?"

"Your Majesty, it is my honor." I paused and mastered all my courage to ask, "Your Highness, may I seek a remedy for my confused mind?"

He beckoned me to speak further.

"Your Majesty, as we all know, you are a benevolent King and liberator. But why do we engage in any combat?"

King Cyrus beamed. "We go to war and conquer other countries to free the throngs who are under the ruler of tyrants calling themselves 'kings' and 'leaders.'"

"Your Majesty. Please forgive me," I ignored my pounding heart. "in the way of Ahura Mazda, killing is a sin."

"I am well aware of that." He placed a piece of meat from his plate onto the Queen's plate, grinned at her, and turned to me. "Tell me, how do you get rid of slave drivers without confronting them? Do you think disregarding the people's lamentation is the way of Ahura Mazda?"

I had no words. However, I did not doubt that Ahura Mazda sent King Cyrus to defend the oppressed people worldwide.

➤ ✴ ⋖

I opened my eyes, looked around the room, and understood I had to make a glorious robe to impress King Cyrus. So, despite exhaustion, I started a new robe for my imaginary lover who lived only in my dream. *A slave girl like me to meet a king one day? Impossible.*

This time, more cutting to do—five pieces, two for the front, one for the back, and two sleeves. The royal robe became authentic by attaching some leftover gems in the shape of an angel with opened wings—the same emblem I'd seen on Ormazd's cap. In addition, from the last long piece I had to cut from the bottom of my robe, I made a belt—the harmony of blue and yellow brightened my heart, like the sun and sky.

To my amazement, this time, the fabric slitting did not bother me as much as the first time; nor did the uniting of the pieces intimidate me. Instead, the beauty of the robes put the silkworms in the distant past.

I put mine on, carried the royal blue one on my arm, and looked around the room. It was messy no more.

In Cordelia's room, I could not help but laugh and turn around, showing off my creation.

In return, she could not take her eyes off me. Smiling, she said, "You look just like a princess. Did you use all the fabric?"

"Yes. Now the room is neat and clean." I showed her the royal blue cloak with a sun-color belt. She pointed to it. " It's regal. Who is this for?"

"For my whimsical lover—King Cyrus, perhaps," I

verbalized the secret in my heart without any apprehension.

Cordelia raised an eyebrow. "You do know that he died about 500 years ago."

After a pause, however, I ventured, "Can a slave girl wed a king?"

"Of course, if she is brave and strong enough to go after it."

"But, to a Persian king, soooo far out!"

"Go after what you want," Cordelia said with great pride, "and don't let the stones in your path block the way. Jump over, go around, or even through them. Stop at nothing until you're where you want to be."

Again a smile embraced her face when my exciting voice filled the room, "Do you mean I passed?"

She gave a benevolent smile. "Of course, my child. Go and rest for now."

While I stepped away, Cordelia called after me, "Remember, the silkworms paid the price with their life for you to have the luxurious robes."

I stopped and turned around. "The commoners believe our Emperor doesn't own any silk robe."

"He owns several, but he's forbidden to wear one when attending a formal ceremony." She then left some breathing space. "He isn't a king to show off his wealth by trumpeting his luxurious outfit." She rolled her eyes.

"So the folks won't think he has a lavish lifestyle. Very tricky."

CHAPTER 11

Rome

18 BCE

W hen I opened my eyes this morning, Cordelia stood before me, carrying a few white items over her arms. At first, I thought she wanted me to dress as the Persian religious leader. But the outfit consisted of baggy pants, a shirt, and a robe. Without a word, she gestured to me to change and left.

I yearned to run out; no locked door prevented me from escaping her place. I ran through some options in my head. No home to go to ... except living in the wilderness and sharing the beasts' food. Nowhere else was left for me. Perhaps when my mother wanted me to go to the East, she meant for me to be here. For sure, the Eastern star, *Vega*, guided me to Cordelia. Of that, I was confident.

In her hub, life was different for me. I wondered why she was adamant about me learning all the various lessons. I could never use any of them—an enslaved girl! No way, no how! To leave and live as a wanderer in the wilderness would always be a choice. I had the strength to survive wherever. But would life living with animals satisfy me?

After clothing myself with each piece, I had to fold the two sides of the torso-length shirt together and fasten them with the belt knotted in the front. Its long loose sleeves gave me the freedom to move my hands quickly. Despite not knowing why Cordelia wanted me to look like a man, I felt at ease in my new outfit.

Drowned in my thoughts, filled with confusion, wishing I could reach through time and give the blue robe I made to King Cyrus, suddenly, Cordelia appeared before me. Her words jarred my ears for the first time: "Today, you must learn some combat techniques."

"Remember!" My loud voice echoed in the open space. "I'm not Princess Atossa, with King Cyrus as my father. I'm only a slave girl, discarded from the Emperor's Palace."

She only confronted me with silence. Then, calmly, she gestured to follow her to a patio on a prairie. Like a sheep, I walked behind her.

The morning was balmy, a soft breeze touching my face and the pleasant sun warming my heart, when a short, muscular man turned around and faced me. His slanted eyes set deep in a round face were all signs of him being far from Rome. *An Easterner in the West—a long way from home.* His outfit was identical to mine, except his belt was black. With a friendly smile, a nod, and a hand gesture, he invited me to step into the middle of the rug covering the floor. He then bowed to me.

He must think I'm from a royal family.

Before I even could blink, with a swift move, he grabbed my shoulders and, with his feet, cut into my legs, destabilizing me. I lost my balance and fell flat onto the mat. I was flabbergasted. How can a man shorter than me knock me down?

Thinking of how I landed on the floor prevented me from getting up swiftly. The coach extended his hand and pulled me up. Then, to my surprise, he bowed to me again.

Over the next several months, becoming agile was the primary purpose. My teacher showed me how to use the right versus left or a significant outside move in a swift motion. I quickly used my right leg to unbalance him at one point. That gave me satisfaction beyond my belief—a girl overcoming a man. *Unbelievable!* At this time, I became as strong as a bull but agile as a cheetah.

One day, at the end of practice, or an *exam,* he handed me a black belt and wanted me to put it on. I could not believe my ears when in the Roman tongue, he said, "Now, you're a master too."

My mouth fell open. I couldn't believe he had made me think he could not speak.

He replied to my questioning expression about why he had never talked to me all these days. "Talking destroys concentration." He bowed with his palms together before his face and said, *"Namaste."*

He impressed me with his strength and was courteous to me—a slave girl. The same night, when I went to my room, a joyful feeling enveloped me through and through. But, an eternal question in my mind kept knocking on my head. When or how would I use all these skills as a woman in Rome? Cordelia did not need my assistance. Despite not confronting anyone else, no one else was here to need my help. Everything was always prepared for me. Recently, I felt some movements like a breeze or shadows passing by me. But, in reality, Cordelia was my only companion. All these confusing thoughts pounded through my head over and over.

At the end of the year, I had to learn sword fighting and how to attack and use a shield to protect my upper body. The thought of Cordelia's intention to make a soldier out of me and send me to battle the Persian forces hammered me. But, in this country, a woman could never have a chance to be a soldier.

My favorite drill was archery, different from the way I'd seen it in Rome. But first, I had to master riding a horse before learning how to shoot an arrow while riding. I had no idea why she wanted me to be like the riding-archery men in the Persian army. *Cordelia must think I'm a Persian girl or going to Persia—only in my dream!*

Being proud of my past life, as Mithra, annoyed me. My present time had nothing to do with my life as Thea. *Why does Cordelia continually train me as if I were a Persian girl?* I was baffled.

"You're so wrong, dear!" Cordelia's voice banged on my head. "If we choose, we can train our soul to dip into our past and use our past skills in our present life."

"As you know, I've done some. How can I continue seeing myself in the past?"

She led me to the stable, saying, "My child, whatever you do, concentrate, concentrate, and more concentration on that specific task." Then she stopped before a stallion. "This is yours."

I smiled broadly. "Hello dear, you're gorgeous."

Indeed, he was a unique white horse with patches of dark spots on his loins, hamstring, and left shoulders. I looked into his jet-black eyes only to find my special *friend*. He made me joyful beyond my wildest dreams.

Cordelia grinned. "What would you like to name him?"

Without thinking, I shouted, "Sattar!"

"Like Atossa's horse," Cordelia murmured. "Did you hear when she called her horse?"

I shook my head. "I've no idea when or how I learned this Persian name. Somehow it just popped into my head." After thinking for a moment, I said, "Maybe I read it on one of the piles of your papers."

Every day at dawn, I put on my simple soldier outfit—brown pants and a red jacket with heavy bull skin boots, then rushed out to the stable. Sattar neighing was music to my ears. After feeding him and giving him a couple of sugar cubes, I walked him with a rein around the same prairie where I took my combat lessons.

After a few days, I slowly mounted him when I felt his vibes were in tune with mine. But my calculation was wrong. As soon as he felt me on his back, he moved so harshly that I lost all control and fell. *I was too confident.* Hearing Cordelia's belly laughs added to my misery. But by bathing in the bull's blood every month, my body stayed strong, and I had no broken bones. Several times, I tried, not only on that day, but every day for over a week. Each time the result was the same. Finally, as Mithra did, I learned how to ride in my present life.

For several days, I rode Sattar while standing up. One day, I sat on his back. He moved and shook endlessly. I kept on holding to his rein. Then, at sunset, he accepted me as his master. Of course, by this time, I also ignored the pains and aches in my hips and thighs. Halfway through my riding practices, amazingly, they disappeared for good.

I began taking him out of the prairie into the woods for short rides. After several days, I managed to gallop for the day-long rides. And the click-clack of Sattar's hoofs became music to my ears.

So then I steered him faster and faster. Sometimes, even without any saddle, I held on to his long black and white mane while enjoying the wind blowing through my hair. The cool air on my cheeks made me feel as if I was free as a canary escaping to freedom.

When Cordelia witnessed my newfound skill in riding, she took me back to the prairie. While I was sitting on Sattar's back, she wanted me to stop before a colorful bull's-eye circle. I had already seen how the hunters used bows and arrows to aim at animals and kill them. But how to ride and shoot simultaneously was still a mystery. My thoughts were interrupted when a young rider approached me.

He reined in beside me. Without getting down

from his horse, he removed an arrow from his quill, set it in the needle, and held his right hand steady. While maintaining his breath, he kept the arrow firm and pulled his left hand to his back without turning his torso. In the next moment, he breathed out and released the arrow. It seemed so easy. *Not for me!*

Day after day, he demonstrated to me and, in return, wanted me to practice. At last, one day, I became a great archer while sitting on Sattar. Next, I had to mirror him in slow riding and shooting, then progressed to faster and faster in riding and shooting arrows simultaneously. Finally, one day, when I did better than he did, he said, "Now, you are even better than any Persian horse archer."

One night, after my *military* training, soothing music wooed me in. I entered and saw Cordelia playing the lyre. Her fingers moved through the thin strings like magic, producing a heavenly melody. I stood in awe and listened as if the strands were pulling my heart. In an instant, she looked up, stopped the music, and murmured, "Let's learn how to play the lyre for the pleasure of your soul. You must strengthen your body and soul together for a balanced life."

She believes in souls like Persians!

The magic lyre melody caused me to hear the trumpet sounds at King Cyrus's court. Princess Atossa rushed to my chamber and excitedly announced, "Lady Mithra, would you like to join our military force to battle the Babylonians?"

The possibility of meeting my father, Harpagus, excited me. "Of course, I would love that." The King sometimes took his family to the battle as a Persian custom. "Dear Atossa, you're still a child. Aren't you afraid of going to war?"

She laughed. "Lady Mithra, we're not going to the front. We ride behind the military forces. But, one day, when I get older, like my brother, Combys, I hope to go to the front with my father."

Before reaching the city, King Cyrus instructed the troops not to loot or destroy the temples. Amazingly, there was no resistance from the Babylonians. On the contrary, the magistrate openly welcomed the King and the Persians. After we rode through the city and witnessed the people's cheering, two Persian soldiers took me to my father's house.

When I entered, I saw a bald and blind man sitting on a thin mattress, but no sign of my father, the Median Commander-in-Chief. Instead, my eyes searched for a man as tall and robust as a juniper. I was about to ask where I could find Harpagus when the old man called me, "My Mithra, come to me and let me touch you."

His words shattered the image of my father in me. But I rushed to him, hugged him, and uttered, "Father, how did you know it was me?"

"I felt the warmth of your light." He swallowed. "Your steps sound just like your mother's."

I was delighted to spend a few days with him. "Father, King Cyrus told me you smoothed his way to conquer Babylon."

He nodded, and a wide grin showed his toothless

mouth. "Wished I was with the King when he went to the cave where the slave driver, Astyages, had prisoned a huge number of Jews." He looked at the space as if he were with the King. "King Cyrus went to each cell and broke the chains from every individual." Harpagus' excitement reached the sky like a young man. "I even heard the Jews called King Cyrus *Messiah*." Father reached for my hand and, holding it, said, "My dear, now my life is complete."

"Father, you've made Mother in heaven and me on earth proud."

"Dear Mithra, your mother was right. I chose Ahriman over Ahura Maza. Darkness over Light. You and her living far away from me devastated me."

"Father, you've made up for your past sin by paving the way for King Cyrus to liberate the enslaved Median nation."

"His Majesty," my father's joy had no end, "King Cyrus even gave them back their sacred vessels and a considerable sum of coins and gold from the Persian treasury to build their temple in Jerusalem." After a pause, he exclaimed, "King Cyrus must be an angel sent to us by Ahura Mazda. His task is to cleanse our land from the tyrant Astyages and other authoritarians."

Suddenly, I saw my father's chest go up and down rapidly. I helped him to lie down. When the sun dipped into the horizon, his life also went with it.

≥ ✲ ≤

"Thea, your smile shows you must be delighted with my music." Cordelia's voice brought me back to her, and she had stopped playing. After pulling the soft blanket over my shoulder in bed that night, I closed my eyes, desiring to return and stay forever in Persia during King Cyrus's time.

CHAPTER 12

Rome

16 BCE

C ordelia's clapping woke me up. "Get up! Get up, Thea! It's time to go."

I refused to open my eyes and urged her to leave me alone. I wanted to stay in the past as Mithra during King Cyrus's time.

Cordelia, ambivalent to the new sprouting love within me, pulled the soft blanket away. She had to have a new task or lesson for me. But I could imagine nothing else for me to do. With my eyes half open, I beseeched her. "*P l e a s e!* For only today, Could you leave me alone?"

She shook her head. As usual, she had no response. I read, however, in her piercing eyes: *Not today!*

"After these four years that I've been with you," I implored, "today, I'm pleading with you to give me one day to myself."

She moved her hand in disagreement and gestured

for me to get up. "Today, you must return to your mother at once."

"How come?" I rubbed my eyes. "She left me and didn't want me ever return to the palace."

"She isn't well and wishes to see you."

"Do I come back here after visiting her?"

Cordelia shrugged.

I started to look for my lyre and pack a bag when she murmured, "Your stuff and Sattar are ready for your departure." *Sattar, my companion from Turkmenistan, Persia! He's my token of the majestic land!*

Cordelia stood before me, holding the shirt, jacket, and pants I made from the Kashmir wool after shearing a few Kasmir goats. She had brought them for me to learn how to produce yarns and knit to make a shirt or shawl.

The winter was upon us, so in a rush, I wore them. Then I pulled on my shoes. She also supervised me on how to put them together out of shredded sagebrush bark. Finally, with wide-open eyes, I asked, "Why don't I wear the leather boots? They're the result of my toiling."

Her lower lip covered the top, and her right eyebrow moved up. "What are you talking about?"

"The ones out of the bull skin you killed for me."

"They're in your bag. You'll need them for your future." Then, staring at me as if she could sense my hesitation, she said, "It's okay. Now ... do not make the guard wait for you any longer."

I smirked. "Would Empress get angry if she sees me at the palace?"

Cordelia turned a deaf ear to me as usual.

I climbed onto Sattar with my head up and a heavy

heart to set out to my mother's hut. For a last sight of Cordelia, I turned around. She released a white dove. *Is she letting me go for good?*

On the way, thinking of Cordelia made me very thankful. She taught me all the trades and created a brave and strong woman out of me. For some reason, Cordelia was eager to teach me both worlds—men and women. I kept wondering why. Today, my time in her cocoon was over.

No longer would I choke to death like those silkworms. *Now I can become a colorful butterfly.*

Upon my arrival, the guard led me to the room next to the Empress' chamber. Before I could even form words, he opened the door. *Unbelievable!* Since my mother abided by her rule, the Empress had advanced her to be one of the maids-in-waiting. As a shell in bed, her pale face worried me. However, to see a slave girl watching over her was comforting.

"Mama, what's wrong?" I sat on the edge of the bed and took her hand. It felt like holding a skeleton's hand. There was a long pause between her breaths.

"My dear Thea ... you look beautiful ... love your red hair." She went to touch my curls, but her hand failed to reach any. "I was praying to see you soon."

"I'm here, Mama, to take you out of this dreadful palace." From her look, I could tell she was struggling to breathe.

Her weak voice interrupted my thoughts, "I've prayed to Asclepius ... to keep me alive ... until I see you again."

My mother is such a believer. She thinks Asclepius, the god of healing, has visited her.

"But ..." Tamara's breathing slowed down, "he told me I'd go to Haydes ... after I see you."

Through tears, I said, "I came to take you with me ..." I finished my thought without any words. *We've had enough of the palace!*

In return, she said with a slight hand movement, "Right now, go ..."

The slave girl finished Tamara's words. "Our Lord, Caesar Augustus, summons you."

I turned a deaf ear, hugged Tamara, and caressed her hair. "I'm with ..." Before I could finish, her breathing stopped, and her eyes went lifeless. Through my wailing, the girl's voice banged on my ear, "Lady Thea, Caesar requests your presence at once."

I had to tear myself away from my mother. The girl pulled the sheet up and covered her lifeless face.

Doesn't a leader allow his slaves to mourn in peace? I had no choice except to drag myself behind the guard to the Emperor's palace.

Before entering, I paused to calm my confusion about Caesar sending for me.

When the guard presented me to Caesar Augustus, I stood by the door motionless. He had his back to me, looking through the only large window, getting attacked by the harsh raindrops. Then, as if he heard my loud breathing, he turned and dismissed the guard. No wrinkles crowded his face yet, and his short curly hair, chestnut in color, and bright green eyes baffled me. The snow-white linen toga draping over his shoulder embroidered around the sleeves and in the front in dark purple attested to his highest authority.

But then, I heard his firm yet friendly voice. "Come, Thea Mousa. Sit by me."

He sat at the giant marble table and showed me a chair near his left. Reluctantly, I obeyed.

He uttered, "Thea. Listen carefully." He poured wine from the decanter into the goblet and continued looking into my eyes. "I've chosen you for an important mission."

He wetted his lips with a sip. "A negotiation between the Persians and us is in progress." He paused and stared at me. "To exchange King Farshads' son, whom we're keeping as a hostage, with the Roman Flag and Golden Eagle. Persians have kept them since Julius Caesar's time."

The Persians possess our national identity—the Flag and Golden Eagle! I screamed in my head.

He continued, "As a friendly gesture, I'm also sending you to the Persian King with the Prince."

With many questions dancing in my head, I knew the protocol. I was not allowed to interrupt Caesar. He read the bewilderment in my eyes and said kindly, "You're a special daughter to us ..."

Did I hear him correctly? Is it possible? Nay! I pressed my lips together.

"So we're sending you as a *gift* to the Persian King in a gesture of good faith." He reached for the giant silver bowl in the middle of the table and grabbed a handful of grapes.

Without paying attention to him, my eyes were stuck on the Emperor's hair color—just like mine. A wild idea knocked on my head. *Could he be my father?*

He, however, was blind to what I was seeing. While

eating the grapes, Augustus' voice came to focus. "Use the skills you mastered at Cordelia's to be our eyes and ears in the Persian Court." He wiped his hand with a napkin.

"Yes, my Lord ..." I swallowed the knot of hesitation.

"We have confidence in you." He rose and paced the room.

Before I asked when I would leave Rome, he uttered, "One of our special guards is ready to look after you during this long journey. Commencing immediately."

Wow! My wish of going to Persia is coming true so fast! The gods must have heard me!

I mustered all Mithra's boldness in me. "My Lord, may I present a suggestion?"

"Of course. What is it?"

"I would like to travel by myself."

My overture shocked him. His eyes became wider and wider. "What? Even without any guards?"

"Yes, my Lord!" I took a deep bow as I'd seen in the Persian courts.

I hope he does not ask me where I learned to bow like a Persian.

"How do you know the practice of treating a king?"

"Cordelia is a fabulous teacher."

"Are you sure? You do know ... Persia is not the next land to us." He grinned. "However, they're trying very hard to conquer us."

I nodded in agreement, dried my forehead with a handkerchief, and said with ease, "Yes, My Lord! I know all the dangers lying ahead of me. I'll take the Silk Route."

"It looks like you're knowledgeable of your path," he

said, impressed. Caesar Augustus picked up a letter with his seal and gave it to me. "I want you to go directly to Tysfoon, the capital. Give this letter to the Persian King—King Farshad. This message is for his eyes only."

"I assure you, my Lord, that I will protect this as if it is my own life." Then, I hid it in my bosom, ignored his smirk, took a deep breath, and said, "My Lord, please stop any negotiation with the Persian King and leave it to me to do so." I felt bold.

His eyes pierced me. "Are you sure that you can do a man's job?"

"Yes, My Lord. Also, may I ask permission to stay for my mother's burial? Unfortunately, she died this morning."

The Caesar's demeanor suddenly changed. He shook his head, blind to my storm within, and exclaimed, "This is a crucial task I am leaving you with." He finished his wine. "We can't possibly waste any more time, Thea. The same guard will accompany you to the Roman border." He then left the room hurriedly, and his footsteps jarred my ears.

Yes, our roads are less safe than the Persians. As a Roman woman, I can't possibly travel by myself, in contrast to the Persian girls.

Without having time to see Tamara's body or say goodbye, I mounted Sattar, blind to the warmth of the tears covering my cheeks. I galloped away as fast as I could.

When we stopped to rest, the guard riding behind came to give me some water, grapes, and olives. "Lady Thea, I'm Linus, and remember you well."

"Do you?" I welcomed the conversation to separate

my mind from my mother's death. So, I invited him to sit beside me on the rocky ground.

At my side, Linus uttered, "Yes, I was one of the guards who chased you. Each time I had to leave you, a little girl, in the dungeon hurt me so much."

"That wasn't the right punishment for a little kid, was it?"

While looking at the ground, he continued, "But, I'm a coward not to stand up and disobey the higher-ranking order."

"The rulers have the heart of stone, except one."

"Who is that, Lady Thea?"

"King Cyrus."

"Who is he?"

"He was a Persian King over so many years ago."

"How do you know him, My Lady?" His eyes were getting bigger by the minute.

"I used to live before and during his time." I looked into the space as if *King Cyrus stood before me.*

"What?" Linus looked at me quizzically. "Your words do not make any sense."

I had no explanation for him.

"Without any of our rulers, we won't survive," Linus stated as a matter of fact.

"You're right, Linus. They train us to be dependent on them. The rulers pound our heads like slices of raw meat," I sipped some water, "shaping us the way they wanted us to be. So very sad."

"Lady Thea, you're right. I can do nothing except listen to commands and follow them."

I agreed, and he returned to his horse, saying, "That's all I can do, nothing else."

I recalled how horrible life was when Cordelia wanted me to learn a new skill and become a master at it. "As much as it's tremendously difficult to learn a new task," I breathed out, "it gives us a sense of accomplishment."

The cold wind on my face put me at ease. Leaving Caesar Augustus' Palace gave me freedom, regardless of what I faced during my journey. I wished Sattar was a unicorn to fly me to Persia. *But, of course, nothing happens in an instant.* However, I welcomed and admired the Emperor for giving me such an essential duty without knowing my longing to journey to Persia.

On the way, I worked out the road map in my head. The best way was to reach Alexandria, a city south of the Mediterranean Sea in Egypt. During Alexander's reign, he used the Persian wealth and built the beach city, helping trade between the East and West.

In my mind's-eye, all the walls and borders melted, and I saw myself standing before the Persepolis Palace three hundred years after King Cyrus's death. The statues of gold lions with wings on each enormous column overlooking fields of wheat and sycamore trees, trumpeted the glorious Persian time, loud and clear to friends and foes. Life could not be any better. Our ancestors fought numerous wars and created a marvelous society for us to enjoy years of prosperity and happiness. As a result, our Empire was glowing in the world like a gem. Our number one enemy, the Greeks, were mesmerized by this jewel, dreaming of its possession.

As Mithra, I was blood-related to Ormazd and Amaya and first Mother Mithra, the Wise woman at the Astyages' court. These days, I was in charge of the main temple in midtown after my father's death. Every day, I, as Reverend Mithra, put on the white priesthood robe and arranged my long wavy hair woven into one braid down my back.

"Dear Mithra!" I heard my husband, Kaveh's calm voice. "I'm summoned to deliver an urgent message to the Anatole satrap." He was already in his riding uniform, dark trousers, white undershirt, and brown tunic. The gold emblem of a king with two wings stretching out was a sign of him being one of the royal messengers.

"What's going on?" I gasped. "Suddenly, the King is sending you to our border with Greece."

Standing still, he said, "A Greek leader, Alexander III of Macedonia, ventured beyond his border, infringed on the Persians' territory, and subjugated one of our cities."

"What?" I had to dismiss Alexander as a threat. "He can't possibly battle the Persian forces for long."

He nodded and, without any more words, kissed me on my lips and rushed out.

Soon, the talk of the town was to rest assured. The mighty Persian King was decisive in caring for this Western intruder in no time. But, then, we learned His Majesty did not even bother to lead the Persian forces—the navy and army. Instead, he left the task to the regional satraps and governors to deal with the Greek leader—*the Kid*.

For several months, no news from Kaveh worried

me to no end. At last, one day, he returned with a weary face. After removing his jacket in silence, I guided him to a chair. Like a madman, he suddenly slapped his face and mumbled through his teeth, "I just delivered some eye-opening news to the King." He got up and started pacing the floor.

My patience boiled over, and the words jumped out of my mouth, "Tell me, dear Kaveh," I failed to hide my anxiety, "what's happening to our beloved land?"

He stopped and sat down without touching the hot black tea. The loud background noise of our ten-year-old daughter, Delbar, and her brother, Amir, two years younger, quieted. They knew when their father arrived home to keep their noise to a minimum, leaving room for Kaveh and me to converse.

"After Alexander defeated part of our forces," Kaveh's angry voice broke the stillness, "and occupied the region," Kaveh hit his cheeks, "King Darius III sent him a peace offering—some jewelry and gold coins." He took a deep breath. "Proposing to Alexander, take the gift and return to your country."

I kept my lips closed, afraid to hear Alexander's reaction.

Kaveh continued even louder, "Our King knows the Greeks aren't as rich as us." He swallowed hard as if trying to get a hold of his anger. "The King had hoped the chest of gold and precious gems would make Alexander's mouth water." He paused.

"Based on what we're hearing, Alexander is still advancing into our territories," I uttered.

With a smirk, he replied, "Even our King, much older and wiser than young Alexander, thought he

would grab the offering and run away to his hole."
Shaking his head and hitting his forehead again, Kaveh
continued, "Instead, Alexander kept everything and
attacked our cities one after another."

"Lady Thea? Time to go." The guard's voice
interrupted my daydream.

It was over a month since Linus and I left Rome.
When we reached the outskirts of Sicily, the last point
of land before crossing the Mediterranean Sea, Linus
wished me farewell in my distant journey. Sattar and I
were amused by the mystifying horizon ahead of us.

CHAPTER 13

Sicily

L ate at night, Sattar and I embarked on a raft to the fishermen's village in Sicily. The life path became like a fork before me. My confused mind did not leave me alone. I urged myself to get lost and not to continue as a woman *gifted* from Caesar Augustus to the Persian King. Why didn't he send one of the Princesses if this was an important task? A voice within kept nagging me to forget the West or the East and jump into the deep Sea. To leave Sattar, however, did not seem a sound decision. But then, this was the chance of a lifetime to see Persia, where I was born as Mithra. *How could I throw it all out?* To repeat the city's name, Alexandria, my destiny after Sicily, transported me to Persia during Alexander's invasion.

An unending thunderstorm and lightning kept Delbar, Amir, and I awakened. It had been several months, and I had yet to hear from Kaveh. It was late at night when the children fell asleep. My worries about my homeland were challenging to settle. For me, ignoring the remarks on the street was impossible. *The Greek Boy is asking His Majesty for an unprecedented punishment.* A knock on the door alerted me. After opening it, Kaveh standing in his soaking-wet uniform, mumbled, "Hello, my dear Mithra."

His shiny dark eyes were dimmed, and he looked much slimmer. "Dear, are you all right?"

After stepping inside, he took off his jacket and boots. "I wish ..." He sat in front of the holy fire with his head down.

"What's wrong?"

In a shaky voice, he said, "Now Babylon is under the thumb of Alexander's forces."

"Where's His Majesty?"

"I'm ashamed to serve such a coward King."

"His Majesty left Persepolis for Babylon a few months ago."

"Yes, he was in Babylon!" Kaveh's piercing eyes frightened me when he continued, "At last, the King confronted the Greek army like a mouse facing the cat. Instead of attacking, he turned his chariot around and fled the battleground."

I had all intention of keeping my cool. "Did you see anyone approach him before he took off?"

Kaveh looked afar. "Yes, I was close enough to see the Chief Commander with a few soldiers approaching him and murmuring something in the

King's ear. After a moment, the three soldiers escorted His Majesty opposite to Babylon toward the east."

"His Majesty and Alexander are both new rulers ..."

"But, our King must be in his middle age, not a young boy like Alexander."

"Yes." I swallowed hard and continued, "the commander asked the King to leave?"

"To think of it, you're right." He paused. "If memory serves me well, this is the King's first war."

"King Darius doesn't have a son as his successor yet. So, if something happened to him, our Empire would be in disarray."

As if he did not hear me, like a volcano, Kaveh spewed the words of agony, "When the King escaped the battlefield, the soldiers also ran the opposite way of Alexander's forces..." he slammed his cheek and cried out, "So, our second Capital stayed defenseless and also fell into the Greek's forces."

I could barely open my mouth and speak. "Do we know when Alexander will stop devouring our land?"

Kaveh shook his head. "No! Like a pitbull, he doesn't let go. Right after Babylon, he and his soldiers attacked Susa, our first Capital. He rode through it without resistance. Its Satrap shook hands with Alexander and let him and his forces enter the city."

I felt a trembling take over my body. At the same time, wiping my tears to imagine what could happen to our second capital and my ancestors' hometown. Kaveh's words pounded me, "As we speak, Alexander and his hordes are on their way to Persepolis!"

Horrified, not wanting to witness what could occur in Persepolis, I opened my eyes to the sound of a few men's conversations. The raft had stopped, and the men were disembarking in a hurry. Sattar and I were the last ones stepping onto Sicily, my first unknown land.

The village was the spot for cargo ships—a port connecting Rome to Alexandria and the Silk Route. They would dock here to unload and load their merchandise. I had hoped to convince one of the shipmasters to let Sattar and me board his ship on the way back to Alexandria.

After taking the rein, I took my bone-tired body with my four-legged friend and dragged him toward the only light in the village. The men's belly laughing sounded like a group of drunkards. Before entering the tavern, I wrapped the rein around a nearby colossal tree and entered.

The place was quite hot. My arms and body started itching. I still wore the original Kashmir outfit since I left Cordelia's home. In addition, I had hidden my long curly hair under a cap covering most of my forehead. No one paid attention to the newcomer among ten or twelve tipsy men. Then, at one glance, my gut feelings picked the least sweaty and quietest man. So, after hunching not to flag the attention of anyone, I quietly slid onto the bench next to him. He said under his breath, "Beer or wine?"

I murmured, "Wine."

"Where are you going?"

In a resounding voice, I said as much as a man could, "Alexandria."

As if my response shocked him, he turned and

looked at my face. "Lad, why so far?" He did not even take a breath. "Are you traveling for a long time?" He turned his torso away and mumbled, "You stink."

I moved my head in agreement when he gestured to a cheerful woman in a fisherman's net robe. She glided in my direction. On a closer look, underneath, she had one piece of cloth wrapped around her breasts and one around the waist, matching her robe in sea color. Then, while pouring wine, she whispered, "Hey, boy. I'm available if you want to learn some movements in bed."

I hope no one notices my red face.

For a while, my mind took me to Neptune, the god of water, and his wife, Salacia, bringing me to the god of wine, Bacchus. I took delight in thinking. *This tavern very well can be their gathering.* For sure, I was in my fantasy world. But then, the man broke into my thoughts, "I'm Albina. Who are you?"

After I had a sip, I put the goblet down and paused.

He ignored me and continued. "One just left a few days ago. We won't expect to see another one for a long time." He then looked at me with pity. "Do you have any place to stay?"

I shook my head while drying the sweat from my forehead and wiping my mouth with the stingy sleeve. "I have a horse, too."

"It's easier to sell your horse here and get many coins. They're lighter to travel with." A huge smile covered Albina's face from ear to ear.

As if he were a thief, I hollered, "He's my friend! No way anyone can separate him from me." Imitating a man, I tapped my chest.

Instantly, the crowd became quiet. *One woman pretending to be a man, an eye-sore!* I read in their eyes.

"Sit down!" Albina pulled down on my sleeve and forced me to take my seat while instructing, "Let's get out before they attack you."

We rushed outside. At the sight of Sattar, he whispered, "Handsome stallion. No wonder you refuse to sell him."

Albina took us to a courtyard. As a master of fishermen, no doors were locked to him. After opening the gate, he took the rein from me at the open-space stable and led Sattar to a few other horses. "Now that the weather is not too cold, we let them be out under the sky."

When I insisted on sleeping beside Sattar on the grass, Albina stood firm on taking me home to his wife. "We've no idea when the next boat arrives ... maybe weeks or even months."

While walking next to him, he mentioned, "No human sleeps with an animal."

I countered, "To my eyes, Sattar isn't an animal. He is my partner and friend." Then, with hesitation, I left him behind and, with Albina, walked toward the house on the highest hill.

He and his wife, Helen, had no children, even though they had been married for a long time. On the way, he pointed to a massive boat with its shiny wooden red hull and all the nets hanging under a tower. "This is my boat, ready to go to the Sea, day or night."

Outside his house's slim blue entrance door were several clay pots in different shapes, like soldiers on guard against the wall. The planted shrubs and colorful flowers in their fat bellies signaled in receipt of undivided attention.

As soon as he opened the door, the small circle of the community room made me think they believed in the god of Aion. *He is the god that moves time as a circle, not as a straight line.*

A low round table with four chairs around it, accompanying a freshly made bed covered with snow-white linen, wooed my body. Losing control of my sack when it slid out of my hand reminded me that I'd been on the road for almost two months, hardly eating or sleeping. But then, the sound of my body hitting the bare floor was all I heard.

I woke up from the sun's warmth and a soft woman's touch on my head. It had to be Helen, Albina's wife. Her blonde hair and blue eyes came into my focus. In Greek, she said, "What's your name?"

When I hesitated to answer, she asked, "Do you understand me?"

I nodded. "I'm Thea."

"A Roman girl. Hard to tell." Right away, she took me outside to a place surrounded by a short wall with one opening. After washing my filthy body in the shallow river, she gave me a thick cotton robe, brown like hers.

I could not wait to check on Sattar, worried a thief might've stolen him. Helen, however, convinced me, "Your horse is fine. I checked on him this morning. We'll go after you eat."

The fried fish, freshly baked wheat bread, and some green olives tasted so delicious that I finished every morsel. Afterward, I rushed to Sattar, who showed his happiness with a neigh. The beauty of the open stable was that every horse could reach and eat from the fresh plants and bushes around them. No one needed to feed them.

Every day, before sunrise, Albina went fishing with a helper. Meanwhile, Helen and I strolled around the village market. She exchanged the fish in the basket with their vegetables, fruits, and flour. Back home, we waited for Albina to bring us fresh fish for dinner. However, sometimes, he had to stay out all night to catch even more fish when we needed wheat, beans, and olives.

Albina and Helen were shocked when they heard me say, "Albina, I would love to come with you fishing upon regaining my strength."

He dropped his mouthful of fish on the tin plate and jumped up. As he left the house, he yelled, "A woman wants to fish. No way!"

Helen was shocked, too but kept quiet for a long time, watching me with her horrified eyes. At last, she murmured, "Dear Thea, can you do a man's job?"

"Of course!" My firm voice echoed in the room. "What's the difference between them and us?"

Helen looked at the floor and had no response. But then, she looked up and stared at me. The line between her eyebrows became deeper. "No woman has gone fishing before, though."

I was shocked at how hard it was for Romans to understand that women could do everything a man could. Of course, with proper training. I stepped into the past.

≥ ✼ ≤

I saw myself as Mithra with my younger sister, Shirdokht. She was fencing with the neighborhood boys. But, as the oldest child, I practiced the three religious essentials: *Good Thoughts, Good Words,* and *Good Deeds.* To be the spiritual leader after my father pleased me to no end. "There is no difference between a boy and a girl." I heard him say over and over.

At age 18, Shirdokht came to me. We were at my house with Delbar and Amir. Kaveh was gone to deliver his message to one of the Satraps, warning him of Alexander's attacks.

I watched her put on her uniform—a long-sleeved tunic studded with precious stones. I said when she went to put on the golden necklace, a token showing she belonged to the Immortal Unit soldiers, "Wow, Sis! I'm so proud of you for being part of the elite corps of the imperial army."

She looked in the mirror to ensure her uniform was all in order.

"Dear, are you sure the military is the calling in your life?"

She turned to me. "What do you mean?"

"Don't you yearn to marry and become a mother? Not that there's anything wrong with being single."

"Of course," she responded casually, "perhaps, one day ... as soon as we defeat and chase Alexander and his military forces out of our land. Then I can marry and have many children. But not now."

"Dear, in a battle, we must kill or be killed." I

swallowed. "Why do you want to be part of it?"

Shirdokht moved her head in agreement. "Sorry, Mithra, but this isn't the time for us to close our eyes to Alexander's invasion and ignore his threat to our land."

Before I could reply, her firm voice broke in, "If Alexander attacks Persepolis, I'll be ready to take him down with all my mighty force." She made a fist, brought it close, and squeezed it in my face while exclaiming with bravado, "I'll fight a good fight."

"But, dear, aren't you afraid to lose your life?"

She burst out loud laughing. "Mithra, if it weren't for our brave men and women fighters, people like you couldn't sit back safely and only think about the spiritual life."

"I appreciate our brave men keeping Alexander in the distance as long as possible. But, there is a job for every woman to give birth and ensure the human race will never perish."

Before I could utter any other words, Shirdokht darted a bold glance at me over her shoulder and rushed out.

A roar of hoofs galloping through the streets of Persepolis rang in my ears. It was a month after Shirdokht had gone. I rushed to gather Delbar and Amir. Then we stepped outside.

Watching Greek cavalry in their bronze armor at dusk hurt my eyes. The town butchers with bloody aprons and knives in hand, bakers covered from head to toe in baking flour, farmers, stone cutters, and carpenters joined in to watch how an enemy was looting and destroying our land. I understood when the Western aggressors took over our beloved Persepolis, covering it with a blanket of darkness. *This is how the West meets the East!*

Suddenly, a young rider in his full armor and helmet with a red cape surrounded by a few soldiers cantered toward the Palace. Delbar pointed to him and shouted, "Mom, he must be their leader."

"To grab the wealth of our Empire!" an old man called out.

"Where is our King?" an old woman wailed.

When no foreign soldier was in sight, I saw Kaveh walking toward us in a disheveled outfit. His jet-black hair had turned white. I ran and embraced him. "Dear Kaveh, how are you? Any news of our King?"

He remained quiet as if trying to swallow a massive knot in his throat. His quivering lips worried me. I murmured in his ear, "What's the matter, dear?"

"My Mithra, I have to tell you something ... but don't know how ..."

"What is it? Is our Majesty dead?"

"No, but much worse." He sighed deeply while holding me tight. "Shirdokht ..."

"Is she all right?" I held my tongue and kept hoping for good news, but my inside voice told me differently. I barely heard Kaveh say, "She's ... dead."

I hung on to him to avoid falling and said through tears, "Shirdokht's braver than our King, lost her life defending our country."

He caressed my hair. "Your sister, the last courageous soldier standing, protected the Gate of All Nations. This brave sister fought against more than ten Greek soldiers."

Through my tears, I asked. "Where is her body?"

Then without even waiting for an answer, I started walking.

When I saw the gold emblem of a lion with a bull's flank in his mouth, I knew I had reached the Persepolis gate. The blood of Persians and Greeks had soaked the parched land. From far away, her gold necklace announced her body. "She's dead, and no one ever knows," I murmured. Yet another soldier replaced her to keep the unit at one thousand. *No wonder it's called Immortal Unit.* I ran, sat, and held her lifeless head on my lap. Only then I realized I was holding onto an empty shell. When I looked up, and saw shining stars glimmering; among them, one star closest to the moon was the brightest.

"Shirdokht battled courageously," Kaveh's voice brought me to him, "until her last breath, defending the Persian Gate." His warm touch made me feel peaceful.

"Much braver than our King," I muttered.

≥ ✹ ≤

"Dear Thea, why are you crying?" Helen implored.

I shrugged and wiped my tears.

After a few days, Albina softened under the fire of my tenacity. Finally, he agreed to take me as his assistant the next day.

The following day, I found two rags; with one, I covered my breasts, and with the other, I wrapped it around my waist like the other fishermen. Then I waited at his boat. On that day, he wanted me only to watch him.

He was skillful in aiming and throwing the spear to

stop a fish or stick a trident into an octopus or eel's body. But in casting out the vast net, he needed my help.

Only a short time after, Albina let me have my boat. On the first day, I caught a strange-looking eel, much longer than a ladle but more grandiose than a usual eel. Nevertheless, its blue radiating body looked majestic.

"Neptune had to choose you for catching such a special creature," Albina said excitedly. "From tomorrow, I'll give you a bigger boat and send some of my fishermen to follow you so they can be as fortunate as you."

"And Thea brought us luck too." Helen grinned.

The villagers gathered when I played my lyre that night. We sang, danced, and drank. But, standing alone behind the circled crowds, a girl leaned against the stable gate and never participated in our celebration. And no villagers talked with her or invited her to join our festivity as if she were invisible to all but me. She kept gazing at me with daunting eyes. Like a sun under dark clouds, her round blank face had no shine. Part of her wavy dark hair was out of the blue cap, and the rest was stretched down to the shoulders. *She must be from somewhere else.*

At one point, I stepped toward her without drawing anyone's attention. She could speak no Roman, but she said under her breath in Greek, "My name is Gigi. I am a gypsy."

"Where is the rest of your group?"

As if she read in my eyes my urgent feeling that I was a friend, not a foe, she kept talking, "Somehow, my heart tells me I can trust you." Finally, she whispered,

"I crawled out of the last cargo ship while it was anchored here."

"From Alexandria?"

She nodded. "I'm starving, hiding under the hay, surviving on the animal's food."

No wonder, since Sattar and other horses were moved to the regular stable, he was gobbling everything I cupped in my hand. I felt sorry for her and agreed to secretly take some fish to her if she promised to keep an eye on my horse.

Holy beholds! As if the gods knew I had to feed another mouth. Every day, not only a school of fish turning, twisting, and forming a circle in the water around me, but a shoal of sea creatures also gathered and competed in jumping into the boat. There was always plenty of fish for Helen's exchange with the farmers' goods, so they never knew some cooked fish were missing. Once in a while, Helen mentioned, "Dear Thea, since you work like a man, you start eating like a man, too."

My smile was the only answer for her.

CHAPTER 14

My days went by quickly. I spent them fishing from sunrise to sunset, and thoughts of Mithra's life never left me after Alexander's conquest of the Persian Empire. One night I had a dream ...

Delbar and Amir were sleeping, but my eyes were empty of any sleep. Suddenly, the banging on the door shook me. I picked up a small, dimly lit lantern and crossed the hall, where I opened the door to a royal messenger. His loud voice put a lid on my utmost worries about the fate of the Persian Empire. "Lady Mithra, Princess Roxana summons you at once."

After braiding my long hair in the back, I put on my fresh white robe and rushed to the Palace. On my way to the Princess's chamber, I had to calm my disappointment. Princess Roxana and other royal women made peace with our enemy, Alexander. Instead of the uprising against him, they all crawled deep into the Palace like worms. The royal families were ignorant of how my sister, Shirdokht, and other soldiers paid with their lives to defend our land. But, the princesses, lower than any animal in the jungle who safeguards his den, welcomed our enemy.

My footsteps, bouncing off the walls decorated with friezes in the muted hall, jarred my ears. And the tapestries interwoven with gold and silver threads blinded me.

"Reverend Mithra," the Princess, fixed up with blinking jewelry, shamelessly ordered, "I want you to marry me to Alexander."

Her words shook my core. "Our number one nemesis, Your Highness?"

Roxana moved her head in affirmation. "Very likely, the nuptial is the only way to bring peace to the two countries."

I let silence fill the chamber for a while. But soon, she questioned me, "What do you say?"

In a firm voice, I exclaimed, "Your Highness. Alexander believes in many gods, not One as we do."

With a smirk, she commanded me, "Convert Alexander before the ceremony."

I was bewildered, not believing my ears. *The Princess dances like a monkey to any tune Alexander plays.* At last, I spoke up, "In our religion, Your Highness," I paused, "it is not allowed."

"Who cares?" She got up and fluffed her colorful silk dress. "With your approval or without it, the marriage will happen," she sneered. "Then my father, the King of Persia, will return, and Alexander, as his son-in-law, will be my father's successor."

The Royal women had put shame on all of us. Like her father, Roxana, the daughter of the King, found an easy way out. With my head down, maintaining silence, her order exasperated me.

"Will you marry us, or..."

I bowed and, without waiting for her dismissal, left the Palace.

At sunrise, in the street, the people's jargon pounded my head. "Alexander wedded Princess Roxana, sealing the unification between the East and West. Hurray! Hurray!"

> ❧ ✻ ❧

When I opened my eyes, I wondered whether the sound of Persians or the hustle and bustle of the Sea landed on the verandah—my sleeping place. For an instant, I thought we had a storm and closed my eyes. Rest assured; we wouldn't be fishing that day. But, the noise was not the Sea's, but men's mumbo-jumbo.

I stood up. In the light of dawn, squinting my eyes, I saw the sight of a Tall Ship with some men disembarking and running toward the land, which excited me to no end.

To continue my dream journey to Persia is within my grasp!

It had to be about six months ago when the cargo ship had left Alexandria. Indeed, the vessel delivered silkworm cocoons from China, spices from India, and expensive wine produced in the Persepolis vicinities. Some horses, famous for their speed and agility, came from Turkmenistan, Sattar's homeland, presently under the satrap abiding the Persian King. The goods had to stay on the ship until the Roman merchants arrived from Rome to Sicily, about another two to three months.

While waiting for the traders to bring the goods, I have yet to have a chance to talk to or even meet the shipmaster, Marcus. After a day of fishing, he and Albina went to the Tavern where men bonded, with no place for any woman to interfere. Each time I asked him whether he had a chance to relay my desire to sail with them, Albina answered, "Wait, my child. No rush." Then, he would kiss Helen and leave the house. We saw him no more for several days.

Finally, the Roman merchants arrived with numerous containers of silk fabric, iron swords, spears, gold, and silver jewelry. Again, I felt some light of hope warm up my heart.

In the following days, everyone, including the fishermen and all the villagers, did nothing but transfer the boxes from the Tall Ship and load them onto the enormous wagons pulled by horses and mules. Throughout this time, I rushed to get close to Marcus, but he had no time to waste on listening to a woman. To the men's surprise, I also started to help with the unloading and loading.

Whenever I moved toward Marcus, Albina rushed, pulled me back, and whispered, "Not the time yet. Leave it to me."

"But, I must know," I protested.

He shook his head. "No worries. I'll make sure Marcus knows how strong you are."

As a close friend of Marcus, Albina was confident that he would devise a way to set me up with Marcus to sail to Alexandria. I had to be patient and abide by his rules.

After several weeks, the Tall Ship was ready to sail. On the night before the departure, Marcus finished checking the ability of the vessel to make the long voyage, and Albina invited him to a farewell dinner at the house.

In the evening, Helen and I decorated the round table with fried fish, eel, eelblenny, tomatoes, melted cheese over the eggplants, and some rye and wheat bread. After gathering, Albina raised his goblet and cheered Marcus, wishing the Tall Ship to have yet another successful excursion. We all raised our goblets in his honor as Marcus' friendly voice filled the room, "Thank you, Albina." He then turned to Helen and me, "You, two ladies, for making such beautiful dishes. Smells scrumptious."

I kept my mouth shut and did not reveal that I had added some of Cordelia's spices while Helen was not in the kitchen.

When dinner was finished and the men had consumed a few wine decanters, Albina grabbed the right moment. "Marcus, what do you think if Thea and her stallion tomorrow come with you?"

Albina did not expect such a horrified reaction. Marcus roared as if Albina had cut him open with a sword. "No way! I can only be in control of my ship!"

I dared to mutter, "Sir, I'm a worker."

He ignored me and yelled again, "The hungry men I'm in charge of haven't seen a woman for months and months." He turned to Albina and shouted, "It is impossible to guarantee any protection ..." he didn't even stop yelling and spitting, "What in the hell does she want to return a Turkmenistan stallion? We just brought here a bunch of them."

Albina got up and filled Marcus' goblet to the rim. "Don't get angry, my friend. Let's talk it over."

Staring at the bare ground, I said, "He's mine, and I don't want to leave him behind."

Marcus picked up his goblet. "Who said you are going?"

His angry words did not sit well with me. However, I mustered all my strength and chose respectful words, "Capitan. What if I dress as a Roman cavalryman accompanied by my horse, and slave woman returning to Alexandria?"

Marcus glared at me, then looked to Albina and exclaimed, "What is *she* talking about?"

To defend me, Albina uttered, "Thea is a remarkable, brave girl."

Helen jumped in, "Our Gods send her. Since she came to us, our village has been thriving."

With a gesture, Marcus turned to me and commanded me to stand up. After looking me up and down, he claimed, "I guess you're as tall and lean as a soldier. But, ney! A sailor's nose is sharp to the scent of a woman. Sooner or later, some can tell."

"As much as we hate to see Thea go," with a sad face, Helen said, "we should help her continue her journey. She's a very dear friend." She turned to Albina. "Tell Marcus how hard Thea worked shoulder to shoulder with other men."

Marcus responded, "You all care about her and want to help. But I'm not sure taking her is a good idea." His wrinkles deepened, but seeing our unhappy faces, he muttered, "Let me think of it for a while." He took a drink of wine while rubbing his forehead. He even stepped outside to the Veranda for some time.

I calmed my thumping heart and dipped into deep silence while we waited for Marcus' decision. At last, he ended my longing and returned—no way to read his mind from his somber look.

He sipped on the wine and wiped his beard. "Albina. You and I are long-time friends, and we count on each other. I trust you and your judgment."

Albina agreed. "Thea is an exceptional girl."

Marcus flinched. "I guess it works."

"Thank you." I quivered before asking, "Are you taking Sattar too?"

"Now that the traitor, Marc Antony, is dead, and our Caesar Augustus is the ruler of Alexandria ..."

Albina finished Marcus' thought. "It's feasible for a Roman soldier to voyage there."

Helen turned to me with piercing eyes and broke her silence, "How do you know a slave girl? We have none."

"I'm so sorry not to tell you sooner." I got up, picked up the empty dishes to avoid their grimaces, and continued, "The other day, I stumbled over one." I grinned and hoped the sound of piling up the plates muffled my words. "She's from Alexandria, and I promised to take her back to her homeland whenever I go." I paused and swallowed hard. "She's in hiding. Her master left her here. He couldn't afford to have an extra mouth to feed."

"Why didn't you bring her to the house?" Helen insisted. "We'd love to meet her."

"Dear Helen," I explained, "she's timid and only comes out when it's time to embark on the vessel."

Marcus scratched his silvery beard. "But, there is one more problem ..."

In a ghastly voice, I asked, "What?"

"Where do you get a soldier's uniform?"

"Marcus," I looked directly at him. "don't you have one somewhere on your ship?"

He shook his head. But Albina gestured to me with a hand motion. "In the boat tower, I have a soldier's outfit. You can use it."

I had seen it one night while snooping around and tried it on, knowing it fit.

When Helen agreed to take the dishes to the kitchen, Albina took me to the tower and gave me the soldier's outfit. "I hope it fits."

"I hope so too."

I put the metallic wool tunic over the linen undershirt and wore the metal helmet with cheekpieces on my head. A protrusion covering my forehead was on the front, about three inches above the rim. I was excited—a slave woman in a Roman soldier's outfit. *Unbelievable!*

When we returned to the house, nobody could hide their surprised eyes. Helen cheered, "Fantastic! No one will suspect that you're a woman."

Albina could not cover his enthusiasm and gleefully said, "It's a perfect fit...Zeus must be watching over you." He wet his lips with a sip of wine and turned to Marcus. "Now, you shouldn't have any reservations about taking her."

"Hmm?" Helen and I exclaimed.

Marcus looked at me from head to toe and said, "It'll do."

I sought confirmation again to ensure, "Do I have your word?"

"Yes. Now, as a Roman soldier, what's your name?"

"Theo, Capitan Marcus!" I saluted him.

We all laughed and cheered while finishing the rest of the wine. To get used to my uniform, I kept it on.

Later that night, after everyone went to bed, I snuck into the barn. At first, Gigi was apprehensive and scared. She thought a Roman soldier was coming to drag her away. She hid behind the mounds of hay. In a cheery voice, I whispered, "Gigi, come on out!"

At first, she did not trust her ears until I removed my helmet. After revealing my plan, she became so thrilled that she jumped up and hugged me.

To be free was within my reach. All night, I pressed my eyes together without any sleep while holding onto my helmet.

When the crimson sky showed up, I rose and took Sattar to the clean horse box on the ship. Marcus took the lead, embarking while the rowers behind him went below the deck to position themselves with their oars. I fetched Gigi. She had covered her face with a piece of cloth. While taking her underarm, I led her to the deck and left her in my cabin. As a Roman soldier, I had the privilege to have my private place next to Marcus—not to be cramped with the rest of the workers.

Helen and Albina came to say goodbye. While hugging me with a smile, she whispered, "Thea, I'm carrying a baby."

"Wow! It's marvelous!" I kept it secret about the herbs I had been mixing with her fish for the last few months. They were Cordelia's. *Indeed she has remedies for everything.*

Helen asserted, "You brought Tyche, the god of fortune, to us."

"I'm so pleased. You two deserve the best." After touching the future father's shoulder, I saluted Albina. Then, I boarded the ship to continue my uncharted voyage.

CHAPTER 15

Alexandria

O ur excursion had started several weeks ago, and the vessel had made excellent progress crossing the Mediterranean Sea. So far, the Sea was calm and pleasant. The soft breeze helped us move steadily with enough strength through the sails. However, to expect the rest of the way would be the same was a short sight.

I asked Marcus, "If we go the same speed and the weather remains calm, how long will it take us to get to Alexandria?"

"Hard to tell." He stood up from his dented seat behind the steering wheel. "If everything stays the same, it'll take about six months, give or take ..." His hesitation was evident in his voice. "It usually takes more ..."

I finished his line, "Nothing stays the same in life, does it?"

"True ... true."

Every night, Marcus invited me to his cabin for dinner. He and I joked around while eating and drinking. He challenged my refusal whenever he insisted that I take off my uniform.

"Your red hair is gorgeous," he said, "don't hide it under the ugly cap."

I removed my cap and said, "Marcus, this is the only piece I'm going to take off."

His belly laugh was so loud that it reached the Sea. "We shall see about that!"

Whenever he tried to touch my legs, I pushed him away and did not think he would move toward me like I was a woman. He had no idea what I was capable of. To his eyes, I was only a weak woman at his mercy.

One time, after dinner, he stepped toward me with his goblet and went to grab my breasts. While sitting, I pushed him away so hard that he fell flat, and the wine spilled all over him.

"Captain Marcus! Remember," I whispered while extending my helping hand to him, "you permitted a soldier to board your ship, not a woman."

Every night he would drink until he passed out—*his way of damping his frustration*. I also took pleasure in accompanying him. I, however, kept my guard on him like a cat watching her kittens. Then, I stumbled to my cabin by dawn, removing my uniform, changing to the linen robe, and crawling in beside Gigi.

One night, I had difficulty closing my eyes, tossing, and turning. To escape into a dream, I shut my eyes tight.

⋙ ✲ ⋘

I was in Pasargad Palace as Princess Atossa's governor. I found myself sitting with the Princess. At age eighteen, she grew to be tall and slim in stature like King Cyrus. Her face was a reminder of her mother, Queen Cassandane. Her chiseled cheekbones with a wide jawline and angular hairline gave her the same refined beauty. The shine in her dark eyes declared that she was on the path of Ahura Mazda.

She whispered, "Lady Mithra, I want to unveil my heart's secret to you."

"Dear Atossa, you're like my daughter. Our bond is unbreakable, and your secret is safe with me."

"I am in love." She stopped, motionless, as a little dove landed on the edge of a pool.

"My dear, who is the lucky man?"

"Combys' adviser, Darius." Before I could speak, she continued, "He and I are planning to marry."

"My child, this is wonderful news. When are you planning to make His Majesty aware?"

"When he returns from battling Scythes."

"Scythia? It's even farther north than Armenia. It will be a long time before he returns."

"I meant to tell him the last time he was here, but his stay was short. I also hesitated."

"Since we lost the Queen during childbirth, your father has made his utmost responsibly to liberate the enslaved people."

"Also, Father Cyrus is not very fond of Darius."

"Why not? He is from a branch of your family tree."

She only shrugged.

I then perceived myself in my loose shoulder-length hair and night robe, strolling in the rose garden by my chamber. Instantly, a majestic eagle flew over my head and sat on the wall closest to me. I was mesmerized by its shiny brown feathers and the white feathers that looked like a ring around his neck delighted me. I went to smile at the bird, but suddenly, some scruffy-looking group's uproars horrified me. They started attacking the eagle. After several aggressive moves, one successfully captured the eagle. He immediately snapped its neck and threw the dead body on the ground. The mob rushed and crushed the strong bird's body. To see them flatten its chest bones sent a painful shock through my frame.

I opened my eyes in horror and heard the sails banging the mast. The calmness of the Sea and the rowing sounded like lyre music. The sun was almost in the middle of the sky when I wore my uniform without a helmet. Instead, I hid my curls under a cap. Taking Sattar out of his compartment and grooming him on the deck became one of my pastimes.

However, the Sea did not give us long-lasting happiness. After several cloudy days and rough waves, one night, Marcus and I walked to the deck carrying our goblets filled with the best Persian wine from his last journey. He looked at the sky and warned me, "Hey, lad," the wrinkles on his forehead became more profound, "see those dark clouds approaching us? Not a good omen."

However, we ignored the gods' warning, and neither stopped drinking. Even at the first drizzle, we kept cheering on each other until the huge raindrops beat our bodies. But after some more clinking of our goblets and laughing, the pouring rain forced us to rush back to our cabin.

That night became much longer when suddenly, Poseidon and Neptune unleashed their wrath on the ship. The high waves hammered the hull harshly, making it move erratically, uprooting it as if the waves pulled out its keel. These two gods joined forces with Ares and Ira, gods of anger and hate, determined to annihilate us all. I wondered when Poseidon would send beasts from the Sea's murky depths to take us to the underworld. Or perhaps, the gods were angry with the Romans for killing our men on the battlefield to conquer more territories, and we had to pay the price for it.

The Tall Ship became a ball in the gods' hands. Gigi and I were violently slammed into the opposite wooden walls. We had no time to catch our breath before we were thrown against the previous divider. With our churning stomachs, we believed the ship floating on the Sea like papyrus paper would become shredded at any moment.

I held on to one of the posts, watching Gigi throwing up. I refused to give in to the gods' fury when I thought I should check on Marcus. He might need an extra hand. But he had taken this route several times, and this storm was not his first. So he knew what to do in this dire situation. But not when he's severely filled with wine.

I caught up with him on the way to the deck; we both tried to reach the steering wheel. Each time a towering wave poured water on our faces, made us blind, and took us a few steps farther from the wheel. I was thankful for the soldier's helmet I had on, which somewhat protected me from the rain and waves attacks. The Tall Ship was in desperate need of leadership. Marcus was too drunk to be able to rescue it. The horrific, lofty ripples had made our massive vessel full of cargo like a feather moving aimlessly, getting us farther away from the southeast toward Alexandria. At one point, Marcus' scream hit me by the skin of my teeth, "Hold on to the steering wheel!"

Wow! Marcus must be desperate to put a woman in charge of his ship.

He then stepped to the left mast to change the direction of the sail. After reaching the rope, he went to release it. Unfortunately, he accidentally pulled the wrong one, and the front sail shot toward him at lightning speed, lashing out at his head and knocking him overboard.

I rushed to pull him out of the water and bent over, looking and shouting, "Marcus! Marcus!" My voice disappeared in the thunder and lightning, and my yelling fell to no one. My eyes could see nothing except angry high waves and the harsh movements of the ship. The hungry dark hole of the Sea had swallowed Marcus instantly—the shipmaster was gone—no sign of him, as if he never existed.

On the deck, I stood alone, letting the seawater wash over me and hoping the god's rage would soon subside after taking Marcus as the offering. My only safeguard was the helmet. Keeping Marcus's death a secret became a priority. Under no circumstances could the rowers know that Marcus was dead. So it had to be kept under wrap.

When the sun finally found its way through the clouds, the Sea gradually calmed down, and the rain stopped. I held on to the wheel and corrected our course. At sunrise, before any man walked up to the deck, I locked up Marcus's cabin, called on the rowers' leader, and announced, "Marcus caught a dangerous disease. To have any contact with him is forbidden. I'm the only one taking care of him. Nobody can get close to his cabin. We must prevent the illness from spreading."

No enslaved men dared to question the authority of a Roman soldier. The entire boat dipped into a somber silence. I appointed Flavius, the man one rank under Marcus, as the new leader.

I wore the soldier's outfit daily and hid my hair under a sailor hat instead of the helmet to show my presence. Every time for dinner, I picked up Marcus's food after eating mine and ate it in his cabin. I even slept there to ensure no one was checking on Marcus.

After a few weeks, it seemed no one remembered the ship master. They stopped asking about Marcus, and we had no significant storm either. One night, a banging on the door woke me up. I rubbed my eyes, pulled the nightcap over my head, and cracked it open.

Flavius was standing before me with a horrified face. I asked, "What's the matter?"

His voice shook like he had seen Orcus, the god of terror. "A pirate boat is approaching us at an unbelievable speed."

"I'll be right up." I closed the door behind him, hurriedly put on my armor and helmet, and then marched upstairs. Before quite making it to the deck, *BANG!* The Tall Ship came to a complete halt. I increased my speed to the top and heard the men yelling, "Those bastards ... the pirates hit us again!"

A strange-looking boat, much smaller than ours, had blocked our way. Both sides remained quiet. As the sun started to come out, I whispered into Flavius's ear, "What do they want?"

"They're looking for our gold and silver. Usually, they hit us first. If we don't offer them anything, they jump onto the ship and get their hands on everything they can."

"So, they blackmail us," I said incredulously. "We aren't afraid of the pirates, are we?"

After a pause, he uttered, "We don't have any man capable of fighting them." He took a deep breath and continued, "They terrorize us. Believe it or not, they're more dangerous than any beast in the jungle." He swallowed hard. "We can't afford to lose any of our rowers."

"Okay, let's wait and see what they do."

Five short, mean-looking men jumped onto the Tall Ship when it was almost dusk. The vexation on their faces reminded me of devilish gods: *Typhon, Orcus, Hades, Ereus,* and *Phonos.* Orcus, the most vicious of them all, had to be the leader. He stood at the front. His face, arms, and naked chest were covered with numerous scars and some fresh raw wounds. He stepped forward and stopped within my arm's reach while hollering, "Where's your master?"

Imitating an angry soldier's voice, I unchained my words toward his face, "I'm in charge. What do you want?"

Angry foam appeared on his lips. "Give us some gold, or my men will kill you and take over your boat."

Stepping closer to him and entering his space, I seethed, "How do you dare talk with no respect to a Roman soldier, a representative of Caesar Augustus!"

His smirk was annoying when he claimed, "I don't care about your Caesar. You're not in charge of this boat. Marcus is." He hollered, as if I was invisible to him, "Where is he?" With a grin, he howled, "Marcus! Marcus! Come on out. Your friend is here."

In my deep voice, authoritatively, I said, "I'm here to defend this boat and everyone in it. To get to Marcus, you must first go through me." I pushed his chest.

Like a stump, he barely moved. Instead, he rushed toward me, intending to attack me. Confident in my agility and the lessons I had learned, I pulled his hand toward me in a swift move. In one motion, I was triumphant in unbalancing him. When he landed on the wooden surface, his scream filled the Sea.

One of the men rushed to help the leader to get up, stretching his hand, and the rest gathered around me with eyes full of anger and hate. After I knocked down two more of them, with a smirk, the chief moaned, "No fighting! I never knew Roman soldiers could be so quick and strong."

"Hurray! Hurray!" Some sailors' voices broke the silence

"Let's shake hands." Flavius approached the pirates' leader, Orcus, raised his hand to him, and said, "And be friends from now on."

I tossed him a sack of silver and gold. "Watch for the cargo ships coming to this route. The Emperor is counting on you and your people for their safe passage."

The next day, while grooming Sattar, Flavius came to me. "I never knew your name. You've been instrumental in rescuing the ship and caring for Marcus."

I said, "Theo," at the top of my lungs.

"Hmm?" He twisted his long and thick mustache. "A Roman soldier with a Greek name."

I proclaimed, "Roman father and Greek mother."

He moved closer and questioned, "Are you telling me what happened to Marcus? Or do I have to break his cabin door?"

Without looking at him while brushing Sattar's back, I uttered, "A few weeks ago, I told you all."

He shook his head, then went around to the opposite side. Sattar's body blocked him from getting closer to me, but his voice reached me, "his cabin is empty."

His sneer disturbed me. "Will you go away now if I promise to tell you everything? Come to the deck tonight, alone."

Under the sky's darkness, I disclosed to Flavius the unfortunate event of Marcus's death.

The space between his eyebrows became more profound. He wiped his eyes and said, "Marcus was a beloved master to all of us."

"Yes, it was an unfortunate accident. Now, this ship is yours."

"No one will accept my leadership for long if they don't know he's dead."

"We don't have a body. So what do we do?"

"I'll find a way."

One day at dawn, the ship stopped moving. I looked out, and the water still surrounded us. I rushed to the deck. Flavius and all the rowers had gathered for the funeral of their beloved Captain Marcus. Everyone was standing around a body shrouded in stained white linen, held by chains on a board. Marcus's cap, the only familiar item, was on the chest.

Flavius recited words about Skipper's greatness and how sorry they were to see him go. With a gesture, he commanded the two men guarding the body to tip the board to the Sea. He said reverently, "Marcus, we give you back to the Sea where you lived most of your life with grace and honor."

The men released the body to the bottom of the Sea. I broke the silence a minute later and exclaimed, "We all lost a significant man and flawless Captain." I took a deep breath. "But now, another great man, Flavius, is replacing him, who was trained by no one but Marcus."

Everyone's cheering reached the sky.

When our ship anchored in Alexandria, I took a deep breath. My secret had been safe for over half a year. Gigi and Sattar disembarked, and I went to Flavius to say goodbye.

He looked straight into my face. "We're so sorry to see you leave."

"Me too. I'm glad everything worked out." I touched his shoulder. "Enjoy your ship, and good luck carrying the precious cargo safely back and forth."

I could never bring myself to ask how he found a

body, neither did he divulge to me. *Perhaps it's a dummy.* I wondered.

"Have a safe journey, Theo."

CHAPTER 16

Silk Route

15 BCE

A fter separating from the vessel, we walked toward the land in Alexandria. The first sight of camels was a sign that we were getting near a caravansary—a place for Persian merchants to arrive and exchange their goods with the Romans.

I left Gigi and Sattar in a crowded courtyard and entered an adobe building. A young fellow pointed out to me the Chief of Merchants, Sohrab.

"Good day, sir." As soon as the words left my lips, he stood up, turned around, and said, "Since when can a Roman woman be a soldier?"

My deep voice did not fool this Persian man.

He gestured to a stool in front of him. I took the seat. He sat and asked, "What can I do for you?"

"Are you a good secret keeper?" Despite his puzzled eyes, a few strands of white hair made me trust him. "I must get to Tysfoon. What is the fastest way?"

"My caravan will get you there."

"My horse and slave wouldn't be a problem, would they?"

Sohrab offered me some wine and said, "If you have a horse, you must know how to ride like a Persian girl."

I nodded and shut my mouth, not wanting him to think of me as a delirious woman. *I used to be a Persian girl in another life.*

When he heard no words of mine, he continued, "You're fortunate. No speed of camel can come close to a horse."

According to Sohrab, not to be bogged down by the caravans, I needed to travel north, along the Mediterranean, and eastwardly in the Sahara for a few days. "Make sure to pick up plenty of water at the last caravansary."

After tolerating the heat of the Sahara, the Persian Royal Roads were available to us. They were the best part of the Silk Route, thanks to Darius the Great, Atossa's husband, for being instrumental in constructing them.

Sohrab also suggested changing into a Persian male outfit and buying a decent robe for Gigi. "Persia doesn't have enslaved people walking in the street. Some only in the palaces."

Staring into his eyes, I asked, "Am I able to pass on as a Persian lad?"

"You speak Parsi well. With your green eyes ..."

I interrupted him, "I can be a mix of Persian and Greek." His approving smile and a nod were my answer when he continued, "To travel as a husband and wife, people are more inclined to help." Sohrab left a good word for me with the inn owner, so Gigi and I had a place to stay overnight. Sattar, however, had to stay beside the camels in the courtyard.

When I left Sohrab in the tavern, I had heaps of respect for him. He did not drill me about the nature of my travel to the Capital, or why I disguised myself as a Roman soldier. On the contrary, he saved me from some lying abhorred in the Mithraism religion.

At the market, I exchanged my armor for a pair of long pants, a long-sleeved tunic in gray for myself, and a soft green linen dress for Gigi. I kept my dagger and sword in my sack.

Later, Gigi helped cut my hair short with only the curls covering my head. It had also been long since I had used Cordelia's potion to make it red. "Now," Gigi declared, "you look more like a young Persian man."

She, however, was not happy about wearing a dress. While changing, she murmured, "How do you want me to ride without trousers?"

"Well, you can wear your dress over them."

A shrug was her approval.

Before we left Alexandria, I asked Gigi, "Would you like to continue your path with me?"

"You're not leaving me here! Are you?" Her horrified eyes at the same time were full of admiration, and with a nod, she said, "I have no one here. You're my guide. I follow you wherever you go."

Following a big breakfast, filling up the water jugs and taking some flatbread and goat cheese, with heaps of hope on our side, we left Alexandria's hurly-burly. Alexander built this city, opening up the Silk Road to cargo ships. However, he burned Persepolis, the magnificent creation of the Persians. To forget the long route ahead, I drowned myself in the past.

≥ ✳ ≤

A harsh smoke smell awakened me. As Reverend Mithra with my husband, Kaveh, I rushed outside, and so did most of our neighbors, to confront a thick black cloud hanging over our heads. We were all in awe.

"PERSEPOLIS IS BURNING!" Someone shouted. Shockingly, no one within the Palace even attempted to put the fire out, as if everyone inside were dead. I and some residents refused to let this majestic building burn to the ground, a survivor of our King Cyrus and Darius the Great. The throngs lined up with buckets, pots, and pans. We made a human chain from the Pulver River to where the fire started. We decisively poured water over the flames spreading to the gold rugs, tapestries, paintings, and statues. With our sweaty faces and wiping our foreheads, we successfully salvaged part of the walls, columns, and lions with wings.

When the sun pushed its way through the dark cloud, a voice in a foreign tongue mumbled something from one of the balconies closest to Kaveh. He touched my arm and whispered, "That's Alexander, ordering his soldiers to help us extinguish the fire."

I turned and looked at our new ruler.

Alexander carried one of the King's gold goblets with a crown emblem. He constantly sipped wine. I disliked this Western man with dirty blond hair, fair skin, and livid eyes. But I was ashamed to let the feeling of hate get into my thoughts.

"It appears," Kaveh's voice brought my attention to the fire, "Alexander got drunk while celebrating his victory. He ordered his men to make a bonfire out of the ivory tables, stools, gold tapestries, and colorful cushions made of silver and gold."

While passing the bucket of water to me, an old man shouted, "All out of jealousy!"

I mopped sweat from my forehead with the back of my hand and added, "Very likely, Alexander wants to show he's the one who strips the Persian Empire of its glory."

$$\geqslant \text{🙰} \leqslant$$

I repeated aloud, "How does a weaker force bring down a more powerful force to its knees?"

"Thea, what're you talking about?" Gigi shook her head. "Why are you shouting?"

I stared at her momentarily, then turned to the road ahead. The farther we got from Alexandria and the Sea, the vegetation became more and more scarce. The desert heat was unbearable during the day. We stopped traveling and only started back on the path as soon as the sun went down. Not to make Sattar too tired, most of the way, we walked and took the rein leading him.

One evening, a large pond with a few palm trees appeared in the distance. We dragged our bone-tired bodies toward it. While struggling to reach it, I said, "It must be a mirage, like Cordelia's fire." When I heard no response from Gigi, I turned to her, ensuring she was okay, and asked, "Do you think this oasis is real?"

She barely made a sound, "Aha!"

The waterhole became a reality when Gigi and I splashed water all over our bodies. Even Sattar wet his feet. I felt so pleased that I spread some water on them too. She also returned the favor.

"The beauty of this place is," I said, exhilarated, "we can take our time under these palm trees for several days."

"No! No!" Gigi shook her head. "This oasis must belong to a tribe. And I bet they live nearby. They'll kill us when they see a couple of strangers wasting the water."

"Ney," in disbelief, I tried to convince her wrong, "we haven't taken any vicious act toward them ..."

Without letting me finish, she blurted, "We wasted *their* water, and we're not part of them."

Gigi's anger baffled me. Not believing my ears, I asked, "How did we do that?" But, instead of waiting for her answer, I proceeded, "We didn't steal any water, did we?"

"Any drop of water is sacred to the nomads. It's as precious as blood ..." She was too weak to continue.

I led her under one of the palm trees to lean against it. Upon sitting down, she picked one of the brown droppings from the tree, sank her teeth into it, and took its stone-hard seed out. Chewing and swallowing the rest, she offered me one.

"What is it?" I examined it all over. It came softly with a hard seed in the middle. "I've never seen or eaten one of these."

"Dates. The fruit of these trees. Eat at least ten or twelve if you want to regain strength. Especially since we haven't eaten much for the last few days."

When Gigi witnessed me eating the dates, she talked about how living in the Sahara differed from anywhere else.

This oasis, where we made its water *dirty* by washing our bodies and taking our horse into it, had to belong to a tribe living nearby. The members created this beautiful spot in the middle of nothingness by laboring for several weeks. They had to travel through the parched land until they arrived here. Then, they dug a reasonably deep hole during the rainy season and planted these few palm trees around it. Doing so would protect the manmade lake from the direct sun's heat with no mercy.

"Wow, Gigi, I had no idea."

"Of course not."

"A fisherman doesn't know what hard work it is to live in the Sahara."

"And it's true the other way around too."

No wonder it was tough for Alexander's soldiers to live in Persepolis, created in the desert. I didn't dare to say my thought aloud. I closed my eyes.

≥ ✤ ≤

At dawn, I left my lonely bed. A few years ago, my husband, Kaveh, went to deliver a message to the satrap of Babylon and has yet to return. Amir and Delbar had both wedded and now had their own families. I pulled back my jet-black hair with some stranded white hair in one braid and wore my white robe and belt. It had to be at least five or six years after Alexander had conquered our land.

I walked toward the newly renovated temple with a pond in the middle. After Alexander's conquest of our land, he destroyed many cities, but let us keep our temples and practice our monotheistic religion as our ancestors did. I took a deep breath.

The high temple, a quadrangular building with four open arched gates on all four sides, made me feel free yet protected. I passed a corridor built with raw bricks inside and baked bricks outside. I stopped under the dome, where the holy fire was lit all the time on a stone reaching right up to the sky. I hadn't even started praying when I heard someone's footsteps.

"Reverend Mithra, may I speak with you?"

I turned. Gordieh, one of my followers, stood before me. A few years ago, I had married her to one of Alexander's soldiers, George. Since his marriage to Princess Roxana, Alexander encouraged his soldiers to take a Persian wife, so our advanced culture could rub on them too.

I swallowed my words not to ask about her husband's well-being when I detected unhappiness in her eyes. To see a young newlywed woman in the temple so early, instead of being in bed with her husband, baffled me. I fixed my gaze on her dewy face.

She exclaimed, "Reverend, help me, please!"

"Dear Gordieh, what's wrong?"

She stared at the ground. "I have some difficulty with George. But, maybe, you can talk with him."

"I'll be more than happy. But, tell me more."

She could barely get the words out through the knot in her throat. "George and I were getting along for the first few months after our wedding. But now, life with him turns out to be hell." She swallowed hard. "The worst part is that…as you know, we don't understand each other's tongue."

"When can you bring him here?"

"He's home sleeping. I can go and bring him over now. Is it all right with you?"

When the sun lit the temple, Gordieh and George sat before me. Without greeting, he slurred in his bloodshot eyes, "Tell her," He pointed to Gordieh as if she was merely a stranger. "If it weren't for Alexander's order, wanting his troops to marry Persian girls, I would never have wed her."

I kept staring at him. With a smirk, he said, "I must confess." George turned and pointed to Gordieh's hair. "Her curly waist-length hair and voluptuous figure, she's much prettier than any Greek girl." Then, he mumbled, "The Persian lamb kabob and fluffy rice with Saffron are to die for." He put his fingers and lips together and sent a kiss. "However, I still miss my Greek wives, children, and country."

I moved my head in agreement with him. "Now, Persia is your land too. So why don't you listen to your leader, and learn the language of our land?"

His angry voice reverberated throughout the temple, "I never learn the tongue of the defeated barbarians. You all need to learn Greek."

Shush! Gordieh sounded. "Don't raise your voice. You're in a sacred place."

I swallowed my exasperation, even though he kept staring at me with no shame in insulting us. "George, if we're barbarians, why does Alexander pay you all some incentives from the Persian treasury to marry our girls?"

George stood up to leave. Gordieh took his hand and pulled his slim body down.

I continued, "Your Master attacked this country, saw this magical land, and married our Princess. So he commanded his soldiers to do the same."

He cried out as disgust rushed to his milky face, making it the color of beets, "Not all of us agree with him! It is his dream of conquering the entire world, sitting on top like Zeus, and being our great god."

I answered honestly, "Alexander is mesmerized by our civilization. His marriage to our Princess shows he's planning to stay here."

George moved his hand as a sign of disapproval. "Lady Mithra, I doubt if Alexander would stay anywhere. He's merely a wanderer dragging Greek soldiers behind him." He paused. "Let me tell you, he was born in Pella, and no school in Athens or anywhere else admitted him ..."

In shock, I interrupted him, "But why? Isn't Pella part of Greece?"

He nodded. "Now, after Alexander conquered Athens. As a Macedonian boy, he was inferior to Athenians. So his father, as the satrap to the Athenian ruler, hired Aristotle to tutor him."

I exclaimed, "Now, Alexander wants to prove to the world that he's worthy of respect like your gods."

>✹ ⋞

The sound of women and children wailing and crying awakened me. I rubbed my eyes. The red sky and the rising sun signaled that Gigi and I had missed one night of traveling. We crawled to the dune behind us and were stunned at the scene before us. Several horsemen in black outfits, looking like ghosts, were carrying a few horrified women and children on their horses, trying to escape while other men were sword-fighting with their opponents.

Gigi hit her cheek while sliding down and pulling me down with her. "Such a horrifying sight! They're robbing this tribe and grabbing the women and children."

"Why are they taking the women and children?"

"They, too, are considered commodities—to sell them as slaves."

"Is this how we buy humans like cows and sheep at the market?"

Gigi nodded with teary eyes.

I hurried to my sack, feeling like all my blood had rushed to my head. After taking out the dagger and placing it on my back in the belt, I carried my sword, running to block the two horsemen ahead of everyone else.

Ignoring the heavy smoke burning my eyes, I jumped before the two horses preventing them from getting away. I was confident in Cordelia's oil on my face that the horses would not crush me. So I came as close to them as possible and let them easily smell me. Suddenly, they neighed and shook so frantically that the riders, women, and children fell to the ground. In horror and motionless, I deftly wielded my sword and dagger. The men's angry voices sounded like wounded wolves, knowing they were losing to a stronger attacker. Soon their wounds were so significant that they could no longer get up from the ground. One more time, I was triumphant in fighting with men.

I'm pleased that Cordelia, being aware of the present, past, and future, trained me for my future.

My bravery encouraged the tribal men, and they, too, started lashing out at the robbers, stopping them from putting more tents on fire. At that moment, I had to decide whether to kill a few or get killed myself. Each time, it was an easy decision. Saving the women and children and warding them off from being enslaved was the only thought in my mind. Safeguarding my own life never occurred to me.

While the men ran the aggressors out of the land, the women and children had to put out the enflamed tents. Finally, after the village was cleansed of aggressors, I set out to leave, but I heard a man's voice, "Hey, mister. Please stop ..."

I turned around. A wrinkled face with bright eyes continued speaking in a different tongue. Finally, with my hand gestures, the man understood. He asked, "Do you speak Parsi?"

I responded eagerly, "Yes! Yes!"

His tone of voice warranted me he was a friend. "I'm Ehsan. I thank you for saving the tribal women and children."

"I'm Theo." I stepped closer to him, and we shook hands.

After my fight, he never would believe I'm a woman.

Turning my face away was impossible when he uttered, "We want to thank you for what you did. Come! Come, and break bread with us."

In my most resounding voice, I said, "But I'm not alone. My wife and horse are behind this mound."

"They're welcome too."

Ehsan walked with me to the oasis. Sattar was where I had left him, but no sign of Gigi. "Gigi, where are you?" I kept calling her and thought she might have been scared of seeing me with a stranger.

We looked around and found her sitting behind a sturdy palm, almost motionless.

I whispered in Greek, "Let's go. The enemy is gone, and Ehsan is inviting us."

Without any words, she pointed to her left thigh. When I lifted her skirt, a swollen wound on her thigh protruded through her trousers. "What happened?"

"I think," she breathed, and I had to get my ear close to her mouth to hear her, "a tarantula ..."

"Lie her down!" Ehsan said and pointed to my dagger. "We must take the poison out immediately. Otherwise, she'll die soon!" He then opened the wound, ignoring Gigi's screams, and started sucking poison out—one breath at a time; and each time, he spat it out. Finally, he tore part of her skirt and wrapped it around the wound.

When Gigi opened her eyes, Ehsan asked, "Can you walk?"

She nodded while reaching for my hand, and with horrified eyes, she stood up. After only one step, her trembling body crashed to the sand. Ehsan and I took her underarms and led her to Sattar, where we laid her face down on his back. Ehsan guided us to the enormous tent in the middle of the few unburned tents. His wife and children came out, helping us get Gigi inside, and lay her on a thin mattress in the corner.

In his tent, Ehsan and I talked while drinking black

tea. "In Persia, the court language is Greek. Is it true?" I asked.

"Yes. After Alexander's death, his generals divided his territory among themselves. The one by the name of Seleucus took over the Persian part."

"What about the ruling Persian King now?"

After a shrug, he said, "Oh, extremely interesting. Have you heard of Cyrus the Great?"

"Who hasn't?"

"He was killed by a tribe named Scythians ..."

I nodded, and he continued, "After over three hundred years, some of their successors rose against the Seleucids and took over the entire old Persian Empire."

"Are they the ones calling themselves Parthians these days?"

"Yes."

"Ehsan, how come you know so much about Persia?"

With pride in his voice, he told me: His father was a Persian merchant during the Greek holdings. After many years of traveling through the Silk Route, he became old and tired of it. Ehsan took over his trade. Once, his caravan was caught in a sandstorm. They lost their path to the Silk Route. When they dug themselves and goods out of the sands, he decided to stop the madness of commerce. Instead, he built an oasis for travelers.

"Fantastic! Your oasis saved our lives." Under my breath, I murmured, "Please forgive us for wasting your water."

"No worries." Ehsan's big smile put me at ease. "Ahura Mazda brought you here to save our women, children, and some tents. Whatever we have left, we owe it to you."

Ehsan's wife entered, carrying a bowl full of milk

while smiling, "Master," she stared into my eyes, "here is fresh goat milk. Have some, and give some to your wife. It'll help heal her wound and strengthen both of you."

I lowered my head. "Thank you, ma'am."

We had to stay for a few days until Gigi was strong enough to travel. Meanwhile, we consumed lots of dates. Eating the flatbread made of date-flour seeds with fresh goat cheese, and drinking goat milk to wash it all down, gave us enough energy for our trip.

One day I asked, "Ehsan, how did you not prefer a wealthy merchant's lifestyle to your simple life in the middle of the desert?"

A wide smile from ear to ear enveloped his face. "The joy I feel, and see in my family, is worth more than the entire Persian treasury."

"As a merchant, you were gone most of the year ..."

"Yes." He moved his head in agreement. "My family is a priceless gem to me. And in my absence, I could not protect them, which was not a joyful life for me."

The day Gigi started helping with the household chores, I knew our time with Ehsan and his tribe was over.

Ehsan drew the path in the sand to show me the faster way to Tysfoon when we were ready to leave at dusk the following day. "Within a day or two, you'll pass the Dead Sea. Continue north, in the Mesopotamian territory."

"Is it where I can take the Royal Roads to the Capital?"

He agreed while continuing to draw. "The Royal Roads became the same as the Silk Route. The current Persian King's ancestor, the first Mithridates, who rebelled against the Greek ruler, connected the Royal Roads from the extreme northeast of Persia to Alexandria over two hundred years ago." He turned to me and said, "Why didn't you take the Silk Route from Alexandria? You could find resting stations for the Persian messengers along the road."

"Not to be bogged down with caravans and the camels."

"The Sahara is hostile. Of course, you didn't foresee the unknown events of life either."

I concurred, and he continued, "But, Mesopotamians are friendly folks, especially now that their satrap's abiding the Persian King. They welcome any newcomers."

As Gigi, Sattar, and I left Ehsan and his family, he shouted, "After the Dead Sea, the rest of the way is a breeze."

CHAPTER 17

Dead Sea

D uring our journey, sometimes I rode and carried Gigi on Sattar's back, and sometimes she was alone on his back. She and I walked at night and rested by the shadow of a dune in the daytime.

After two nights, we could see the eerie Dead Sea in its blue water with white edges. Before us, the multiple holes in the mountains looked like the gods opening their mouths in awe at the Sea. At one point, I left Gigi and Sattar outside under the moon and shining stars, then entered the nearest cave while carrying the dagger.

I was walking with my dagger at the ready when I heard some noises far away, as if from beneath the ground. The first sign of life since we left Ehsan's oasis.

Some lights radiated below when I walked forward, igniting a mixture of hope and despair. I mustered all my strength, determined to find the place. With my eyes alert, cautiously, I stepped one at a time. In an instant, the path's edge gave way and, in a whirling motion, threw me on the flat land but still far from the light. After checking the bones in my body, I stood up, pleased that I could still walk toward the light. Not very long, a snaky path sliding to the right caught my attention. It took me even lower and lower. I'd never been so deep in a cave before.

A torch on the wall shined on two men, blocking the path before me. "Stop!" If he hadn't gestured for me not to move, I would've had no idea what he'd said. Only part of it came familiar to me, "... Roman, Persian, or Greek?"

I had yet to decide which one to choose. I remembered that my outfit resembled a Persian man with a wife. In Parsi, I replied. "Persian."

I was so close to them by this time when the other one exclaimed, "With a set of green eyes, how can you be a Persian?"

"Well, my mother was Greek," I offered.

"That explains it," The other one said.

"Can you speak Greek too?" the first man asked.

"Yes, I prefer it to Persian."

With a smile, he responded in Greek, "Welcome to the town of Petra. I'm Noah, and this is Jacob. What's your name?"

"Theo."

"Are you traveling alone?" Jacob inquired.

"Not alone. I have a wife and a horse waiting outside the cave."

Jacob brought the torch to my tired face and stared at me. My muddy face prevented him from noticing any lack of beard. He thought I should rest and drink wine before returning to fetch them.

I thanked them and started to leave when Noah's voice hit my ears. "Wait!" He rushed after me. "Are you a hard worker after some rest?"

"Of course. What do you want me to do?"

"Well, if you agree to work with the rest of the men during the day, you and your wife are welcome to stay with us as long as you wish."

Jacob announced, "And you'll get paid handsomely too."

"I'd love to help," I replied.

Noah accepted my promise and continued walking with me in a direction where the road was smoother than the one I had taken.

Outside, the sun, almost in the middle of the sky, shocked me to find the underground city had taken me so long. Before the mouth of the cave, Sattar stood there without Gigi. I panicked.

Noah's words caught my attention. "Are you sure you left her also at this spot?"

"Of course, I did not want to be far from them."

Noah knew the area well and took me on a shortcut to a place with a few palms. She had sat down under one. "Gigi, what are you doing here?"

She thundered, "You were gone for too long ... I wandered looking for you." She sounded harsh and put me at odds. Just a short moment later, she screamed, "My eyes! My eyes are burning ... I'm going blind!" Her swollen face shocked me immensely.

"Oh, no!" Noah shouted. "Your wife put some water from the Dead Sea on her face!"

"Gigi, did you do that?"

In a wailing voice, she replied, "I was so hot. I thought to wash my face with the Sea water and not waste any freshwater!"

Noah rushed to take a sack from his belt and splashed her face with fresh water. "The water from the Dead Sea is very salty. It burns our eyes and sometimes can even blind us."

Noah scooped up Gigi and dashed ahead.

As Sattar and I trailed behind, I heard no strength and rhythm in Sattar's gait. An examination of his hoofs revealed all the leather straps were torn or had fallen apart. Very slowly, he and I lagged. On the way, in a loud voice, Noah called out, "You'll see a stable on your left in a short while. Leave your horse with the other animals."

I left Sattar in the stable with plenty of food and rushed to catch up with Noah. Inside, he laid Gigi on a cot. I immediately started mixing some of Cordelia's herbs with water to make a paste to cover her eyes and face.

Noah asked, "Are you a medicine man?"

"No, no." I stopped and looked at his face. "During the trip, I picked up some herbs that might heal certain wounds. But I don't know if the paste will save her eyes."

Before leaving with Noah, I decided to go to the stable and fix Sattar's shoes. "I'm worried about my horse."

Noah pulled on my sleeves. "He'll be fine as long as he doesn't walk on them any longer. You can fix them before leaving."

He and I headed toward where I had heard noises and music from. Indeed, Petra was a town built belowground, with houses made out of sand. Noah took me to the community room, where more than 200 men, women, and children gathered, eating, drinking, and dancing.

"Do you all ever go to sleep?" I asked in amazement.

"This part of the city never sleeps. A few ones stay up while some others are working or sleeping."

Noah and I joined the rest of the townspeople, and over a glass of wine, I asked, "How come you all can survive in this abyss?"

He smiled. "Did you see the path that I took you up?"

"Yes, it was smooth and shiny, not dusty like others. It looked different."

"The secret is that the Persians learned the most-kept Egyptian secrets when King Cyrus the Great conquered Egypt."

A lady set down before me a bowl of porridge.

While eating, I thought he did not hear me. I repeated, "What's the secret?"

He was busy eating and drinking. After scratching my head over the cap, I repeated, "What is it?"

He swallowed his wine. "I heard you the first time. But I'm trying to explain it to you." He paused and took a deep breath. "In contrast to its name, this Sea is not dead. It has natural asphalt. It floats to the surface, and we harvest it with nets ..."

"Like fishing."

"Correct. During the Pharaoh's time, only a few handfuls of Egyptians learned that by heating asphalt, they could embalm the dead royal bodies."

"So, is this your business?"

"Yes. If you would like, come with us, and you can participate in catching asphalt that floats on the Sea." He paused. "Recently, we lost some elderly and are shorthanded."

"I'd love to. But I can only stay until Gigi's eyes improve."

"Why are you in a rush?"

"I'm tired," was my excuse. I left the party to go to rest. On my way, I wondered, being underground, how they would know it was time to go and start their harvesting.

I was fast asleep when a knock on the door made me open my eyes willy-nilly.

Noah's voice was clear: "Theo, time to go."

We walked up the road, and he explained that today was his turn to go early and stay for half a day. Two other fishermen would go and carry on until sunset. After that, the other couple would go and work all night. Then, he gave me an extra jug filled with fresh water. "If you touch your face, especially eyes and lips, right away, wash them with this water." He also gave me a hat similar to a cone to protect my head from the sun's heat. Since I already had my cap on, I took it and carried it with me for the next day.

Harvesting asphalt was much easier than catching a fish—no need for any boats. The beginners like me are only required to have a giant sieve with a long handle. No one could drown or have to know how to swim, either. A perfect situation for people who live in the desert. This water never swallowed anyone. *The Dead Sea keeps them alive.*

We walked up to the waist to start collecting the pieces of asphalt. I could acquire many parts of asphalt early in the morning, but I felt tired and woozy when the sun became so intense. Working as diligently as the men, I breathed deeply and shut my mouth without any complaints.

I must survive the heat and hard work to get to King Farshad's court. Of course, Caesar Augustus wanted me to be his eyes and ears. However, I desire to be his wife, the Persian Queen. But, the King already has the Queen, many wives, and concubines. Would he choose me as his Queen when he and I meet? I wondered.

Planning for my future life motivated me and made the days go much faster. After several days, Noah trusted me with a huge bowl as large as the others. That way, I could carry the sieve to the shore each time after filling it. At last, I verbalized my perpetual question, "Noah. What do you do with these huge loads of asphalt?"

He explained. One of their best advantages was being on the Silk Route's edge. After collecting and packaging a whole bunch, they usually caught up with the merchants in a caravan. And if the price were right, they would sell it to them.

"And if not?"

"We transport them ourselves, directly to Cairo or Alexandria." Noah sounded confident.

I witnessed a few men covering the road with hot asphalt while Noah and I were leaving. I pointed it out to him. "Is this how you cover the dust and rocks in the street?"

"Yes. That's how Persians learned to make the Royal Road, connecting East and West. The best roads in the world."

"It makes them shiny, too."

"Roman Caesar pays lots of gold to buy these. So now, he's our best customer."

"Yes, Greece, including Athens, is part of the Roman Empire. So many roads to cover." With a smirk, I added, "The Emperor refuses to leave many sacks of asphalt for the Persian King."

Noah agreed.

After several days of working with them collecting asphalt in different shifts, the sun's heat no longer bothered me. Whenever I thought of my future lover—King Cyrus, a wave of joy would run through my heart. Then, laboring intensely did not agonize me.

Meanwhile, Cordelia's potion improved Gigi's eyes, and we were getting closer to our departure. It also expedited the healing process when I doubled the mixture each time following my shift. While Gigi's eyes were improving, I spent some time fixing Sattar's shoes. In Petra, I also learned that the horsemen used woven plants, unlike in Rome, where they made them from leather straps. Noah taught me how to utilize the outer tree's bark if Sattar needed a shoe change later during our trip. I spent a day or two inside the stable—a good excuse to avoid the dire heat.

When Noah saw Gigi's eyes healing, and I finished with Sattar's hoofs, he called on me one night after work. "Hey, Theo, I want you to come with me."

He flared up a torch, walked toward the highest mountain, and I followed him. We climbed and stopped before a narrow wall that looked like a temple. However, the human faces carved on rose-red walls announced, it was a graveyard. With my big eyes and curious mind, I urged him, "Shall we go inside?"

The heavy sizeable wooden gate creaked and cranked open. We stepped inside the belly of the mountain. A few pigeons and bats flew over, barely missing our heads, taking me by surprise.

"This is *Al Khazneh* or the Petra Treasury," Noah's voice echoed back. "There are many other groups like us in Petra, living in caves and collecting pieces of asphalt."

"Is this man-made or natural?"

"This treasury belongs to the entire Petra region, half-carved and half-built into the mountain."

"Was Persepolis your model?"

He turned to me with his wide-open eyes and shrugged.

We stepped farther, and the inside scene put me in awe. On the walls of the mountain, there were many unknown riddles. Noah pointed out a statue in front of a hole in the wall. "This chieftain's body occupies this space."

It's good Cordelia is far from here and can't pulverize human bones!

Noah walked to the other side, toward a few closed chests, and opened them all. One was full of gold coins, the other with gold bars, and a few others filled with gems and jewelry. "Take as much gold or silver as your heart desires." He reached in and took out a few necklaces and earrings. "Here, take these for your wife. She'd love you even more."

When he saw me with my mouth open, he claimed, "It's your compensation for working diligently with me these days."

"Knowing and working with you and your community is my reward." I held onto his shoulder. "I don't have any use for these coins. They're heavier than they're worth. Thank you for rescuing Gigi and welcoming us to your home."

The day he saw the three of us were ready at sunset, he provided us with some cheese, goat meat, and plenty of fresh water. Once refreshed and reasonably contended, we continued our journey.

We caught up with the Royal Route. Our traveling was, in truth, a "breeze," galloping through Mesopotamia. While riding through the Royal Route, I remembered King Darius and Queen Atossa's court.

≥ ⚹ ≤

My daydream melted into my past. It was about 400 years before my time. As the King gathered the Persian forces to liberate Athenians, Queen Atossa expressed her desire to me to accompany them with the other family members. Despite not being enthusiastic about witnessing bloodshed, I put on my white robe, pulled back my silvery hair, and rode my horse beside the Queen. I loved Atossa as a daughter, so I never wanted to miss an opportunity to be close to her.

We had started from Persepolis, the southern part of Persia, toward the Northwest, passing through Mesopotamia. I felt proud of our Queen. She was a partner to the King, just like her mother.

We camped after arriving at the narrow Bosporus strait, separating the Black Sea from the Mediterranean Sea. While I was resting in my tent, the Queen walked in. With a big smile, she said, "Lady Mithra, aren't you happy?" The Queen continued without giving me a chance to respond, "Now, vast portions of Eastern Europe are part of our Empire. Our troops connected the Eastern and Western world for the first time."

"How wonderful." My words carried a lack of enthusiasm. *Not without creating a bloodbath!* Instead, I swallowed my words.

In her eager voice, she said, "Now, we have only one hurdle to conquer. Athen."

"What's that, my dear?"

"The King and I must find a way to cross the strait."

I knew it was only possible to tie the Eastern and Western land together with a bridge. However, not desiring to say a word of discouragement, I uttered, "You and the King are brilliant. I'm sure you both will devise a triumphant plan."

At dawn, I was awakened by the soldiers' footsteps and the horses' neighing. I ran out of my tent. As far as my eyes could see, hundreds and hundreds of boats and ships were anchored along the strait. Then, hand in hand, the King and Queen pranced from the first deck to the last ship. I could barely hold back my fervor, clapping and yelling, "Bravo, my Queen!"

"My Queen ... my Queeee ..."

"Thea, what are you saying?" Gigi's voice finally reached me.

Finding a place to stay in Mesopotamia for Gigi, me, and Sattar was not a hurdle. The city's hustle and bustle showed us it was the trade center. Its wealth and power were apparent everywhere we went. The palm trees on both sides of the road, with lush gardens, ornate houses, and markets loaded with exotic goods from India, Arabia, and Egypt, filled our hearts with great pleasure. All signaling that we had reached the upper part of Mesopotamia.

We stopped at one of the Royal messenger's stations, where the man gave us the best news: "From here to Tysfoon, the Capital of Persia, is only one day ride."

"Hurray!"

CHAPTER 18

Tysfoon

14 BCE

M y eyes took in the bull's flank under a lion's teeth, carved on the colossal north wall of the palace iron gate—a replica of the *All Nation Gate in Persepolis.* I wanted to cheer my triumph, but the parched lips, a gnawing stomach, and the rain-drenched outfit kept me stoic.

Last night, I had to say *goodbye* to my friend, Gigi. She followed me like a faithful dog throughout the numerous months on the road and never asked any questions about why I was going to Persia.

"Dear Gigi," I said before she went to sleep. "Tomorrow, you and I must go our separate ways."

She stared at me with her large dark brown eyes filled with sorrow, "Why?"

I gave a heavy sigh. "I have to go to the Palace, and going alone gives me a better chance to get in."

"Persian Palace? Really!"

The silence occupied the space until she threw more questions at me, "But why? What's your business? To see the King? Ha-ha-ha!"

I swallowed hard. "I'm sorry. I'm sworn to secrecy."

She shrugged, dashed to bed, pulled a pillow over her face, and squealed, "And I thought I'd be with you for the rest of my life."

I apologized to her repeatedly, then left her in the room at sunrise.

In front of the gate, I dismounted Sattar and stepped toward a single pacing guard. When I got close to him, he stopped and yelled in my face with red eyes as if his eyelids had been cut off. "What do you want?"

I decided not to talk in a deep masculine voice because Persian men respected women. On the way here, I also noticed some women, like men, wore pants and tunics to walk the street. So with my regular voice, I replied, "To deliver a message to His Majesty."

His angry voice jarred my ears like I had said a forbidden word. "Stop! Stop! Aren't you a cook helper? Or a cleaning girl?"

I shook my head. "I ..."

He did not give me a chance to finish. In a swift move, he pulled out his sword.

I felt its sharp point on my stomach as he hollered, "Who are you trying to fool?"

"No one!" I gulped down the knot in my throat. "I had to change my clothing to fit for the long way I came from."

As if he did not understand me, he continued howling. Most of it was not audible to me. Finally, he pointed to my cap. "It's a man's, not a woman's!"

I hurriedly took it off. For a moment, the guard was mesmerized by my curly wine-colored hair pouring over my shoulders. But soon, he took control of himself and yelled again, "A foreign woman in a Persian man's outfit! What's your business here?"

I mustered up all my strength, ignored the sword pain, and stepped even closer to him. With a calm, relaxed face, staring him in the eyes, I grasped its edge and pushed the blade away from my belly. The guard's mouth opened as a cave; his eyes, vast as a dark sea, attempted to devour me. In a firm voice, I exclaimed, "I have a direct order to see His Majesty, King Farshad!"

His loud laugh brought a few nearby standing guards closer to us. "I didn't hear you." He cupped his ear. "Who're you here to see?"

Grunting like a hungry bear, I shouted, "I have an important message to deliver to the King!"

As if the presence of the extra guards nearby made him stronger, he kept bashing me with his questions. Finally, he did not even wait for me to respond and yelled, "Who's your master?"

"If you step away from me and give me a chance to calm down, we'll talk like two civilized persons." A slight push on his chest propelled him two steps backward.

He had yet another excuse to continue blocking my way. "Why do you think His Majesty will give an audience to a little girl like you?"

I kept my lips shut like a bashful maiden to avoid laughing. I was taller than all of them! No idea why he called me little. Instead, I pulled the letter with Caesar's seal out of my sack. I took a deep breath and waved it at him. "Look. I'm a messenger of Emperor Augustus. And I must give this to the King in person, immediately. Forget my vagabond clothing..."

"Give it to me!" He rushed toward me to grab the letter. "I will make sure His Majesty receives it."

I pulled my hand briskly away and declared in a deep and controlled voice, "From the hand of Caesar to His Majesty's eye."

"No! No! You can't possibly be the messenger sent by your Emperor." His fast-moving hands were dismissing me.

"Check it out." I tapped on the seal. "I was in his presence when Emperor Augustus wrote and sealed the letter before my eyes."

"I don't know any Emperor's seal. And I do not trust you at all." He angrily demanded, "If you're so important, why don't you have some guards?" He again moved toward me to grab the letter.

In an agile move, I stepped away with my right eyebrow raised. "Over my dead body!" I safeguarded the letter on my chest and pressed it hard, setting the other hand over it.

The guard stopped short and uttered, "Your Emperor sent a host of guards with his envoy to the court not long ago. How come no one is with you?" He made a show of glancing behind me.

I said confidently, "He trusted *me* to do the job myself."

The guard let loose with a loud belly laugh again. "Do you want me to believe the Roman Emperor has nobody else at his disposal except *you*?"

"I requested to travel alone, like a Persian girl."

He replaced his laugh with a smirk. "Not a good reason."

When he blocked my way through the gate again, out of desperation, I lowered my voice and murmured, "What do you think ..." I stepped closer to have his ear. "What do you think the Emperor will do to your land when I return the letter unopened to him?"

He scratched his head. "For sure, it'd be a huge problem." While staring into my eyes momentarily, he turned to a bystander guard, gestured to escort me to the chief guard, and let him decide what to do with me.

I had no luck with him, either. I suggested, "How about sending me to His Majesty's corresponding secretary? I'm sure he recognizes the Emperor seal and validates its authenticity."

His eyes were tired and frustrated. He wanted the same guard to chaperon me. We walked for quite some time. Finally, when we reached a courtyard with many buildings, he mumbled, "I believe you." He pointed out to one of them in the middle, "That's his place. There is no reason for me to come with you any further."

"How come?"

"Well, an imposter envoy would fold, or pass out, right by the gate as soon as the guard put his sword on her stomach."

"Thank you for believing me."

"Go there. That's the Chief Secretary, and talk to Javid."

Yet another guard pointed to the wrong place. After asking several times, finally, I was led to his workroom. Before entering, I shook my head and ensured my red curls were still like a waterfall pouring down my shoulders.

The open door, without a guard, was an invitation to walk in. The floor was covered with books and papers, so like a rabbit, I hopped to avoid stepping on them. Heaps of books covered with cobwebs were scattered on a few tables. The vast wooden walnut table at the end of the big room, near the mantelpiece, was also cluttered with massive loose papers and books. They obscured me from seeing anyone behind it. A perfect reminder of Cordelia's desk, where I found books and learned about the bygone Persian kings.

I called out, "Hello! Is anyone here?"

Instead of a response, a chubby gray-bearded man stood up. To see an older man with a massive hunchback in such a critical position was mind-boggling. The words out of his mouth were in Greek, "Such beautiful hair—wine-color, so unusual." But then, a huge smile showed his toothless mouth when he approached me.

After introducing myself to him, I pulled the letter from my bosom and said, "Do you recognize this seal?"

"It's Caesar Augustus' seal…well-kept," he replied confidently with a grin.

He has to be Javid. My happiness reached the sky, and a huge smile broke across my face from ear to ear. "I must deliver this letter personally to King Farshad."

"You sound like you're fluent in Greek."

In a firm voice, I answered, "Yes."

"Well, on the administrative side, we speak only Greek."

"Why not Persian?" I pretended not to know it.

He shook his head. "Most of the time, His Majesty speaks Greek, especially to any foreign envoy. And even sometimes to his advisors," Javid pulled a wrinkled handkerchief out of his pocket. "when the King doesn't want others to understand him." He blew his nose. Meanwhile, he never took his eyes away from my face. "No problem, I can present you to His Majesty, but ..." he stopped with squinting eyes. "Do you read and write in Greek too?"

"Yes, I do. In addition to Roman."

He said his assistant had gone away several months ago and had yet to return. While looking around, Javid said, "He wasn't a good one, as you can see." He pointed to the disarray of the room.

So it was up to me whether to accept or reject his offer to be his deputy. The work involved managing all the correspondence, mainly in Greek. In that case, he would have an excellent reason to introduce me to His Majesty as a new addition to the administration. In return, however, I had to keep a secret that I was a Roman girl.

"What's wrong with being a Roman?"

"His Majesty isn't very fond of you all these days." He stepped closer to me. "Let's see how well you do the task." His deep breath brushed my face.

"Why isn't the King fond of Romans?"

"Romans tricked us. They promised they would return the Prince, Ardalan, but they haven't yet."

"Caesar is waiting for the return of the Roman Flag and Golden Eagle held by the King."

He ignored my words and claimed, "Persians threw

out Augustus' forces from Armenia in the last war. To everyone's shock, Romans still took the Prince with a couple of soldiers as hostages."

I repeated, even louder, "You haven't returned the Roman Flag and Gold Eagle either!"

With tired eyes, he asked harshly, "Would you like to work for me or not?"

"I would love to as long as you promise to introduce me to the King."

"First, we need to clean you up to be presentable."

"Sattar's waiting at the main gate. I'm going to fetch him."

"Who's he? Your husband?"

Smiling, I said, "No, he's my horse."

"No worries, the stableboy knows what to do."

"My horse won't follow a stranger."

After taking care of Sattar, Javid housed me in the same facility that belonged to his former assistant. All the rooms around the courtyard were under his control. He, however, lived much closer to the Palace.

That night, after settling into my new home, I took a deep breath and crashed on the soft bed, wondering about Gigi.

For several weeks, I worked as hard as a horse to show Javid I was worthy of meeting His Majesty. However, whenever I asked him a straightforward question about when he would introduce me to King Farshad, he confronted me with a shoulder shrug. Or he ignored me, walked out of the room, and his best response was, "Soon. Soon."

His workroom, worse than a battlefield, was one of many I had to put in order. In addition, several other rooms were filled with mountains of papyrus letters. Bodies of thick books covered the desks and floors. To start with, I had to read or look at each entry in the ledger line and ensure that the previous assistant had sent a response. Then, according to the dates, I had to catalog it into a book downstairs in the basement. Otherwise, I had to pile it up separately and ask Javid whether to send an answer or if there was still time. Even as diligently as I worked daily, it still took me a long time to manage the heaps of letters and tablets.

If Cordelia had not trained me to bear the hardship of life, I'd have escaped immediately. After several months, a guard gave me news on Gigi. She worked in one of the taverns close to the Palace. I rode Sattar and visited her.

After a glass of wine, she described how she entered the city. No guards gave her a hard time. On the contrary, they were so sorry for her being a destitute young girl that one of them even guided her to the tavern, where he knew they needed a worker. Fortunately, the pub was not far from the Palace.

I was blessed to have a friend who shared my journey's hardship. Drinking wine with her soothed my heart while waiting to meet the King.

She's my only friend to have my back while walking toward the lion's mouth.

Gigi and I loved the taste of Persian wine as it was the best in the world. "Naturally," I raised my goblet, "these people were the first to learn how to make wine by crushing the grapes," I claimed after wiping my face with my bare hand. "No wonder Roman royals drink only Persian wine and pay dearly for it."

"Persians also learned," Gigi dished out her recently acquired knowledge, "if we let the wine ferment even longer, it'll produce a very sour fluid."

"Oh, yes! It gives a delicious taste in contrast to the sweetness of any dish."

"How do you know that?" Her mouth was wide open.

The silence was my answer. I turned to a cavalryman sitting next to me and started having a small talk with him.

The other day, a woman in a snow-white robe stepped into the workroom when Javid was out, and I was sitting behind his desk. Like the sun, her big smile and bright face made me jump up and hurry to get closer to her.

"Somehow," she said while walking toward me, "I had to meet you when I heard Javid hired a new woman as his assistant. I'm Mithra."

Wow! Now, Mithra in the flesh! With my surprised look, I stared at her waist-long black hair and her face as bright as a goddess. I replied in the same tongue as she, "Mithra, I'm Thea."

"I'm so pleased to hear you speak Parsi too."

Here, they call their language 'Parsi'!

"Why did you want to meet me?"

Her kind smile sat on my heart. "Well, these days, we won't have any woman in the administration."

"I thought Persian men and women were considered equal in this land."

"We did." Her smile disappeared. "Not anymore."

"How come?"

"Sorry, I'm in a rush. We'll get together soon and

talk." She waved at me when she left.

Her gliding gait made me believe Aphrodite had visited me.

When I went to bed that night, I remembered what Cordelia had said repeatedly. *Our souls travel through different times and places.*

She's my present light from my past.

GIGI

CHAPTER 19

Sicily
16 BCE

T he whirl of life mystified me to no end. I never thought one day I would live in the vicinity so close to the Persian Palace and the King would be my protector. Yet, I had no home to call my own for a long time and no pillow to rest my head on.

At age five, my family and I moved to the middle of the desert with a few others. Traditionally, the leader chose a land nearby a town or village after each rainy season for our relocation. The women and children had to walk to the neighboring city begging for food. The villagers called us *Gypsies*.

My mother and I, however, did not need to be beggars like the others. Instead, the town women came to us. She could tell their future by looking at their palms. They stayed willingly in a long line, even when their babies' crying reached the sky. Standing beside her and staring at each customer, I kept hearing, "Such lovely huge eyes you've got!" Or, "A set of mysterious eyes as dark as a starless night!"

One day, a boy a little older than I hid one of his hands in his jacket sleeve. In the evening, he returned as happy as he could be. The people had given him so much bread, vegetables, cheese, and fruit that other kids had to carry them for him. The following day, most children copied what he had done. In no time, the villagers chased them out of their town. Then, we had to pick the tents up and move.

At the new place, after the change of season, my mother and some wives refused to leave. To the chief's surprise, their husbands also turned down the relocation. So no one went away. Three rainy seasons passed. My mother gave birth to my three siblings, and her popularity grew. The housewives demanded to know whether their husbands had any affairs. Or whether their men would leave them for another woman. So, they rewarded our family handsomely with some blankets and clothes, all graciously used. And that wasn't all! We had an abundance of flatbread, cheese, and dates. At one time, a woman brought a live goat to our tent. *I'd never forget the delicious taste of fresh milk.* Life was at its best.

It seemed like the men became bored from staying in one place—no new territory to explore. Finally, after the fifth rainy season, the chieftain who witnessed my family's success ordered us to pick up and set out for new land. My mother again refused to leave the ground where she had rooted. Some other women, in support of her, also remained in place. They were brave not to cry when their husbands left. The ones whose husbands took the tents with them moved in with us or other women and children. My father, the only man in our tribe, was now responsible for protecting everyone who lived in the handful of tents. Our laughs could reach the sky, especially when my father tickled our bellies.

As the season changed, so did my life. At age ten, my life altered from day to night. The sound of women's wailings, and children's crying, tore the dark blanket wide open. I could make no sense of the horror in the darkness of the night. My father picked up his dagger and rushed out. I moved the cloth away from the tent opening. Some tents were on fire. I had to wipe smoke from my burning eyes and stop my siblings from going outside. By this time, my mother had also stepped out. And expecting their return never ended.

When the outside noise became hushed, a man stepped in from the other side of the tent after ripping it as if it was a piece of paper. A dark shirt and pants covered him, and his ear-to-ear grin exposed his ugly yellow teeth. I had to cover my ears when he shouted at the other thief behind him. "Take these toads away! They're yours! Their wailing hurts my ears!"

In no time, the deep silence outside made me understand my siblings' fate. I closed my eyes, ready for the man in the tent to bring down his bloody sword on my neck. But destiny had another plan for me, far from my five-year-old twin brothers and an infant sister.

I opened my eyes without flinching and shouted, "What are you waiting for? Go ahead. I'm ready."

"You, low-life girl. How dare you speak to me and tell me what to do." His belly laugh pounded my head.

Seeing another enormous man's shadow, getting closer to the tent, washed off my tenacity. He glanced at me, and the newcomer sheathed the blood-dripping sword in his belt. He said with a smirk, "Look at her large eyes. They're haunting. Lots of money for her!"

He ordered the first one to leave. While showing his long and crooked teeth, he stepped toward me and howled like a hungry wolf, "Wow! Such frightened, beautiful eyes. You're a keeper!"

His creepy voice unnerved me. I opened my mouth to scream but was unable to make a sound. The attacker locked one hand around my waist and triumphantly picked me up, carrying me on his shoulder like a grain sack. Once outside, he ordered the other thief, "I take this one. You get whatever is left in the tent, including the goat." He tied me to the back of a dark horse with my head and shoulders hanging, then rode away.

We were on the road so long that I had to shut my eyes to avoid getting debris in them, ignoring the rocks hitting my face and arms. Finally, my capturer reined in. He dumped me on a heap of hay and stomped out. The colossal wooden barn door's screech felt like my siblings and parents' wailings.

The stable became my home; my companions were a goat, a cow, a horse, and a few chickens and roosters. The cries, laments, and mutilated bodies crowded my head. For how long this went on was unknown to me.

One day I opened my eyes to see a strange woman dressed like a Lady in a clean, black robe staring at me. She left a piece of flatbread with goat cheese and a jug of water, then went away. I had never seen her before and had no idea how she knew I was here.

There was no reason for me to live either. I wished one of the vicious men had murdered me with the rest of my family right then and there. They all perished in one night. I had no one—not even a friend who didn't have four legs, or was not covered with feathers.

Without a word, the Lady kept bringing me the same stuff daily, as if she was blind to the pile of bread smeared with cheese getting taller. Finally, the pieces of flatbread gathered some big blue spots on them.

At last, one day, after she left me with a piece of freshly baked flatbread, its smell broke down all my resistance. I forgot my bygone family and the wish to be dead. I shoved the entire piece in my tiny mouth at once and washed it down with water like a savage. Then, even the dried pieces could not run away from me! I gobbled them to the last crunch.

Suddenly, the sound of some children playing in the distance and the clickety-clack of hooves reached me. The desire to play like in the good old days excited me. I tried to get up and go to them, but my feet rejected that idea. To think of kicking open the monstrous wooden barn door, double my size, rushed into my head. No will can do. Each time, after visiting me, the woman pushed the giant board back into its place behind the door. So did her vicious Master shut and chain it, making sure my tiny body could not go through it. Several times, I thought of breaking through the wooden walls, especially at the sites with holes. But my hands were too little, and my nails were too fragile to make a big enough hole for me to crawl through.

For a long time, during the Lady's visit, I could only see her lips moving, without hearing the sound, like a deaf girl. I could not conceive of what she was saying. But one day, my ears filled with her voice, yet no way to understand her. At last, she pointed to me and smiled, "Gigi."

Unsure, I repeated. "G I G I?"

She took my hand and put it on my chest. "Gigi ... you're Gigi."

Then, she pointed at herself. "I'm Lady Hoda."

That day, Lady Hoda walked me to the river. After washing the clogged blood and dried mud off me, she clothed me in a robe, socks, and thin shoes. They made me feel warmer despite being bigger than my old ones. My original wrapper, which I had on since the invasion of my community, was torn in most places and displayed parts of my growing body. In the end, Lady Hoda covered my head with a cap. I'd never had one before. It became one of my favorite items.

She picked up my old robe and went to give it to the river. As she was about to throw it away, I jumped and snatched it from her with a strength I never knew I had. In my tears, I screamed, "No way! My mother fitted this for me from her own used cloak!" While I pressed it to my chest, Lady Hoda hugged me and caressed my head. She smelled sweet, very similar to my mother's scent.

"Gigi, you don't need this old one anymore. You have a new one. Later on, I will get you more."

Without saying a word, I stormed to the barn and hid it in an opening of a wall. A few minutes later, Lady Hoda arrived, combed, and braided my hair in two parts—they barely touched my shoulders.

As days passed, the cap that at first came down and covered my face sat on top of my head. Its edge shaded my face perfectly. I loved my new look.

Lady Hoda acted kindly toward me, especially in her Master's absence. Whenever he was away, she allowed me inside the house. It was crowded with rugs, dishes, beds, sheets, and pillows. Helping her with the household chores was my pleasure. And combing my hair and braiding it into two parts became my reward. To have her attention was my delight.

One day, my braids even touched my blooming chest. Finally, my hair ran to my waist when I let it loose. Lady Hoda, amazed, said, "Gigi, your wavy hair looks like a night without any stars, so mysterious, matching your eyes."

I had no idea what she was talking about.

Another night, I went with her to the basement to grab a wine jug. When she took the key from her bosom, I was shocked and asked, "Lady Hoda, did your mean husband trust you with the wine cellar?"

Before opening the door, she turned to me. "Now, you're old enough that I can trust you. I will tell you a secret about my life as soon as I wet my lips." She pointed to one of the jugs.

The roomy place was filled from top to bottom with wine jugs of different sizes. I shook like a twig caught in a sandstorm. "Are you sure it's okay with your husband?"

With friendly eyes and a smile, she responded, "Well, he isn't here, is he?"

She grabbed a reasonably big one, and I helped carry it upstairs. At last, Lady Hoda said, "He has so many. And he can't count," then she burst into laughter.

I scratched my head. "True. Impossible to see one or two missing."

"And, whenever he returns, he has a few more jugs to add to the piles."

Lady Hoda poured a goblet for me and one for herself. The smell of wine made me sick, as if I were in a rickety boat. So, I only pretended to drink. When Lady Hoda was on her second goblet, I asked, "Now, are your lips wet enough to tell me your secret?"

In a tipsy voice, she revealed, "Well, my Master thinks he can fool me." She wiggled her index finger. "No! No!"

Initially, he kept the key with him when he went away. Then, after a few years of marriage, Lady Hoda desired to drink in his absence. Knowing he wouldn't give her the key, she devised a plan.

To find a man selling locks and keys in the village was the first step. The store owner looked at Lady Hoda askew and said, "Lady, no one sells keys to a woman. I can sell you a lock but no key."

With an alluring smile, she whispered, "Keys are only for men." She caressed his hand. "I know that, sir."

When the store owner pulled his hand away, she beseeched him so much that her face was covered in tears. "Sir, I want to lock a few dates away from my other sister-wives for my only young, sick daughter."

"Why don't you share them with everyone?"

"My Master gives whatever he has to them." Through her tears, she continued, "I have to set aside my share. He hates me for not giving him a boy."

The shopkeeper could not resist her tears and blue and black arms and legs. So he even offered her two keys in case she lost one.

One night, Lady Hoda took a chance and changed the lock when her man had passed out after emptying many wine jugs. The next day when he woke up, Lady Hoda offered one of the keys to him and confessed in a whisper with some flirtatious moves, "I found this on the floor by you this morning. What key is it?"

With his eyes half open, he grumbled, "Where does this go to?"

She only shrugged.

Growling, he snatched the key and pulled her to bed, believing he was the only one with the key to the wine cellar.

"Very clever, Lady Hoda!" I was proud of her.

We sang, danced, and drank all night long. As we finished the wine jug, Lady Hoda and I lay on the floor, playing with each other's hair and arms, and drowned in our joyful world.

Suddenly, the door banged open, and her husband walked in. He was so humongous that the ground shook while he was walking. A cold sweat took over my entire body to hear him growling. He also kicked our heads with his boots one after another.

At last, I could get up, but not Lady Hoda. Instead, he leaped over, held her down, and hollered, "My woman is lying next to another woman!"

Her loud voice hit the roof, "Stop! Stop it! You're

the only one I love. I came from far away to be yours, didn't I?"

The sweet talk made her crawl out of his grasp and jump up. She kept her distance from him while straightening her robe. Her words carried lots of fear and were choppy, "Wow! You're ... home ... long time!" She swallowed with difficulty, "Sit, dear. You must be exhausted." Her trembling was apparent when she stepped toward him. She held on to his shoulders and steered him to the cushions on the other side of the room. With one hand, she propped them up and sat him down. "Gigi!" She called to me with a loud voice, as if I was outside.

"I'm here," I mumbled while trembling.

"Pour some wine for Master." Lady Hoda removed his boots. Somehow, she made him believe that he was the only one who drank the wine—not she. So, he thought the jug was the same one he had left her last time. When I put a goblet before him and stepped away as fast as possible, he grumbled, pointing at me, "Who is she?"

In a cheery voice, Lady Hoda responded, "She's Gigi. Don't you remember her?"

"Hum." As if he was looking into his mind-eye, he responded, "The little girl I brought to you a few years ago."

"Yes, I named her Gigi."

He looked me up and down. This left a bitter taste in my mouth, like a cucumber butt.

He thundered, "I had forgotten all about this girl." His vast mouth opened like a cave as if he would devour me, and his howling shook the entire world,

"What's she doing inside the house?" Without wasting any time, he flew over, grabbed Lady Hoda by the hair, and after punching her repeatedly, he screamed, "She must be in the barn, not in the house!" As if I were a lowly animal.

There was no end to him beating her. Even her robe and face soaked in blood did not make him stop. With the door wide open, the thought of running away came to my mind. But to escape into the darkness was scary. More importantly, how could I leave Lady Hoda behind? She was my friend, and I loved her so much.

Wishing he would stop, I recalled she had divulged to me some time ago that she played dead when the hitting became unbearable. And just like that, his beating stopped when she moved no more. He left her on the floor and came after me, huddled in the corner, trembling like a caged canary waiting for the wild cat to devour me.

Master grabbed my two braided-hair and pulled me on the ground behind him to the barn. He was deaf to my wailings. Finally, he stood motionless, staring at the two hair braids in his hand. "This is the place for you!" He looked at me with a cold face. "A woman with your eyes means many coins are waiting in the bazaar for me. Too bad, now you have short hair." Without letting me breathe, he ripped off my clothes with a strange smirk and dropped his pants. I could do nothing; except to pull my cap over my face. I refrained from wailing and tolerated the excruciating pain when he forced himself on me. I only tasted my bleeding lips quietly—not to give him the satisfaction of a triumph.

The following day, as if he was blind and deaf to

Lady Hoda's weeping, he took me to the bazaar. The robe he ordered me to wear exposed most of my breasts and thighs. At that moment, I had the urge to run away, and if he caught up with me, he could imprison me. But at least I would be with Lady Hoda. My heart was in pieces for her. I wished she could break her invisible chains and come with me.

Sometimes jumping into a fire beats staying safe in the shade.

At the bazaar, the Master pushed me to stand up on the stage in a lineup with other men and women to be auctioned off to the highest bidder. Surprisingly, I didn't have to tolerate the shame of being half-naked for a long time. In the blink of an eye, a heavy-set elder immediately bought me. His head was wrapped in a white cloth. His bid was so high that no one else could afford to go higher.

It's shocking, a man paid so many gold coins for me!

Amazingly, without hesitation, he covered my naked shoulders with a linen shawl. Unlike others who took the slaves to a carriage or wanted them to walk behind the horses, the man walked side-by-side with me to an area filled with palm trees. Without a word, he left me under the shade of one. Meanwhile, I was ready for anything, wishing a beast would devour me and end my misery. Finally, close to sunset, he showed up with two other men. I was not able to pinpoint their tribes or countries. Wearing armor, they possibly were soldiers from the Roman army, especially with their blond hair. They couldn't be Persians.

In shock, I felt my original owner's gentle push in my back nudge me toward them. A short ride on a raft took us up to a gigantic ship full of iron boxes. We embarked. The two soldiers gave me a pair of pants and a shirt to change into.

Neither one ever acted like they were my owner. They even introduced themselves to me as Justus and Titus. On the boat, Justus even offered me a mattress, all to myself. My horror dreams of waiting for them to make a move on me never became a reality. Instead, both protected me during the trip, ensuring I had enough to eat and drink. They never talked with me. When I asked whether they were my Master, Justus, the taller one, shook his head. "No!" And walked away.

After several days, nights, and possibly months, one night, finally, the boat anchored. The harbor was filled with joyful music and singing. "These people must have no care in the world," I said.

Before getting out, Justus uttered, "This is the place we get parted."

I felt like my body had collapsed. "Didn't you pay for me? Aren't you my new Master?"

He whispered while he stared at me with his blue eyes, "Listen, we will leave you in this harbor. If you want to escape the world of slavery and not starve to death, make friends with a fisherman named Theo or Thea."

I was baffled. "Who is he or she?"

Justus pointed to a person in the distance.

"Become her friend," he said emphatically. "Go wherever she goes. Be her shadow."

"She's your salvation," Titus uttered.

"Hard to tell whether it's a boy or a girl playing the lyre," I observed.

Indeed, Thea was my savior. Without her, I would

have been dead. I was her companion until we arrived at Tysfoon. In the inn, she left me all by myself. But I never lost sight of her, especially when I befriended one of the Palace guards. I knew exactly what she was up to.

Thea, bold as a bull, but soft as a morning breeze

THEA

CHAPTER 20

Tysfoon

12 BCE

T he royal horn trumpeting His Majesty's hunting trip woke me at dawn. The uproar of barking dogs, striding hoofs, and men's mumbling beckoned me to the outside. In the distance, I saw the man riding ahead in the middle of four other riders. It made my heart miss a beat. *He must be King Farshad.*

His upright stature with broad shoulders gave him royal dignity and an aura of self-confidence. This was despite his identical tunic, trousers, and robe with a plain rounded cap, similar to the other cavalry. I had the urge to rush to him and introduce myself. However, I used my inner rein to stay and keep my legs from running.

When they rode out of sight, I rushed to my room and put on a Parthian archery rider's linen outfit. The long earth-color scarf covered my head, neck, and face.

My eyes were the only central bare feature. I mounted Sattar to chase after them and left the workplace. Getting permission from Javid wasn't needed. Today, like most days, he was a no-show. Since I did not need to ask him questions, he would come in only when he had to present an urgent message to the King.

I rode after them but kept my distance, as far back as I could still see the last King's guard. They proceeded north along the Tigris River. Dense trees and bushes helped me stay hidden. The King and his entourage were moving at a snail's speed. It looked like the King's hunting trip was not a simple outing. So many horses, carriages, and wagons looked like they had uprooted most of the Palace.

By sunset, they were close to the King's camping area. While His Majesty was resting at a station, the men in charge of setting up went ahead. The men erected the royal camp by the river bank, replete with trees and plants of all sizes, absent of weeds or harmful shrubs.

This place must be a man-shifted nature only for the King.

Upon His Majesty's arrival, the royal camp shone like a gem in the middle of the forest. They had to be close to the dens of wild boars. Sattar and I, however, maintained our good stretch from them.

While everyone was sleeping, I walked far from the guards' eyes around the camp until I located several wild boars in a flatland. Sattar and I hid behind a hill close to them. They were even more dangerous than any lions and tigers. *They're the wildest beasts in the wilderness,* according to Cordelia.

I snuck next to their dens after rubbing some of Cordelia's oil on Sattar's body and mine to tame the wild animals. The potion made it as if we were invisible.

No wonder so many of them were gathered here. They were lured or transferred by the King's men. During the spring, the male boars had to prepare their habitat under the poplar trees for the birth of their babies—boarlets. They would pull tremendous amounts of leaves and branches over their heads to create a canopy for shelter near the stream.

With the first rays of the sun, the camp's buzzing was a sign that His Majesty was getting ready to start his day. Soon, the riders, including the King, became visible with numerous Bone-Mouth Shar Pei—the only breed capable of scaring the beasts. However, before everyone in the group had assembled, the King galloped his Arabian stallion well ahead of the others toward one of the dens. It was hard to tell whether it was the horse's will or His Majesty's.

How come he doesn't know about the enormous danger he's facing? Or, he thinks his men trained these beasts too.

Suddenly, a male boar ran out and picked up his speed toward the King. The horse's loud neighing made it apparent that His Majesty had lost control. When his men realized the King was in danger, they released the dogs. But the boar ignored the dogs and sped toward the King even faster. Unexpectedly, His Majesty fell off his mount. At this instance, the King's men started galloping toward him. They were too far and too late to save the King's life—the boar had almost caught up with the King. At once, Sattar and I sprinted from another direction, and like an archery rider, I shot the boar with not one arrow but two. Moments later, all of the King's men arrived. The boar's lifeless body lay before His Majesty's feet. Two of his guards right away escorted the King back to the camp.

A few others who stayed behind had concluded that the two arrows were meant for the King, not the boar. They blocked my way and yelled, "Whoa! Stop! Stop!"

One of them yelled even louder, "Hey! Lad! You're not going anywhere!"

I reined in Sattar.

The man riding next to the King yesterday dismounted and gestured for me to do so too. In a calm voice, he said, "How did you know the King's life was in danger before anyone else?"

I shrugged nonchalantly. "I was closest to the boar and had a much better view than the other royal men." My response needed to be more adequate. He still questioned me and even, at one point, accused me of trespassing in the area designated only for the monarch and his men.

"I was traveling at night. I did not recognize the forbidden land." I leaned against Sattar's body and continued, "I am a master archery rider. My aim is precise. My arrow was only meant for the boar, not otherwise."

When he understood that rescuing the King was my ultimate desire, he said, "You saved the King's life. How many gold coins would you like for your reward?"

"Zero."

He rubbed his chin. "A sack of gold coins, maybe?"

I shook my head. "I'm delighted to save His Majesty's life."

He looked at me with disbelieving eyes. "Wow, I never came across anyone who refuses gold coins."

No words came out of my mouth as I stared into his eyes. However, the vultures' joyful cries, soaring over our heads, were all signs of their celebration. They could not wait for the feast on the ground. *Losing a life is a gain for others.*

Tired of waiting for dismissal under the direct sun, I stepped to Sattar, set my left foot in the stirrup, and was ready to mount when his voice made me turn around.

He rubbed his forehead and said, "Name your prize."

I came down, faced him, and in a firm voice, I claimed, "A private meeting with His Majesty."

"Wow! Wait a minute." He tapped his chest. "I'm His Majesty's confidant. He and I grew up together. He rarely gives me any time alone with him."

"Well, this is what I want as my reward. Nothing else." I turned away and mounted. I trotted away when he roared, "Come to the Palace and ask for Babak. Maybe I can do something." His voice stretched out in the distance, talking to the other men. "Unbelievable! Have you encountered anyone who declines some gold coins, even a sack?"

A few days later, from work, I walked to the Palace, draped like a Persian girl: A long colorful dress showing the curves of my body.

I addressed a couple of guards blocking the massive iron door. "Where can the King's advisor, Babak, be found? There is a confidential letter for him." I showed them the letter.

One of them, with a stern face, said. "Who are you?"

"I'm Javid's deputy."

"How come he didn't bring it himself, as usual?"

I shrugged. "Today, he was too busy and wanted me to be his messenger."

As if they heard the magic word, the one closest to the door let me inside without further questions. I walked a long way through the long corridors and halls. The hanging tapestries interwoven with threads of gold and a delicately sculpted frieze around the walls were impossibly luxurious. Still, this one was a hut compared to the glory of the past Persepolis Palace.

By every closed door, two guards were standing. Finally, I asked one, "How can I find Advisor Babak?"

"Turn around," one guard directed me. "At the end of this corridor, go right. The tenth room is Advisor Babak's."

When I got there, the security guards prevented me from entering. But after showing the letter, one of them announced my presence as Javid's deputy and asked permission to enter. I entered.

Babak jumped up from his desk and, in a surprised voice, said, "What can I do for you?"

"I brought you this." Then, I slid the letter onto his desk. He stared at me briefly, then asked, "Where's Javid?"

"I'm Thea. Today, he wanted me to deliver this to you."

He looked into my eyes and murmured, "Do I know you from somewhere?"

Smiling, I said, "Perhaps."

"Your green eyes are very familiar."

"Do you remember the archery rider?"

His joyful voice filled the room, "You are the one who saved His Majesty's life."

Babak must be from the same tribe as King Cyrus, Aryan, for not being shocked that a woman saved the King's life.

"Remember? That day, you invited me to the Palace. To see how you could arrange ..."

He exclaimed, "Yes, I recall now." While scratching his head, he continued, "Wow, I'm sure His Majesty would love to meet the person who saved his life." He went to the big table and poured some wine. "Would you like some?"

"No, thank you."

"Don't tell me, as a Westerner, you don't drink."

"I do, but not while working."

After going back and forth for some time, he devised a solution for introducing me to His Majesty. "King Farshad will attend the feast for his twenty-second anniversary on the throne in three days. Come as my guest. I'll do my best to introduce you to him."

I frowned. "Then, it won't be a private time with the King."

"Only His Majesty decides on that. He will allow you to have an audience with him if he chooses."

His offer was the most solid one I had ever received.

The day of celebration came like a snap of the fingers. After combing my curly red hair to get ready, I took part of it to the right and kept it away from my face with a gold and emerald ornament enhancing my green eyes. I let the other side run to my left shoulder. My look became ravishing, especially after I wore the silk robe—my creation while living at Cordelia's place.

The roaring of the upbeat music, including drums, throughout the Palace and beyond was my guide. The enormous main hall was crowded with men and women in fancy clothing, mostly made of silk. They were dancing or drinking. It was easy to distinguish each group by the color of their outfits. The bunch in red were warriors. Magi, the religious ones, in white robes, belts, and caps with the royal emblem of an angel spreading his wings. I recalled Ormazd's uniform. And wealthy farmers in rustic blue.

Amazingly, the King's formal robe, a mixture of these three colors, was made in identical triangles, pointing up to the sky, a work of art. His robe showed His Majesty's authority over the three estates, as each triangle is unbreakable. His hair was neatly pulled away, tucked in the back where the diadem crown set. His coiffured mustache and beard almost covered his facial wrinkles.

Next to him, the Queen's most colossal jewels in the hall seized my attention and hurt my eyes. I stayed close to the door but within Babak's eyeshot. He sat next to the King, talking with a lady beside him. Upon seeing me, he acknowledged my presence with a nod. Babak took the hand of the same lady and walked over to me. "Thea, this is my wife, Nur."

I bent my knee, a sign of respect. He turned to her and murmured in her ear. With a smile, she said, "Marvelous! A woman saved our King's life."

In a loud voice, Babak offered, "Let's go and introduce her to His Majesty."

The three of us walked two steps up. Nur and I stayed behind when he whispered into the King's ear. Babak turned his torso and gestured for both of us to step forward. Nur willingly stayed one step behind and gently pressed her hand on my back to go ahead. I proceeded toward the King and bowed. I made sure my mouth was close to his ear and whispered, "Your Majesty, I seek your private audience to reveal everything to you."

In shock, he turned his head to me with wide-open sharp eyes.

I continued, "I have a message from the Prince for you."

He nodded and murmured, "Of course."

Without wasting time, the Queen murmured into his other ear, drawing his attention to her. The Queen's head, decorated with the royal crown, was regal.

Shortly after, the King left the feast when he finished his conversation with the Queen. I became occupied talking with some people and made friends with those who were not shy to speak to a once-enslaved Roman girl. With the Queen still present, the festivity continued as strongly as before. I was about to leave when a guard approached me and murmured, "His Majesty commands your presence in his chamber."

As I followed his steps, I could not miss the Queen's stern eyes staring at me. I ignored the voice within me; *I'll wear your crown one day.*

QUEEN JEWEL

(as told by Kam)

CHAPTER 21

The vexed Queen Jewel witnessed that King Farshad had summoned Thea to his chamber—an infuriating event to her. When she stood up, I, as her confidant eunuch, abided Her Majesty's desire and followed the Queen to her chamber.

Two maids helped her remove the cumbersome gown with many gems sewn on it. The Queen ordered me to take a slave girl to the black hole beneath the Palace.

"Which one, Your Majesty?" I mumbled. "A few new ones just arrived. They won't know what awaits them." Avoiding her fierce eyes was my best remedy when I heard her shriek: "Kam! Choose the prettiest of them all!"

She threw on a pair of trousers, a shirt, and leather riding boots, all in black. Her joyful face masked the dark sea within her. Before opening the heavy iron door to the dungeon, she chose the thickest and widest whip among the rest.

Knowing Jewel's habit, I had already ordered a trusted servant to chain the slave's hands with the legs wide open, facing the wall, and her dress was ripped in the back.

The Queen never wanted to see the face, not to be haunted by their eyes. "To see those sad, hopeless eyes is not my cup of tea," she mumbled.

To feel sympathetic toward them was all I could do. I uttered several times, "Your Majesty, have mercy on them."

She said through her teeth, "They're only hopeless and helpless creatures."

"What do you want them to do, Your Majesty?"

"Fight ... fight ... and fight!" Her anger was evident in her words. "At the end, they'll die anyway."

My answer to the Queen's blind eyes was: "But they're all tied up! How could they?"

"They could gnaw, growl, bark, or at least wiggle to show some resistance, not hang there like a piece of meat!"

"Would you then release them?"

She shrugged. "So far, I haven't seen anyone who wanted to rebel against me." A wide smirk covered her face.

Instead of going back and forth with her, I kept my mouth shut without verbalizing my thoughts. *But enslaved people aren't as vicious as Your Majesty. They think if they obey, you'll stop.*

After banging the heavy wooden door open, Jewel started flogging the girl nonstop, so forcefully that soon the floor gathered her blood, turning the dust and smut into red mud. The Queen turned a deaf ear to the girl's wailing and crying.

When the hitting became faster and more vicious, she beseeched the Queen through tears, "Your Majesty, what did I do wrong to deserve your punishment? Please stop!"

The Queen's answer was to bring the whip up and down with her mighty strength even faster. Finally, when the girl's back was slashed so profusely that the backbone was on display, I could keep silent no more. "Your Majesty, she is only one breath away from death," I uttered while trying to take the strap out of her grip.

I warned the Queen several times. She finally turned to me as if my voice awakened her from a deep trance. "Kam, why are you trembling?"

I closed my eyes not to see the Queen's face spattered with the slave's blood. Then, in dread, she stopped and stared at her hands in disgust. With my trembling hand, I took the whip away from her. Under her breath, she uttered, "Free her."

Now, the Queen feels good about herself. She freed a slave girl.

Later four maidens pampered and soaked Jewel in the warm camel milk at her Quarter. She screeched when they started to clean the blood from her face with the softest sponge. "Stop! Stop!" Queen Jewel slapped the maid's hand harshly and ordered, "Don't use that! Use the coarsest and hardest one!"

None of them dared to cause the Queen any harm and backed off. Jewel, however, blind to their quivering like leaves on a fragile tree, snatched the rough sponge herself and scrubbed her face and hands. Suddenly, she looked horrified at the slave's blood mixed in with the milk. She shrieked in horror and leaped out, screaming, running, and scratching her cheeks and forehead. Petrified of her royal blood and an enslaved girl's mixing, she could have bled herself to death.

Though feeling woozy, I had to grab her hand to

stop the Queen from hurting herself any further—no one else dared to do so. I led her to bed where she hid under the cover and pulled it over her head. After that, she did not leave bed for two days, and I sat quietly beside her.

Another day, the Queen's jealousy flared up again. She was baffled about Thea. A Western girl was getting close to the King's ear, undermining Jewel by not making friends or contacting her. Babak introduced Thea to the King only. He went against all the Palace protocol and failed to bring her to the Queen at the feast.

Compared to the King's women living in the Quarter designated for them, Thea stood alone, far from the rest. Unlike other of the King's women, this one was no dummy and much more challenging of a nut to crack. She wasn't just a pretty face. Thea spoke Parsi and talked in Greek with the King and everyone around him. It was yet another reason for the Queen to be upset.

As a teenager, many tutors tried to teach her Greek. None tolerated her two-year-old behavior. And after a few lessons, they all quit. So, she had no idea what that girl murmured into the King's ear.

Thea's youth and stature, almost as tall as the King, also opposed Jewel to her short and chubby body. Right away, Thea had a place at the court. The Queen had hoped that after Thea spent the night in the King's chamber, she would move to the Women's Quarter to be under Her Majesty's rule. But that did not happen. Jewel thundered when she heard Thea had saved the King's life by being faster and better at shooting than any man. The Queen was worried sick over Thea's future in Persia.

The Roman girl arrived alone and quickly entered the King's chamber. The robe she had on for the celebration looked pretty expensive. Jewel kept wondering about Thea's business. Several times, the Queen screamed, "A Roman, rich girl landed in the Palace without any other members of the Roman Court!"

"Your Highness," I counseled, "she's brave enough and doesn't need any man's protection."

"Nonsense! A woman always needs a man's backing!" Jewel's red eyes were full of anger. "She must be a Roman spy!"

Spy or not, she was a threat to the Queen's position. And Jewel's eyes were glowing with malevolence. So, for the time being, she let anger run through her like bad blood.

To me, Jewel was like a cloth I witnessed being woven. I was born to one of her mother's maids and raised in her family to be a royal servant. Unfortunately, Jewel's mother died right after giving birth to her. Without any siblings, she was the apple of her father's eye. So they castrated me to be with her in the Women's Quarter, to protect her like her father, and be her nanny and confidant.

I'm her shadow—a eunuch living through her.

Queen Jewel grew up like a princess, despite not being born to a queen or king. One of her ancestors was the right hand of Mithridates, the first man among the Scythes tribe to uprise against the Greek rulers in Persia. He was instrumental in building a colossal temple in his homeland, near the Caspian Sea, in the extreme northeast of the land. He named his dynasty Parthian and presented our religion as Mithraism. Its priests became known as Magi. And the Persian past flourished with a new face throughout the land.

For over 200 years, Jewel's forebears were embedded with the Parthian kings. Ever since they became privy to the kings' secrets. I was present when Jewel's father revealed King Farshad's secret to her. He was not supposed to be our current King. But, he was sneaky enough to get rid of the two other legitimate princes, who rightfully could become kings. No one knew exactly how each one after another met their Creator. Farshad mingled with many of Ahriman's friends, who did not mind doing His Majesty's dirty work. And Jewel's father played a significant hand in it.

The King's mother, an enslaved girl, never was allowed to marry the previous king and become the Queen. Farshad remained in line for the throne as an illegitimate King's son. At the time of the last King's passing, no other successor was left except Farshad. So, Farshad grabbed the crown and became the King of the Persian Empire in a fascinating coronation ceremony.

The young Farshad married Jewel soon after he became the King, an arranged marriage by her father. To everyone's amazement, at the wedding, His Majesty declared her the Queen of Persia for life. While Jewel's father was alive, as one of the closest advisors to King Farshad, he ensured Jewel's position as the Queen would be as solid as a rock. Jewel learned from her father how to keep King's skeleton in the closet.

For everything in life, there must be a price to pay!

Jewel also had to pay a hefty price for being the Queen. She closed her eyes to His Majesty's four-time marriages. He had a good reason. Each wife was a satrap's daughter of such a land that became part of the Kingdom. Or, to deny her hurtful heart, he often summoned concubines or slaves instead of her. The Queen tolerated them all. But, somehow, she could not close her eyes to Thea's existence.

After twenty-two years of marriage, she failed to give the King and the nation a successor. Farshad had an eighteen-year-old son, Ardalan, by a concubine. The King officially appointed him as the Crown Prince. During the last battle, the Romans somehow captured and kept him hostage. If Thea had been here during that time, Jewel would blame her for it.

Before Thea showed up at the Palace, life was good. Parthians were urgently decisive in bringing King Cyrus's glory back. They were successful in the trades connecting the Eastern and Western worlds. But, the Parthian kings continued to rule like Alexander's successors. They encouraged the merchants to bring enslaved girls and eunuchs from abroad.

Hoping not to give Thea a chance to seep into the King's heart, Jewel was busy thinking fast and hard to find a way to get rid of her. Finally, one day, she gestured for me to come close to her earshot and ordered everyone else out. Jewel disclosed a few plans to rid herself of Thea while I sat before her on a stool. In case one would not work, she could implement the other. Hearing them one after another, I finally jumped up; and with horrified eyes, I browbeat her, "Please, Your Highness, I don't want to hear any more of your plans."

Lying on the plush couch, with a smirk, she murmured, "Remember! She is our enemy. And we're entitled to kill an enemy while she's in our territory."

THEA

CHAPTER 22

U pon opening my eyes this morning, the time I spent in the King's chamber last night came to focus. The possibility of him being my lover was still there. Unfortunately, he did not even come close to looking anything like King Cyrus—a disappointment.

When I entered the King's chamber, he had already changed into a silk tunic. He sat behind a small round ivory table. He did not look propped up while wearing the formal robe. He had a small stature but still was as tall as me. The patches of white hair with so many wrinkles on his face gave His Majesty a ruminative look that a king needed to rule this vast kingdom.

Nevertheless, his authoritative voice sat in my ears: "We must thank you for saving my life." A becoming and kind smile enveloped his face. "We are delighted you were at the right place and time."

"Your Majesty, it was the least I could do," I said and bowed.

He got up and stepped closer to me. "Did you say you have a message from my son, Ardalan?"

I nodded and walked so near the King that his breath fell on my face. I back-tracked myself and took out Caesar's letter hidden in my bosom. With a bow, I offered it to His Majesty.

Breaking the seal, he whispered with a grin, "You safeguarded this very well from the West to the East." But, after staring at it for a moment, he threw it on the floor and, in harsh words, exclaimed, "This is not from Ardalan. It's from your Emperor!" His eyes were angry, and his face became marred with deeper wrinkles.

After bowing again, in the softest words, I uttered, "Your Majesty, let me negotiate between you and the Roman Emperor for exchanging the Persian Prince with the Roman Flag and Golden Eagle." Without waiting for a response, I ignored the gold goblet on the table and stepped to the enormous mahogany table. I picked up a fresh goblet from the other six, then decanted the wine and placed it at the King's reach. "Your Majesty, I urge you to appoint me as your envoy, so I can have the authority to settle the matter with Rome."

The King let the silence hang. I picked up the goblet and offered it to him. Looking squarely into his eyes, I said, "Your Majesty, I can handle the communication between you and the Emperor as quickly as possible."

He took the goblet from me and still stared at me. "Your bravery is proven to us." He squinted his eyes. "I can see the reason Augustus chose you."

"Thank you for having confidence in me, Your Majesty."

He stepped past me and sat on the edge of the bed behind me.

No subject is allowed to have their back to the King! I

screamed in my head and swirled around, ignoring my stormy heart. "I have only your interest in mind, Your Majesty." My eyes could see nothing but gold—the gold-trimmed bed and the canopy fabric were interwoven with gold threads. A soft red silk rug under his feet had to cost a fortune. The King likely did not care for a bunch of crushed silkworms.

Of Course not. A ruler gives orders to crush men; some dead silkworms count for nothing.

The King's eyes were full of sexual desire when he tapped on the spot beside him, inviting me, "Come and sit by me so that I can hear you better."

No one dares to refuse a king's order, especially a woman.

I took one slow step at a time. Upon reaching the same edge, I sat on the other side and kept my distance from the King. "Your Majesty," I turned my upper body to him as near as possible and whispered, "I'm interested in you as much as you are in me."

He looked into my eyes. "Then why are you sitting way out of my reach?"

I was cautious not to raise his anger. "I would love to prove that my only desire is to bring the Prince to you...first!"

He sipped the wine. Then, he reached to a box on his side table and took out an eye-grabbing gold necklace decorated with emeralds from small to the largest in the middle. With a big smile, he mumbled, "Come closer, so I can put this on you."

I got up and stepped toward him. I replied, "Your Majesty, how very generous of you to offer me such an amazing piece of jewelry." I swallowed hard. "Please, forgive me." Continuing, I turned my face to the royal rug. "I won't be able to accept it."

"Are you refusing the King's gift?" he said in his tipsy voice.

"Not at all, Your Majesty! We can be together when I return Prince Ardalan safe and sound. Then I will happily wear this outstanding piece around my neck." I bent my knee and brought my head down. "From my heart, it is my promise to you."

He removed his silk tunic and mumbled like an aggravated lion, "But that'll take soooooo long— I am not used to waiting."

For His Majesty, everything has to be Now or never. Let's see if I can change that.

"I beg you, Your Majesty! I'm here for a task. Let me concentrate and bring Prince Ardalan to His Majesty first." In a firm voice, I said, "With the Persian royal messengers, famous for their speed, at my fingertips, Prince Ardalan will be home in no time."

Each time the King heard the Prince's name, his jaws relaxed. I kept my eyes on him while speaking. "Your Majesty, I dream of the time you will have me."

Without waiting for his dismissal, I returned to the door, opened it, and rushed out of His Majesty's chamber. The exuberant feeling of being in charge, especially when the man was the ruler of the Persian Empire, blanketed me.

All the way, I danced until I arrived at my room. The joyful feeling of refusing His Majesty was UNBELIEVABLE! However, I had a sinking feeling about whether I convinced the King. Or, at any moment, my head would be on a platter like

Bardia, Mother Mithra's son. With rulers, we never know to what extent they would go to take revenge. But I didn't think King Farshad was as vicious as King Astyages.

Javid's banging on the door broke my daydreaming. The sun, almost in the middle of the sky, made me realize that the morning went by quickly. The last I saw him was a few weeks ago. His untidy appearance showed as if he had gotten up from somewhere else and run over here. His spotted, wrinkled robe and long hair, usually tied neatly to the back, were messy as if he was a destitute man and couldn't even afford a comb. His half-open sleepy eyes, thick eyebrows filling the gap between them, screamed his frustration.

In a respectful voice, I said, "Hello, sir. How are you today?"

He took out a keychain with many different sizes of keys and threw it on the desk. After a heavy breath, he shouted, "You went to the King's chamber last night, didn't you?"

"Yes, I did." I said unperturbed. "Where were you for the celebration? I didn't see you at the festivity."

His red eyes and intense annoyance disturbed me when he shouted, "Congratulations! Now with you, the King has added yet another woman to his concubines."

With disbelieving eyes, I uttered, "What? What are you talking about?"

"Don't tell me you did not share the King's pillow last night!" he scowled.

His exasperated voice hit me, moving his hands up and down as if he would slap me. But, being shorter than I was, he missed. So then, like a father, he questioned me, "Was it before you offered yourself on a shiny platter or after?"

And I was at the receiving end of his spitting. In an agitated move, he wiped his forehead and continued with his insulting words, "Stop looking at me with your open mouth as if you had no idea!"

He thinks he is the King, my owner!

Javid had crossed the line, and he needed to be stopped. "Please!" My firm voice filled the room. "No more insults! I have no idea what you are talking about. Whatever went between the King and I is ..."

He interrupted me, howling, "Now, pick up your stuff, go to the Palace, and add yourself to His Majesty's stable of concubines. It's his order."

"I will not go to the Women's Quarter," I insisted. "Even if the King orders it."

With a smirk, he said through his teeth, "How dare you refuse His Majesty's order?"

In an authoritative voice, I responded, "If you don't stop the insults, I will report you to the King. As you know, while living in this country, all the foreign personnel are under His Majesty's protection."

As if he heard the secret word, he murmured, "One of the King's assistants, Hooman, is waiting outside to show you to your new chamber."

"What?" I was shocked. "Javid, what are you talking about?"

He gestured to me. "Go! Go!" Then he mumbled, "Don't let him wait any longer."

Anxious, not knowing where my house would be, and worrying about Sattar, I only asked, "Can I take my horse with me?"

"No idea! Ask him!" But all of a sudden, his voice became much calmer and friendlier. "Why don't you walk over there to talk with him before your move."

The butterflies in my belly were out of control.

I pointed to the keychain. "Javid, I thought you were giving me the keys and going away for good."

His upper lip flinched. "Now, with you not being here, I must remember to lock the doors again."

It's so difficult to read someone else's mind. Of course, I can compete with the bravest men. But, to read a man's mind seems impossible.

While walking with Hooman, disregarding his serious face, I asked, "Am I housed at the Women's Quarter?"

He mumbled, "No."

When we passed the Quarter and entered the vicinity of the King's Palace, I sighed a deep breath of relief.

The move into one of the chambers closest to the King went without a hitch. Sattar was also situated in a royal stable with a large stall identical to the royal horses. The same night, Gigi and I drank a few goblets of wine to celebrate my new position as one of the King's advisors and get a few more steps closer to the King.

"Now," Gigi uttered, "You're as close to the King as Caesar wants you to be."

While leaving the tavern, I murmured, "Not close enough yet."

CHAPTER 23

Tysfoon

10 BCE

D ark ... and dark ... nothing but darkness! I believed the starless night had spread the thickest cover over my eyes. It had to be the longest night of my life. Barely breathing sent me into panic mode. Then, I realized. My stretched body on the ground had nowhere to go, so I started wiggling it to ensure no bone was broken. I went to bring my right hand before my face. It did not follow my order, and neither did the left arm. I tried to extend them to the side, but they only slapped the two walls beside me, causing gravel and dirt to fall over me. And they stayed bent.

My breathing was getting shallower by the minute. After trying to lift my head, some rocks or *bricks* hit it. The steel pain struck me so hard that I could go nowhere except back down to the uneven ground beneath. Meanwhile, wet stones poked me in the spine and hurt me tremendously. Freaking out, I started shouting, "Help! Help!" No reply came my way. Everyone had to be dead.

I was now aware that someone had bricked me alive in the ground. But how? No sickness that I could think of. I might, however, have fainted, and someone thought I was dead. Then, I pushed myself slowly to the right, gathered all my strength, and started digging. The only tools available were my fingers. I wished to have long nails like Cordelia's. But I was too deep in the ground—probably at least six feet under. To make any hole to breathe was my number one urgency. After a long time, I could only dig a few small gaps between the bricks to delay my death. Next, I gathered all my strength in my fists and broke a brick by forcing it out. The soft breeze on my face gave me more power.

I kept digging and digging. After breaking some more damp mortar and spending much energy, the few holes helped me breathe more effortlessly.

"Help! ... Help!" The answer to my shouting was only my voice bouncing back. Regardless of all the shouting and screaming from the top of my lungs ... *Nothing!* The hustle and bustle of capital noise was absent. The grave had to be ways out of town. I urged myself to bring my palms together to pray to Soteria— the goddess of safety. But they failed me.

In this most desperate moment, I refused to admit my defeat—no way I let my life get away. In my heart, I knew this was not the end of me. Death was not an option. Did I come from Rome to Persia and meet so many heartwarming people for nothing, only to die here? Did Neptune help me to catch the majestic blue eel for nothing? Did I learn the Egyptians' secret of using natural asphalt for no use? No! No! I refused to lie here and let worms enter my body and exit my nostrils!

Suddenly, Sattar's and Gigi's innocent faces appeared to me. They urged me to resist and could not wait to see me. Her encouraging smile made me withstand longer and longer.

Soon, however, I came to a grim realization: I had to stop believing my body was frozen.

I would not be in a grave if Cordelia were not in the fire. I only think I am. I held on to the pounding in my head. *I AM THEA! I AM ALIVE!*

To replay the last few months' events in my mind could signify life. Queen Jewel had unexpectedly opened the door of friendship to me. She showered me with jewelry—one day, a gold band; another, a pair of earrings or bracelets and bangles. The other day, she even sent me a silk robe. It put the one I had made to shame. The Persian royals were so wealthy that they did not mind spending many gold coins on the multitudes of silk robes.

A Persian custom dictates not to return gifts from the King or Queen. So, my hands were tied. Jewel's presents were, however, thrown into the bottom of a chest.

Every week I also received an invitation from the Queen to attend one of her parties. Most of the time, I gave an excuse of having to answer piles of letters or have other engagements. To witness the messenger's droopy face carrying the regretful response was brutal for me. Jewel could never hide her fury from me behind a social tapestry that she wove days and nights. Her vicious look at the King's anniversary festivity was unforgettable.

Then, there was much whispering among the court women: "Have you heard?"

"What?"

"Again, the Queen beat an enslaved girl so viciously ... she died shortly after."

And no one was there to prevent it ... how horrific!

Queen Jewel and I played cat and mouse. Whenever she became close, I would seek refuge with the King. But, if I were in His Majesty's presence, a Roman or Greek girl with blue eyes and blond hair in a robe hugging her curves would bring an urgent message from the Queen. Or a messenger would immediately announce that the Queen asked permission for a private audience with the King. She likely bribed some guards to report to her whenever I was in the King's presence.

Later, Jewel even took it upon herself to rush in, breaking the King's official meetings with the advisors or foreign dignitaries. To see me among them made her recoil. In her fiery eyes, her raging anger was apparent. The King finally forbade the Queen to enter his chamber unless he had sent for her.

Even in the darkness of the grave, I remembered clearly, that the last place I went was to attend one of the Queen's parties. The feast was held in the Women's Quarter with only women in attendance. The vast hall was enveloped in a cloud of thick foggy smoke. Several maids carrying around the small braziers reminded me of the scent with a chunky smell Cordelia used once in a while, especially before I went to sleep. A maid had the brazier so near me as if she and I were connected at the hips. While fanning the smoke toward me, and in response to my question about the name of the scent lingering around, she murmured, "Not scent. Hashish smoke."

"How do you get it?" I inquired.

"It comes from the seeds of a plant with beautiful white, but mostly red flowers called ..."

"Poppies! I saw many of them." With a smile, I continued, "At first, I thought the ground was on fire, but ..."

My conversation with the maid about poppies and hashish was interrupted in disappointment when the Queen approached to thank me for attending her party.

I had no idea what had taken over me. I mindlessly drank so much delicious Persian wine. I also consumed mouthwatering food of all kinds: Lamb, deer, and pheasant, accompanied by a rainbow of vegetables, making it one of the best times of my life. No one could sit still or not dance to the drum beats. *Oh!* The breeze-like sound of the flute carried me to the sky. At one point, I even took the harp from a musician, and playing it in my silk robe was a sheer joy. For sure, it was an out-of-body experience—extraordinary. I was hovering toward the ceiling. It was the ultimate joy. To lose control was so much fun. I felt free without trying to impress anyone or attract a man to have fun in bed. To roar to the sky like a happy she-wolf was pure pleasure! And that was the last thing I remembered ... between then and now.

I was still alive in my grave and denied the god of death, Thanatos, to visit me. However, I called on

Soteria again, believing she would save me. As if she gave me strength, I continued howling for a long, long time. Until…I thought I heard a horse in the distance. And then, a woman's voice reached me: "Hey, is someone down there?"

I shouted, "Yes! I am buried down here!"

"Wow!" She couldn't believe her eyes and ears. "Who dared to inter a live woman?"

The mortar on the bricks was still wet, and after removing most of them, she ran to the horse and took something from the saddle. *To travel alone, she has to have something to defend herself.*

Banging went on for some time when she successfully broke some bricks. Finally, she put her hand through the hole. "Can you grab my hand?"

I struggled to no avail. "I can't move!"

She ran to the horse and brought back a long thick rope. After making a large loop at one end, she wanted me to put it through my legs and around my waist. "Try to do it. If you can't, I'll go to town and bring some help. But it'll take a long time."

Pushing and shoving the loop from my feet was not easy. With some moves similar to a snake, I finally managed to get it to my waist. And, while putting all my strength into getting up, she was busy making the hole much bigger by breaking many bricks.

When she saw I stood up like a statue, she connected the other end of the rope to the saddle horn and nudged its flank. As the horse moved step by step, I was slowly pulled out of the grave until I lay on the ground.

The lady's white robe was spattered with dirt. But she did not care. She pushed her long jet-black hair out of her face and, with a smile, said, "I'm Mithra."

I sighed in relief, thanking Soteria for sending Mithra, the Reverend, to save me.

The sun had its first light in the sky when I saw her. I confessed, "Mithra, indeed, you're my light."

"Happy to arrive at the right time in the right place," she responded kindly with a warm smile.

After helping me mount her white horse, she led me to the road, far from where I was buried.

I could barely say: "Why were you traveling on this darkest and coldest night?"

She ignored my question and claimed, "You're shivering!" Then, she pulled her wool shawl away from her shoulders and covered mine, saying, "Your tapping and your firm voice brought me to you."

I have no strength to scream so loud. It must be Soteria.

Mithra turned and looked at my confused face with interest. "Have I met you before?"

I could barely move my head in agreement.

Despite the dirt and mud plastered to me, she uttered, "Oh, yes, You're Thea, the Roman Envoy to King Farshad's court." The rest of the way, the breeze of cold air on my cheeks signaled I was ALIVE!

Before we reached the city, Mithra stopped at a temple with the holy fire always lit. "Let's go inside and clean you up." Helping me down, she said, "Look at your beautiful torn robe."

I muttered, "No worries, I'll fix it."

"Such a talented lady," she said, laying me on a mattress. "Who put you alive in a grave? They should be reported as murderers."

I was too weak to carry on. Mithra attended to my wounds, including a bump on the back of my head. "Thea, you're lucky that the blood from the blow clogged up fast and didn't let you bleed to death." She wondered about the trace of ropes around my wrists and ankles. "You had to be tied up, and someone hit you with one blow to your head."

Now I recalled what seemed like fog covering the entire room. When I got up to return the lyre to the musician, suddenly feeling drowsy, my body dropped to the ground. Two servants rushed and helped me to get up when I barely heard Jewel's voice: "Take her to the basement."

The same two men tied my hands and feet to a pole and ripped my clothes while I faced the wall with my back to the door. Someone came in and started flogging my back. I started wiggling so drastically that one of the ropes holding my hand came loose. Then, a heavy object hit the back of my head.

Mithra finished washing me, then put some warm honey on my wounds.

In shock, I said, "Does honey have the healing miracle too?"

"Oh, yes. And it speeds up the process." She dressed me in a clean robe, then offered me a goblet.

At first, I thought it was wine. *But no!* It was milk. After a sip, I could tell it was a mixture of milk and honey.

"This gets your energy back in no time," Mithra asserted.

Despite doubting what she said, I still finished it. "Hmm ... tastes delicious. I've never tasted the flowery scent of milk. It must be the honey."

Mithra agreed.

One day when I felt better, Mithra explained. That night when she rescued me, she was on her way back from Mithridates, in the northeast of the empire, the original capital of the Parthian dynasty. "The day I met you at the palace, His Majesty had appointed me to be the reverend for this temple. I had to present my papers to the Chief Magi."

Throughout time, the rulers changed the land's religion in many ways. For example, the Greeks did not allow many women to become Magi, except the ones whose ancestors were Priests or direct descendants of the original followers, like Ormazd and Amaya. "So, the Parthian kings also followed the same rule."

"Are you one of Ormazd and Amaya's successors?"

"Yes. I'm so proud of my lineage."

Is it possible that Mithra was me during the reigns of King Cyrus and Queen Atossa? I, however, never verbalized it out loud.

The other day, while helping me to sit up to change the dressing on my head, she uttered, "The present rulers learned from the Greeks in charge of Persia that men are more suited to be in charge than women in all aspects of the government, including the religion."

I mumbled, "In everything?"

"Sad to say," she took a deep breath, "this dynasty isn't Persian, per se."

"But, they're trumpeting the past Persian culture as if they are."

"They're one step closer to being a Persian than Seleucid rulers who took over the Empire after Alexander's death."

I moved my head in agreement. "Taking revenge on King Cyrus's death, Queen Atossa and King Darius attacked and conquered the Scythians' land. Ever since their territory is part of the Persian Empire."

"They hoped the peace treaty would hold." Mithra wiped her eyes. "All these killings for what?"

"So, one ruler feels stronger and braver than others ..."

Mithra broke into my words to fluff the cushions for me to lie down on my face so she could take care of the raw wounds on my back.

I continued, "Or the ruler takes the defeated country's natural resources into his possession."

She whispered, "We're thankful that at least King Farshad's ancestors made us free from the Greeks." She helped me to sit up and said, "Thea, how come you know so much about Persia."

"I read a lot about King Cyrus the Great and how he was decisive in uprooting all the slavery everywhere."

"And liberating the people victimized by the treacherous rulers." Mithra added, "King Cyrus let even the natives govern the conquered countries. His way of ruling was not to force them to change their way of life or beliefs according to the Persian way."

"He was an extraordinary man. In my dreams," I murmured and smiled, "I wish I were alive during his time."

"Perhaps you were," Mithra offered.

"Do you believe in reincarnation?"

"Of course I do." She praised King Cyrus saying, "Many of the Persians wish Ahura Mazda would send him back to us again."

"The world needs more King Cyrus than Alexander or Caesar," I professed.

"Thea, you're so right," Mithra confirmed. "we're sick and tired of these nonsense killings. The rulers want to compel us to their ways."

"Let's pray." I stared into space.

Mithra wanted to ensure, so she asked, "Do you believe in many Gods?"

"As a little girl, my mother sometimes took me to a temple closest to the Palace. On my own, I never went to one." I took a sip of water and continued, "But, believe it or not, my belief is very much intertwined with our gods."

"So, how do you want me to convince you to choose my way?"

"With the force of a sword!" I proposed. "That's what our rulers do."

Mithra could not help but laugh. She said, "It's natural, your belief is what you learned as a kid, and mine is how I learned." A calm smile like light covered her face. "However, both of us pray from *within*."

"Our similarities are undeniable," My words accompanied hers.

She uttered, "Dear Thea, go ahead and sit up; I'm done putting ointment on your back."

With a grin, I said, "Mithra, don't you give too much power to only two male gods, Ahura Mazda and Ahriman?"

"Not really." A big smile broke out on her face. "All the power is in each of us by choosing Ahura Mazda, the ultimate Divine. So if we want to go toward Him, we think only of *Good Thoughts*. If not, then it shows we're getting closer to Ahriman." She came and sat next to me. "By the way, we don't pray to two gods.

The one and only God to us is Ahura Mazda."

"Isn't fire an idol to which all of you worship?"

She let loose with a belly laugh; then her words rang in my head: "We respect fire, for it's an element of life. Greek rulers came up with this and their way of interpreting our monotheistic religion." She paused to sip on milk and honey. "They wanted to show Ahura Mazda is another false god, like the fire we keep in our temples."

"Is this why you all do not burn the dead bodies like we do?"

"By burning dead bodies, we can soil the fire. This way, we also prevent other creatures from starvation. The soul has already left, and the body is useless to us anyway."

I knocked softly on my head. "To your beliefs, is Ahura Mazda *male or female?*"

She shrugged. "I don't know."

"Now it dawned on me." In a joyful voice, I concluded, "The Greek and Roman languages distinguish between *him or her* ..." Mithra interrupted me with her bright eyes. "But not in Parsi." After she sipped milk and honey, she said, "In my family tree, the oldest child replaces his or her father as a reverend."

"Of course!" I shouted excitedly, "No wonder Westerners took your language and changed it according to theirs."

"Yes," Mithra agreed. "My name means light, is a girl's name in our culture ..."

"But, when your religion called Mithraism, after its leader's tribe leader, we, Romans or Greeks, thought 'Mithra' must have been a man's name."

"So true, Thea. for example, *Khorshid*, the sun, is also a female name." Mithra explained.

My excitement could hit the roof when I claimed, "To the eyes of your religion, men and women are equal. Am I right?"

"You're correct, Thea," she exclaimed. "Ahura Mazda creates humans throughout the world…"

"Whether we're from Rome, Alexandria, or Persepolis." I finished Mithra's statement.

We also discussed how Persians believed in "spirit" or "soul." Her words enveloped me: "Every person has a soul and body essential to be alive. Without one, we're only a hollow shell."

"Therefore, it was an unforgivable sin to put a person with a soul in a grave," I concluded.

She asked, "Thea, do you know who put you in the grave?"

After a silence, I said, "For sure, no. But my gut feeling knows, and if I tell you, you'll believe me."

While combing my hair, she said, "I can guess. The person is in a very high position."

Then, she carried the empty goblets out.

Should I tell the King what I believe the Queen did? I had a hard time making up my mind one way or the other.

CHAPTER 24

Once I regained my strength, Mithra lent me her white stallion. I galloped toward the Palace. At the time, there was no doubt in my mind. The Queen had to be the only one who could brick me alive in a grave. She had an entire *cavalry* to pull such a scam, jeopardizing my life.

In my chamber, a letter with Caesar's seal attracted me like a bee to a red rose. Ignoring the dull gray robe that Mithra had garmented me in and forgetting all about Queen Jewel, I broke the seal and quickly read Emperor Augustus' note. The words in his letter made me rush to His Majesty. Without paying any attention to the protocols, I banged open the door. Almost out of breath, I exclaimed, "Your Majesty, I have excellent news!"

He stopped talking with Babak and stared at me. "Where have you been?" His voice filled the entire chamber. After staring at me momentarily, the King asked, "What happened to you?"

I dared to ignore the King's question. After bowing, I stretched my hands and offered him the opened letter. At this time, Babak excused himself and left the chamber.

Without looking at it, His Majesty stood up and started pacing. "What does it say?"

"Your Majesty," I gushed, "as the result of my negations with Caesar, he wishes for a peaceful exchange."

He turned and faced me. "Okay. Go on."

"The Emperor extends the hand of friendship to Your Majesty, and as a sign of 'goodwill'…" I paused out of excitement and swallowed. "Your Honor! He would love to exchange the Prince with the Roman Flag and Golden Eagle as soon as possible."

The King clapped. "Marvelous! We have no objection to that. When?"

"Your Majesty, as your envoy and his, they will release Prince Ardalan only to me when I give them the Flag and Golden Eagle."

The King eyed me with suspicion. "Why don't they bring him to Anatoli's border and do the exchange there?"

"Your Majesty," I explained, "they do not trust anyone except me to receive the Prince and return them the Roman items."

The King said flatly, "We will send the Commander in Chief Jamshid to receive Ardalan."

I shook my head. "Who knows what would happen in between Rome and Tysfoon?"

The King's pacing became faster and faster, making me uneasy. Suddenly, he stopped and turned his head to me. "My people love the Prince. They would never harm him."

I looked squarely into the King's eyes. "Are you certain, Your Majesty?"

Instead of answering me, he stared back into my eyes while I continued, "Your Majesty, the royal lives are always in danger, especially when they're closer to the crown."

"Where does Augustus want the exchange to happen?"

I mumbled, "R ... Rome."

"In Rome? Unacceptable!" the King blurted out.

I looked down at the floor when the King's annoying voice hammered my ear again: "And they want you to travel to Rome to get him?"

The sound of the King's fury was formidable. I pleaded, "Your Majesty, perhaps I can negotiate to bring the Prince to Anatoli as you wish." I looked down again to escape his angry eyes. "If you agree that I'll do the exchange, then negotiating the place would take less time." I gave a moment for the King to digest this. When he looked at me, I uttered, "If not, the negotiation will take months or even years."

The King whispered, "And it's been so long we've been apart from the Prince."

"Yes, Your Majesty. Too long." I agreed.

I hope he remembered my promise to him upon Ardalan's delivery.

At last, he broke the silence, calming my pounding heart: "Do your best for the return of the Prince."

"Yes, Your Majesty." I stared into his face. But then, I said, "As soon as officially, Your Majesty, appoint me as the one to receive the Prince, I'll leave."

With a gesture of a hand, the King dismissed me. "Go and continue the negotiation. Make sure the place of exchange is Anatoli."

"Your Majesty." I bowed. On the way out, I heard him summon some of his advisors.

Yet another letter from Caesar Augustus arrived several weeks later. He agreed to send the Prince to the Anatoli border. It had taken a long time before I became successful in finding the place for the exchange. A few weeks later, the trumpeting of my appointment as special envoy to the Persian King was heard all over the country.

On the same day, I walked into the Throne Hall, built after *Apadana*, the hall in Persepolis where they could gather thousands. I stood next to Mithra, a few steps away from everyone else. With the Queen by his side, the King arrived, followed by his five councils, seven advisers including Babak, the seven priests, the Magi, and the head of the Persian Forces, Jamshid. After the King sat on his throne and the Queen took her seat, so did everyone else.

In her white robe, identical to the other Magi's, Mithra was there for me as a friend; in case she had to attest to my dedication to the Persian Empire. A guard escorted me, and I kneeled before His Majesty.

The King stood up and addressed everyone, "Today, we are gathered to witness the appointing of Thea Mousa as a special envoy to the Persian Empire."

Keeping my head down rewarded me with the escape from Jewel's evil eyes. When His Majesty's gold sword touched my head, he said authoritatively that only a king could muster, "By the name of Ahura Mazda! We choose you as one of our emissaries for the domestic and foreign duties of the Iranian Kingdom."

King Farshad even helped me to stand up. After sitting back on the throne, he claimed, "Lady Thea is devoted to us. She rescued me from a wild boar, and because of her negotiations, she is on her way to bring our Crown Prince back home."

To my surprise, Mithra asked permission to speak: "Your Majesty." She bowed. "Thea served us by putting her life in danger. But she was buried alive. So it was only Ahura Mazda's will for her to be alive today ..."

My eyes followed the Queen, and the eunuch, Kam, leaving even before Mithra finished.

Rubbing his beard, the King said, "We were never made aware of the matter."

No one dared to say anything until I heard His Majesty's voice again, "Lady Thea, is that true?" The King corrected himself as soon as the words left his lips, "Not that we doubt Reverend Mithra's words. Lady Thea, we want you to tell us in detail."

I paid my respect and uttered, "Yes, Your Majesty. If it weren't for the Reverend, I would be dead."

The King's eyebrow lifted. "Do you know who was involved?"

"Not for certain, Your Majesty." I swallowed hard. "Please forgive me!" I beseeched after taking a deep bow. His eyes could not open wider while I continued, "Your Majesty. To bring Prince Ardalan home is more urgent than the event of the past."

The King, without any hesitation, dismissed me, "Go ahead. When you come back, we will pursue the matter."

I was delighted he could not see my smirk on the way out. His Majesty acted as if he had no idea who was behind all the killings of enslaved women in the Palace.

I ran to my chamber and proudly put on a Persian

soldier's uniform—tunic and trousers, all in red, showing I was a warrior for the Persian King. The plain rounded cap hid my long curly hair. I was under the Persian King's protection and an official Persian King's emissary, so I was allowed to wear a Persian soldier's outfit.

Immediately, Jamshid, four Persian soldiers, and I set out to bring Prince Ardalan home from Anatoli.

Traveling on the Royal roads to the Northwest was a breeze. Sattar and the horses loved treading and sometimes galloping on the smooth surfaces. I was delighted to have the Roman Flag and Golden Eagle. Finally, along the way, at dusk, we reached the last station for the Persian royal messengers. They were famous for their unbelievable speed in getting messages from anywhere in the Persian Empire to China, Greece, and even Rome.

I wondered whether, for real, the Persian Prince was in Rome. If so, our wait time in Anatoli could run for several months. But if they'd already moved him to Athens, from there to us would take only a few weeks.

Like the other soldiers, I received a tent with a table, a small basin, with a jug of water to drink and wash up. Soon, a servant brought me a plate with wheat bread and meat. While savoring my dinner, a whoosh sound assaulted my left ear. Was it the stroke of an iron sword that made me look up? With instant agility, I pulled my neck away from the sharp blade, jumped up, and threw my dagger with such strength that it landed deep in the assailant's neck. He dropped to the ground, and blood gushed out of his wound. His face and body were the same color as a starless night. I rushed to him, covered the wound with one hand, and put another under his head. I demanded, "Who wanted me dead?"

Through clenched teeth, he said, "Roman traitor! Go back to your own country. How dare you enter my homeland!"

I put my finger on his lip. "Shush. Say no more. Save your energy."

By this time, the soldiers had come to the tent. No one bothered to pull his mask away before carrying him out.

"Let me know how he's doing!" I called out.

One of the guards responded, "He's already dead, Lady Thea."

"Do we know who he was?"

They all shook their heads, and as they left, Jamshid rushed in. "Lady Thea, are you all right?"

Washing the blood from my hands, I murmured, "Do we have any doubt who sent this assassin?"

Jamshid's sharp eyes, with no wrinkles marring his face, were *All* the King's wasn't. "Lady Thea, having a woman soldier with us doesn't look right."

"I thought in Persia, women, like men, can also be soldiers."

"Women *were* able to when the Aryans were in control. Not now."

I wondered aloud, "How come, in your language, your country is referred to as Iran?"

"Westerners called us 'Persia.' Once the first group of Caucasians, King Cyrus's ancestors, arrived on the plateau of Pasargad many years ago, they named it after their Aryan race, 'Iran.'"

"Oh, then, the Greek historian, Herodotus ..."

Jamshid refused to let me finish. "He called our land untruthfully, 'Persia' when he wrote about many battles between Greeks and Iran." His disturbed voice was evident by his talking without any interval in breathing. "Herodotus did a disservice to the Iranian culture. He even changed Iranian names."

"That's why we know you all as 'Persians' in the West," I said.

"Yes. For example, to Parsi, King Cyrus is King Kurosh."

Then, how do we know he's truthful in portraying the events of the war? I wondered with a dropping jaw. I could not reveal all that was in my heart.

He said, "The Parthian Kings have been trying hard to bring back the Iranian past glory."

"It looks like they've been successful at it."

"Better than being ruled by Greeks, a foreign authority. But, is it possible to bring back the past?"

I shook my head. "A futile task."

Our conversation lasted throughout the night, but understanding his motives was unfeasible. As the Chief Commander of the forces, he was not very supportive of King Farshad. He also had an earful of Queen Jewel and her mischief. Jamshid knew how she tortured and sometimes even killed the enslaved girls. He told me that the Queen's other sister-wives and the concubines planned her death several times. But Jewel still kept on going without her suffering any harm.

She has an enormous evil force, as Orcus does, I surmised.

"However, one day," Jamshid declared, "the truth will come out of the clouds."

As an Aryan, does Jamshid want to rebel against King Farshad? He would make a good partner if my heart weren't set on a higher prize. I had to put a stop to my confused mind about him.

After he left, I could only close my eyes briefly. Upon dawn, we left the station, galloping toward Anatoli.

On the third day, at dusk, we reached the Evros River, the point of exchange. However, our eyes saw no one. With a smirk, Jamshid said, "So, where are *they?*" Without waiting for a response, he uttered, "Aren't we supposed to meet them here?"

In a firm voice, I said, "Yes! They will be here any day now."

Jamshid took off his cap, decorated with a gold band displaying his highest rank, and exclaimed in a harsh tone, "So, in other words, *you* do not know exactly when they'll arrive." He approached my face and shouted, "Do you know if they will even show up? Maybe they've already killed the Prince and are toying with us?"

I had to dry his spit off my face. While pushing on his chest, I uttered in the calmest voice, "Jamshid. Let's not get all huffed and puffed. I trust Emperor Augustus. He informed me they'll be here… so they'll be here."

Jamshid willingly stepped back, and I went on, "When Emperor promised His Majesty to deliver the Prince in one piece, he meant it."

"Wow!" Jamshid conceded, "you have much confidence in Augustus."

For six days and nights, I never left the side of the River, only pacing, thinking, and eating the fruit of the trees—no face to show to Jamshid at the camp. And he left me alone.

If, after seven days, they didn't arrive, I was ready to drown myself. I wondered if Caesar had changed his mind about returning the Prince. Hopefully, getting back the Flag and Golden Eagle was more important to him.

On the dawn of the seventh day, I opened my eyes to the sound of hoofs and men's announcements. I saw a handful of Roman soldiers across the River delighted me to no end. Only one of the men had no Roman uniform, in a simple shirt and trousers. He had to be the Prince. My screaming reached the Persian camp loud and clear: "They're here! They're here." I showed the Roman soldiers the Flag and the Golden Eagle at daylight when they escorted the Prince closer to the river edge.

Jamshid's joyful voice, almost out of breath, resounded throughout the entire area, "Yes! This is our Prince, Ardalan." The Persian soldiers' *"Hip hip, hurray!"* also followed.

As a Roman citizen, I was the only one allowed to ride across the River. After some struggles with the deep areas where the water came up to Sattar's neck, I triumphantly arrived at the other side. I lowered my head when approaching the Prince while still on Sattar's back. "Your Honor. I'm Thea, the special envoy to take you to your homeland. Is everything all right with you?"

His smile reminded me of his father's. "How unusual! A Roman Lady speaks my language." He moved his hands up and down in a gesture of pleasure. "Oh, yes! Can anyone not be fine after being in Rome?"

His deep belly laugh made even his shoulders move.

The exchange went accordingly. While entering the water, the following words out of the Prince's mouth shocked me: "Why did my father send you after me? To live in Caesar's Palace is awesome." He continued as if I was invisible, "With beautiful Roman girls, good wine, and many delicacies." He lowered his voice: "I have no desire to return to Iran. Let me return to Rome. I can fake my drowning. You can tell my father I died."

"Your Highness," I gasped, "don't you think the news of your death will make His Majesty sorrowful?"

He shrugged.

My curiosity didn't leave me alone, and my head was full of questions. "Your Highness, how can it be? Living in the Roman Court was more pleasant than in the Persian Palace with all its glory?"

He looked at me with dopy eyes and mumbled, "No responsibility! And beautiful Roman girls everywhere!"

I guessed the Prince had to be drunk from his tipsy voice and half-opened eyes. While crossing the River, I had to guide and control his horse several times. "Your Highness, you can always return freely after I deliver you to the King. Now we have a peace treaty between the two countries."

"Until then, I'm your prisoner!" he growled through his teeth. "I wonder what your prize is." He galloped toward the capital while I chased him as his shadow.

Upon our arrival, an unusual uproar at the Palace drowned out the announcer's loud voice, letting everyone know that Prince Ardalan was back, safe and sound. Unfortunately, the whispering in the background was more apparent than the accolades for the return of the Prince.

"Have you heard?"

"The King's cupbearer, Mayar, betrayed the King!"

"So unheard of! He had to be the first."

"So, now His Majesty is looking for a new trustworthy one."

"These days, it's complicated to find one."

Mayar had tried to poison the King before the Prince reached the Palace. But, His Majesty's cleverness turned the table on Mayar.

I rushed to the King and asked him to have a private audience. He granted it immediately.

After bowing to him, King Farshad got up and held my arm, raised my chin, and in a firm voice said, "We commend you for what you've done for us. But, misfortune came upon us in your absence."

"Your Majesty, I am at your service and ready to sacrifice even my life for you." I looked down.

It was a coincidence that the King's cupbearer could not have been more successful. Mayar knew that the King always drank wine in his chamber before retiring to bed. When Mayar brought the wine tray carrying the decanter and glasses to serve him, the King looked at his face before permitting him to pour the wine. To the King, Mayar looked ashen and out of the norm. His hands were trembling when he sat the tray down. His eyes were as red as pomegranate seeds. After Mayar poured the wine, the King said, "Mayar, tonight, pour some for yourself too. Let's sit down together and celebrate the Prince on his way to return home."

After Mayar sat down, the King switched the two

goblets, then said, "Tonight, you drink out of my glass, and I out of yours."

"Your Majesty," Mayar objected, "I cannot drink from your glass. It should only touch your lips. Not mine!"

The King narrowed his eyes. "How do you dare to refuse your King's order?"

With a shaky hand, the cupbearer picked up the glass and drank it while the King held on to the other goblet. Crashing on the floor was a clear sign of his treason; he paid an enormous price for betraying the King.

Perhaps, the Queen promised Mayar handsomely to get rid of the King, knowing Ardalan would then be the King. And she had all the power over the young King. Another of Jewel's plots was foiled.

I kept my silence, however.

After I came out of His Majesty's chamber, one of the guards who had informed me about Gigi's place of work a few years ago came to my chamber.

"Lady Thea." He self-assuredly said, "I know someone best for the job."

"Who?"

"Your friend, Gigi, Lady Thea."

"But, never has a woman been a cupbearer for the Persian King."

"There is always a start for everything."

To have him send a message to Gigi was a sign of my acceptance.

She showed up at midday the next day.

Her large shiny eyes were most pleasing. I told her about Mayar's betrayal, then asked, "How would you like to become His Majesty's cupbearer and live in the Palace?"

Her eyes lit up. "For real?"

At first, she thought I was joking. But finally, to my delight, she accepted.

I accompanied her to the King and introduced her. The King was pleased to have a woman as his cupbearer. Gigi was proud to have such an important position. For her to be close to the Persian King was a dream come true. She thanked me profusely, and when the excitement of her new job overtook her, she hugged me too.

CHAPTER 25

I t had been almost a year since Prince Ardalan arrived home safe and sound. I was ready for an invitation from the King to spend a memorable time fulfilling my promise. Every day, my eyes and ears were prepared to see or hear from the royal messenger. Each day started with heaps of hope, and getting up at sunrise was a joy. *Today is the day!* I told myself, over and over.

But at night, going to bed was agony. To lie down like a statue on the bed became a painful chore. What would happen if an invite arrived and I missed it while oversleeping? So I took refuge in walking.

Most of the time, I paced all over the chamber and sometimes even stepped into the lush royal garden. The sweet smell of red roses, some of them like vines growing on the walls, soothed me. The little flowers gave the Palace a never-ending celebration all year round. The birds announcing the sunrise made me join them and sing a hopeful song: *Today is the day.*

Tysfoon summer seemed to last forever! On some occasions, leaving the Palace walls and taking a stroll for the very long distance of the city path felt like the best remedy to calm the storm in my heart. *Now, no guards chasing me, accusing me of being a feral boar.* I

231

could quickly lose myself in the scenery of this capital. The Arch of Tysfoon always mesmerized me—it looked magical under the vast blue sky, fringed by the spread of the Zagros Mountains at the eastern bank of the Tigris River. A Persian architect designed and built the colossal arch to trumpet the past Persian glory. General Seleucia, who received Persian territories after Alexander's death, made this city the capital instead of Persepolis. This city was much more convenient for the Greek rulers to travel to Athens than Persepolis. Walking into the wilderness was not as easy as I did in Rome. Here, riding a horse or taking a wagon was a *must*. This capital was twice the size of Rome. The dawn sun lit the city arch with many rainbow colors. I sat down on a nearby rock. Spellbound, I dosed off.

As Queen Atossa's governess and confidante, I rode from Pasargad to Persepolis with a guard. The city, like a gem, shined from a distance. On an immense tract of land beside the Pulvar River, the Majestic Palace was partly carved out of the mountain and built with open architecture on a vast high terrace, with thick columns reaching almost to the sky. It was a feast for my eyes. The Queen had summoned me to be her spiritual leader in helping her give birth.

The guard and I rode up the multiple wide stairs, which were comfortable for the horses to climb. We dismounted by the massive palace gate made of cedar wood. While passing by, I could not possibly miss the Hall of One Hundred Columns, with friezes and bas-reliefs. It trumpeted the glory and strength of the mighty Persian Empire and was a perfect space to celebrate any grand occasion. My smile showed my pride in witnessing the King and Queen Atossa's success. Bypassing the King's Palace, I was mesmerized by the seedling garden filled with thousands of different plants, including olives, dates, and mulberries. They were evidence that all those countries were under King Darius' parasol. Without wasting a moment, I rushed through the door adorned with the gold pane to the Queen's chamber.

By her side, I kissed her drenched, perspiring forehead and caressed her wet hair. Atossa opened her eyes and, without any firmness, mumbled, "Lady Mithra, so good to see you!"

"My Queen, would you like to hear some lyrics from our holy book?"

Her flat smile was my permission to read:

O Wise Lord, by the Good Mind,
May I reach Thy Presence?
Grant me the blessings in both worlds,
the corporeal and the spiritual,
attainable through Righteousness ...

The midwife's loud voice interrupted me, "Queen, you're doing much better."

Her pale face relaxed, an encouraging sign. I continued:

Thy rewards bring beatific happiness
To the faithful blessed with them.

Atossa moved her lips to repeat and concentrate on the prayers. Soon, her shallow breathing turned into deeper ones. And the midwife declared, "My Queen, one more final push, with all your stamina ... here! Congratulations, Your Majesty! It's a boy!"

⋙ �֍ ⋘

Wow! Is it possible for me to give birth to a boy who will become a king one day? All of it was just wishful thinking. Then, I concentrated on the way of royal life in Persia.

Interestingly, Tysfoon only served the King during the winter when most northern and central parts of the Empire were covered in snow. Every king kept several capitals throughout the country since King Cyrus's time. He and his household traveled during the summer heat to the mountainside where it was more relaxed, like Susa, or in the winter to a warm place, like Tysfoon.

The King journeyed from one to the other. His house was crowded with a group of 'can-do' men who did the miracle. In no time, like a genie, the camp workers picked His Majesty's household up from one capital and set it down in another. To be on the road and riding was no obstacle to a Persian king. He believed living as a nomad strengthened his bones even more. Also, he could observe how his people lived, and the commoners felt close to His Majesty.

However, a Persian king never learned what it was like to live in the hardship of winter and understood how it was to exist like the less fortunate people. His

Majesty kept alive in an endless summer with lush gardens. His world was an empty dream box.

When everywhere else became cold and snowy, Tysfoon's sun became more tolerable. To hear the hustle and bustle of the Palace was a sign for getting ready to welcome His Majesty, security guards, his women, and all the workers. A knock on the door from a few days ago announcing "the Royals are on the way" sounded in my ears. I never considered myself part of the King's "household" nor journeyed with him as part of the "Women's Quarter." I hoped that once the King returned from Susa to Tysfoon, he would get excited about meeting me again.

During the passing days, at one point, I was even scared of His Majesty's arrival. What would happen if he disavowed me as his emissary and ordered me back to Rome?

On his whims, the King giveth, and he taketh it back on his urges.

These days, he had no use for me. The Prince was home, the relationship between Rome and Persia was quiet, and commerce was going well. So how could I create a need in the King to keep me close to him?

Under the Queen's control, the Women's Quarter was filled with beautiful women of different shapes, tastes, and scents. Jewel would send a *new* woman to him every night to make the King forget me. His Majesty's wishes were each woman's commands. Compared to those women, I considered myself a *diamond* among a bunch of glass. Those women could only satisfy the King's body, not his mind. But I was his *partner* and yearned to be equal to him. If every woman desired to look and see herself as capable of any man, even if that man was a king, then we wouldn't need to have the Women's Quarters. And the King could not satisfy his passion every night with a different one. Is it possible for mothers to raise their sons to look at a woman for her beauty and as adequate as himself? Persians practiced this way of living during King Cyrus's reign, but not long enough to yoke within the society and penetrate the West. Or maybe with the death of King Cyrus, the equitable world also died with him?

Upon the royals' arrival, for a few days, I did not expect any invitation from the King. Not only did several days pass, but a few weeks also went by without getting one. The only time I had the pleasure of being with the King was during a formal meeting in the presence of others. He never returned any of my favorite stares, and I had too much pride to throw myself before his feet and beg for a private audience.

One day, however, I sent him an urgent message. Unfortunately, it hit only his closed chamber door. It seemed like the King had carved me out of his life. He kept me waiting and waiting. At one point, even singing with the birds, smelling the roses, and walking could not dent my anguish. I was unable even to enjoy archery or riding Sattar.

The vicious Queen must have influenced the King, covering his eyes with a thick dark tapestry. Oh! Alas! If only I could quell the uproar within me, everything would be all right.

To ride strenuous time is a virtue, I remembered Cordelia's words.

In the highest despair, one day, my ears heard the knock, and my eyes saw the message I had loitered on for so long. King Farshad invited me to have a quiet dinner with him in his chamber.

I started wondering while bathing in camel milk mixed with a potion of love oil made by Cordelia. Then, her avatar image appeared. Her lips moved without me asking any questions of her. Like the old times, she read my mind.

To know your future events is to melt all the excitement of life.

It had been a long time since I did not notice the growth of the dark seed within me. The guards' hollering, Catch that feral boar, made me smile. Indeed I acted very similarly to a wild boar. After all these years, I became complete, not caring who my father was— whether Caesar or a beggar on the street.

Is it possible the dark seed has dissolved under the intense Tysfoon sun? I wondered.

However, sometimes when Queen Jewel's malice was pointed directly at me, there was no way to deny its existence or even prevent its growth.

Perhaps, Reverend Mithra is right. By letting "Good Thoughts" penetrate our minds, we can escape Ahriman.

After brushing my long curly hair, the helper followed my nudging to pin part of it to the side, away from my right ear. I learned to wear my hair from the princesses while living in Caesar's Palace. Didn't I always want to run away from the Palace? But, the Persian Palace was different. I could feel and smell his existence in the air—*my hero,* King Cyrus.

When she tried to make my eyelids as dark as

Jewel's, or Cleopatra, I pushed her hand away. I was not particularly eager to wear lots of makeup. I loved the uniqueness of my green eyes. My creation, the silk robe muted in the maid's hands waiting for me to put it on, was mended just like new after being rescued from the grave. It enveloped my body and soothed my thumping heart when I slipped into it.

Before leaving my room, I rushed to the chest and took out the royal blue robe I had made for my fantasized King at Cordelia's home. The dried red and white poppy flowers on the top reminded me of the field Gigi and I visited on the outskirts of Tysfoon—a beautiful site. The poppies were dancing in the morning breeze. The dried olive branches from Rome were also a gesture of peace from Caesar to His Majesty. I had all the intention to give them to King Farshad upon my arrival. But the events didn't work as planned. *They never do! Now is the time!*

I took a deep breath while approaching the King's chamber, ignoring my still-thumping heart. As I entered, His Majesty's sight astonished me. He was dressed in loose pants and a shirt—both in bone color. He looked much more petite and grayer than when propped up in royal attire. *Am I attracted to him as a man?*

"Your Majesty, how are you tonight?" I opened the conversation.

Before he could answer, Gigi walked in with the wine tray. Her friendly smile and face took the King's attention away from me. While pouring wine, the King followed her with his eyes. Gigi's red glittery head scarf covered part of her long jet-black hair and chest. The gold earrings shaped like Cleopatra's amazed the King when he went and touched one. She hovered around him as if she owned him. Her moves reminded me of the woman who danced in the temple in Rome. My mother and I used to go there and watch the dancer. As if she had no bones in her body, only a head shaped like a ladle. During her flirtatious motion, Gigi and the King shared their breathing. Her oozing voluptuous breasts, partially blanketed with a glittery cloth, brushed the King's arms while she caressed his head and face.

When my patience had boiled over, and I was ready to shout, I heard: "Gigi!" His Majesty's voice became clear. "Tonight, I wish to have no company." Then, he dismissed her with his hand.

Gigi turned around, gave me the same seductive smile that was for the King, bowed to him, and left.

I released a deep sigh of relief for having the King all to myself. "Your Majesty, I have a token of appreciation for you."

After bowing, I picked up the robe from the chair by the door and offered it to him. "Try it on, Your Majesty. It's my creation while I was dreaming of you."

The King put it on and was so fascinated that he stepped toward the long mirror next to his bed, stared at himself, and kept touching it.

In my astonished voice, I uttered, "Very becoming, Your Majesty. It is a perfect fit."

"Did you say you made it?" He turned and stared at me with his wide-open eyes.

"Yes, I did, Your Majesty. In Rome when I was a young girl."

"Without even knowing me? How unusual!"

I then presented him with the flowers and olive branches. "I'm here to offer love, peace, and prosperity." I lowered my head.

In a short while, the servants brought an array of food, all with delicious smells. After eating and emptying several goblets of wine, I had no idea how I ended up on the King's lap.

With his hands around my waist, holding me tight, I dared to open part of my heart to him. "Your Majesty, tonight is the night I fulfill the promise I gave you over a year ago. Do you remember?"

He moved the curls away from my face with a gentle touch. While he stared into my eyes, he whispered, "Such gorgeous green eyes."

My response was a bashful smile.

He grabbed his full goblet, took a sip, and in an incredibly harsh voice, he addressed me, "Who are you? A nymph, a witch, or ..." He put the goblet down on the wooden table with such force that it hurt my ears. He wiped his beard while holding onto my back with the other hand. "We've heard you are a Roman mole in the court. Is it true?" Then, he pushed me away—a harsh signal for me to get up.

I, however, didn't let him go before giving him a wet passionate kiss and murmuring, "Your Majesty, I'm a nomad girl ..." I stopped when he went and sat on his chair next to the gigantic, ivory dining table.

As the gap between his eyes became more profound, the King uttered, "What were you saying?"

I took a few steps toward him and caressed his hairy chest. He did not push my hand away; instead, he closed his eyes. *Triumphantly, I put the lion at ease, not to attack me.* I whispered to him, "The King and I have the same vision."

With his eyes closed, he asked, "You must be a brave woman to have the courage to read the King's mind as yours?"

"Your Majesty, I read much about the Great Kings, like King Cyrus and Darius. I am well aware that great minds think alike."

Not being a princess, I anticipated the King would ask me how I learned to read and write.

His smile and look of admiration delighted me when he opened his eyes. "What did you say?"

"To revive the past Persian glory," I climbed onto his lap, and he squeezed my waist again, "like the times those Kings ruled."

His tired eyes lit up. "Let's drink to that. Cheers!"

"Your Majesty, please do not let the foes destroy your vision for your beautiful people and country." A kiss on his lips sealed my words.

Before sunrise, when I was about to leave his chamber, my vast smile was evident to the world. King Farshad's words sat in my ear: "I've never seen a woman so happy as you are after being with me. It's mind-boggling!"

"Your Majesty. I'm here on my own will, unlike some other women."

The King's sheepish look was a sign of agreement.

Unbelievable! The King does pay attention to his women, or at least to me!

While kicking in the air, I ignored the outside guards' grins.

Not long after my first night with the King, the secret that His Majesty did not desire any other woman in his chamber except the Roman woman became the word of the town. Hearing it made me overjoyed.

"She looks like a woman, but dresses as a soldier, and fights like a man!"

"We don't know...a woman...a man, or another creature from the stars?"

Why can't anyone take me the way I am—a brave, talented woman?

Naturally, I could not be more pleased that the King shared his bed only with me. Each night, he had the blue robe over his undergarments. From then on, I felt I was in love with him, and his love for me was genuine.

One night, before he summoned me, I ran to the chamber without waiting for the guard to announce my presence and banged the door open. Filled with jubilation, I kissed the King and rejoiced without paying any respect, "Your Majesty, I have great news to share with you."

I've noticed recently he dismisses Gigi before sending for me.

While pouring his wine, I said, "Your Majesty, I'm with child."

He set the decanter on the table so harshly that it sucked all my happiness out as I murmured, "Your Majesty! Aren't you pleased?"

He shrugged. "So many princes and princesses have filled the Palace. Another one does not make any difference."

"We must welcome the news," I countered. "This child, whether a boy or girl, will surely tie the East and West together."

If I have a girl, I'll raise her like Princess Atossa. Or better yet ... my daughter will fight and grab her father's crown from the men.

After a moment of silence, Farshad raised his head. "How about if I marry you?"

Resisting the delight in me was hard to do. Finally, however, I challenged the King with a smile. "But why? There is no need for that."

"To the eye of Rome, you won't be a concubine. But a wife of the Persian King."

"If our child is a boy, raised to be fit to be a k ..."

The King interrupted me in a stern voice, "Stop right there!"

"Your Majesty, what did I say wrong?"

"Remember, we already have the Crown Prince."

I nodded but did not keep quiet, "Our son will be in the line of being a king. And who knows what will happen in the future? Whether he will be a ..." I swallowed the rest.

With a smile, he followed my chain of thoughts. "True. No one knows what tomorrow brings—every day is a *new day.*" He continued as if he had planned a battle and wanted me in his corner. "Okay, go on." He also confirmed his words with a hand gesture.

"Your Majesty, you do not need to marry me. A king's child is under the King's protection, just like the King's legitimate children, whether from a queen, wife, concubine, or slave." I took a sip of wine.

"Correct." He looked into the space and justified his decision. "When I wed you, it signals to Rome that we are serious about keeping the peace between the two countries." He got up and started pacing. "However, don't expect me to make you the Queen while Jewel is alive. She is the only Persian Queen."

"Your wish is my command, Your Majesty." I bowed.

QUEEN JEWEL

(as told by Kam)

CHAPTER 26

Tysfoon

8 BCE

"This is what a failure deserves. Isn't it, Kam?" Queen Jewel's angry voice shook the dungeon walls.

She did not waver from hitting herself, even though the blood spattered on and around her bare feet. She was even hitting her own back harder and harder with the chain.

Her breathing became shorter, like a spent horse desiring to win a lost race. But, as the only trusted audience, I could not cheer for her, only watch her and prevent her from going too far in hurting herself.

I murmured when the chaining continued, "Your Highness, please stop. I beg you." I had no stomach to watch the scene any longer. Of course, she turned a deaf ear and struck her upper back with even more vengeance. I was well aware of why the Queen was torturing herself.

Queen Jewel had a perfect reason. Today, the King wedded Lady Thea.

Tonight, she refrained from inflicting pain on a slave girl again. The people's outcries against her tormenting and killing so many girls were heard from every wall in the Women's Quarter and beyond. Once, even the King summoned her in private. I had no idea what went on behind the closed door. Since then, she took her vexation out on herself. I thought very likely she would stop. But, shockingly, her dark soul never let her take a breather.

After meeting the King, she started hissing like a scared weasel. She paced the floor decorated with rainbow-colored rugs interwoven with silk and wool when she bawled, "Kam, who told the King about the enslaved girls?"

I shook my head. "No idea, Your Majesty."

In her red eyes, she screamed, "Be honest with me! Who did?"

After a short pause, I uttered, "Perhaps the guards aren't cautious in disposing of the bodies? Maybe a passerby found them and told others?" I took a deep sigh. "Or they were found by some farmers while plowing."

The Queen inquired, "How do the people conclude the dead bodies are those of the slave girls?"

"Your Majesty, those girls belong only to the royals."

"How come?"

"No commoners can *afford* to buy one."

She took a shallow breath and asked, "Then order the guards to discard the bodies far away from the city."

"Your Majesty, but lately, just about every couple of

days, we have another dead girl before our two confidant guards return to carry them out."

"Damn, Thea!" She cursed loudly. "What can I do to get rid of her?"

Each time Thea became closer to the King, I lost more peaceful moments.

To calm her evil soul, the Queen preferred to torture *herself*. That was the only time she could take a break from planning to obliterate Thea. As if Thea's sharing the King's pillow made the Queen's outrage erupt even more wildly.

The celebration of King Farshad's wedding to the Roman girl, Thea, continued while the Queen lashed herself with her mighty Ahriman's force in the black hole. This girl appeared from nowhere and found her way to the Court, His Majesty's ear, heart, and bed. Thea walked the ladder of success one rung after another unbelievably fast. She had to have a snake bone.

I was the only one who could stand up to Queen Jewel in critical times. And my most important task was to rescue her each time she was lost in the shoreless abyss of darkness.

Tonight, finally, I could close my eyes no longer. As the Queen's faithful Eunuch, I had to muster all my strength, grab the chain, and stop her madness. Swiftly I got a hold of her before she collapsed to the ground. I carried her motionless body while shouting for the two trusted guards. They banged open the wooden door at once.

In her chamber, I went to lay her in bed. She screamed as if thousands needles were pushing their way into her flesh. I whispered, "Your Majesty, allow me to summon some maids to help turn you over."

Her eyes barely opened, and she tried to open her mouth, but no words reached me. I called on the girls anyway. At this moment, the chances of her survival were very slim. I took it upon myself to call the royal medicine man. While he applied some potion to the wounds, I recalled when the Queen forbade me to get help from anyone, not even the man who could save her life. She refused to be seen when she did not look grandiose.

For two days, I had peace of mind and a break from her evil soul. My ears hurt no more from listening to her plans for Thea's annihilation. One of my duties was to point out the impossibility of most of her schemes on a practical basis.

The Queen judged Thea as any other woman was a shortcoming on her side. Recently, Ahriman pulled a thick tapestry over her eyes to prevent her from seeing Thea as she was.

Looking at the wounds and misery the Queen created on herself, I felt like my heart was ripped from my chest. I loved her as if she were the daughter I could never have. But then, I closed my ears to Jewel's nonsense and filled my head with "Good Thoughts."

I was in shock at her. With all the wealth in her possession, why couldn't the Queen find a way to make herself happy instead of letting Thea occupy her mind? Did she believe Thea would disappear from her path by bringing misery to some enslaved girls or harshly punishing herself?

Finally, one day half asleep and half awake, the

Queen started murmuring, "Soon, he'll be sick of her and move on to another ... just like with the other ones."

I extended her a goblet filled with milk and honey. "Your Majesty. Please drink this. It'll prevent the wounds from infection."

Inevitably, she sipped and right away spat it out. While still lying on her belly, the Queen screamed, "I need wine, not this nasty white stuff! Bring it to me NOW!"

I didn't dare to say it was the medicine man's order. "Your Majesty, this helps you to heal faster. After finishing it, I'll get wine for you too."

Soon the pains disappeared when Thea inhabited her head again. Thea was an invincible infiltrator—nothing worked to disarm her. So far, she walked away triumphantly from any trap Queen Jewel had set up for her, including bricking her alive in a grave. Thea was not afraid to stand up to Jewel like a king. Her uproars covered not only the entire Palace, but Tysfoon and beyond. Never before did a woman have such confidence to walk shoulder to shoulder with our King.

As was my duty, I had to be close to the Queen's ear today. After dismissing everyone, she wanted me to come and sit on a stool at her eye level. "Tell me, Kam. How was the wedding?"

"Your Majesty, you need to rest now."

When her scream plastered the entire chamber, I said, "The wedding went fine, as planned, Your Majesty."

She howled, "Tell me in detail."

"Your Majesty, I did not leave your side." I chose my

words very carefully. "I heard many dignitaries from Rome were in attendance. Amazingly, the East and West united in peace for the first time. They shared a joyful occasion, rather than being in battles all the time, resulting in killing each other."

After a high-sounding laugh, she voiced, "Soon, yet another happy occasion they come to will be *Thea's funeral!*" She shrieked again and slapped the pillow.

"Your Majesty, there is another painful piece of news." I paused and swallowed hard.

"Does it involve her?"

I moved my head in agreement. "Your Majesty, I'm not sure you would like to hear it until you feel better."

With a smirk, she responded, "Do you think after almost wiping out my flesh and tolerating the pain of each stroke on my spine, I can't stomach knowing about the Roman witch?"

She ordered the four maids to enter. "I'll show you how strong I am. And that nothing is wrong with me."

The Queen was oblivious to her bare torso on display. Her back made me queasy to see her fleshless spine. She wiggled to the edge of the bed, and the girls took her underarms to lift her. However, halfway she wobbled so severely that they had to help her sit back down on the edge of the bed. In a hand gesture, without almost any breath, she asked, "So what is the news?"

I stared at the white Karakul sheep skin under her feet to avoid her face and uttered, "We heard she is with a child."

"A child!" She turned to the girls. "Go ahead! Leave us!"

"Your Highness," I petitioned. "Are you all right?"

Queen Jewel's expression clouded. "How do you know?"

"The palace walls have eyes and ears, don't they?"

She mumbled, "Isn't that the truth."

The Queen then signaled me to prop her up with several pillows on her lower back so that she could sit up. "Now, we must think of a way to get rid of both."

I stepped back and said, "Your Majesty, as a King's wife, Thea must move into the Women's Quarter which you control ..."

With beady eyes, she completed my thoughts, "Then, right away, we can send both to hell even before the bastard child is born."

"Your Majesty. She accepted Ahura Mazda as her only God, and Reverend Mithra married her to the King. Amazingly, she knows more about our past and present than we do."

The Queen's vicious laugh sounded ominous and wounded my soul. "This is the most ridiculous thing I've ever heard." She wiped her forehead. "The witch knows everything about everyone!"

Perhaps, it's her knowledge that gives her power. I dared not to say it out loud. Without any words leaving my mouth, she took the chance and continued, "Don't you know, we do not allow the soulless people, believing in many gods, into our one-god religion?"

I shook my head, and the Queen said, "Call my scriber in."

When he arrived, the Queen commanded me to be present while dictating the letter:

Dear Thea,
Congratulations on your wedding!
Now that you are part of my family,
I'm extending a hand of friendship and love to you.
As it is customary, a place of residency
at the Women's Quarter is ready
for your occupancy.
I'm here to welcome you with open arms.
Queen Jewel

After her signature and sealing the letter, the Queen's messenger left the chamber.

Several months passed, and Queen Jewel had not received a response from Thea. One day, she called on the Crown Prince, Ardalan.

When the Prince entered, his appearance was shocking. Unlike the time he was an energetic and joyful teenager, he had grown to be a frail young man. He carried his wine goblet, and his shoulder-length hair was disheveled. Instead of having the expensive royal outfit, he wore a long-sleeved tunic that reached his knees, with a linen cloth wrapped around him as its extra part rested on his arm. The soft blue color was, however, soothing.

When the Queen saw the Prince's outfit, she shouted, "Since when did our Persian Crown Prince become a Roman?"

"In this, I feel so carefree." His tipsy voice was noticeable.

Prince Ardalan slumped on the couch and took a sip of wine. "What am I here for?" First, he stared at the Queen, then turned to me. "Kam, did you know Caesars are forbidden to wear silk?"

I shook my head. "No, Your Highness."

Scratching, he mumbled, "Did you tell me why you summoned me?"

"What do you think?" The Queen's angry eyes were centered on the Prince. She still could not wear a regular shirt. Instead, her front covering was a piece of silk fabric attached to a gold necklace. And at the waist, a belt joined it to her long fluffy skirt woven with gold and silver. She asked another question without allowing the Prince to open his mouth, "How was the wedding?" Her angry voice echoed throughout the chamber.

"Please don't shout. I always get a pounding headache each time I see you, Mother." He rolled his eyes and started clapping. "I'm so happy." With a smile, he uttered, "Father married the brave Roman woman who is his partner, rather than sabotaging his governing." The Prince paused to refresh his goblet with wine again. "Now, no one dares to break the treaty between Rome and us."

"Are you in support of his marriage to the Witch?"

"Watch your mouth, Queen Jewel. Thea's as bold as a bull but gentle as a morning breeze. Every man must have one of those."

She laughed so hard that her boney shoulders began to shake.

The Prince interjected, "I was coming to see you anyway."

"For what?"

"Father appointed me to go to Rome and be a special envoy in Caesar's palace." His broad smile showed a set of pure white teeth.

The Queen's shriek made the Prince's smile

disappear. "Her hand is all over the King's decision!"

The Prince asked under his breath, "Whose hand?"

Through her teeth, she exclaimed, "Thea, the Witch of the West! She has fooled you all! You and your father included!" She paused and took a deep breath. "The Roman mole is getting rid of you by sending you to the wolf's den. Ahura Mazda help us if she gives birth to a boy."

Moving his hand as if he dismissed the Queen's words, the Prince said, "Please. Don't be cynical. I hope she has a boy. And I think she would make an excellent Queen in charge of the country. My father has no backbone to rule. And you're in no shape and form either." He rolled his eyes again.

After wagging a finger at Ardalan, she let her words be heard, "But, according to protocol, the Crown Prince is not allowed to leave the country. You are all we have upon your father's death."

He smirked. *Me!* He touched his chest. "It's a pity that all you have is me!"

"Do not forget. You are replacing your father as King of the Persian Empire. No one else."

His laughter filled the chamber. "I don't want any part of it. You all chose me to be the Crown Prince since I was six. And you gave up on having a boy of your own."

The Queen whispered, "I didn't. Your father did." In a kind voice, she said, "You're my boy despite me not giving birth to you ... I'm so proud of you. And raised you as my own ..."

"I have no interest in learning anything that deals

with killing. All the training you sent me bemused me. I preferred to watch wrestling, archery, and fencing while my friends engaged with them. I hated each with all my guts. To wake up one day and be the King makes me feel as if I face my death sentence." He reached to pick up the goblet and brought it high to the Queen's eye level. "But, this magical drink, Roman wine ... keeps me in my dream world. It would be best if you tried it sometime. It's the best medicine for your anger and prevents you from becoming a murderer."

But it has a different effect on everyone! I knew.

The Queen's coolness baffled me; she did not lose her temper. She, however, murmured, "Don't believe everything you hear." However, she jumped before the Prince, holding her walking stick high as if she would hit him at any moment, and lashed out at him, "Stop it! Snap out of your drunken world!" She went on while banging on the table, "I can't believe our Crown Prince, YOU, also siding with our blood enemy."

As if the Prince was deaf to the Queen's words and blind to her outrage, he picked up where she had cut him off, "Lady Thea made me see the difference between her governing and that of my father. Her, as our ally, we can have some stability—no wars and no more killing ..."

The Queen made a fist and exclaimed, "We have no choice but to crush many grapes to make the wine."

After looking at his empty goblet with a disappointed face, he continued, "Right now, because Romans and Persians have united and made one mighty power, no other nation dares to get involved in a battle with either of us. And that's all because Lady

Thea has stretched herself as a bridge between the East and West."

"No one can deny the power of *Unity* to solve our differences in peace." I felt horrible as soon as the words left my mouth. I bowed and asked for forgiveness from the Queen and the Prince.

"Not to worry, Kam. You're right," the Prince said, then stood up. When he hugged Queen Jewel, he had a close encounter with her wounded crimson back. "What happened to you?" He pointed at the lesion that still looked raw. "Is that the reason you couldn't attend the wedding?"

When his question went unanswered, he continued, "I don't think you'll see me for a long time."

She failed to raise her head to look or hug the Crown Prince before he left her presence. She mumbled to herself, "I have lost yet another ally."

While the Queen was healing and brewing another plan to remove Thea forever, the news of giving birth to a boy was like pouring salt on Jewel's wounds. So, she made some more trips to the dungeon.

Soon after the birth of her son, Ardeshir—brave as a lion—a letter from Thea arrived. The Queen gave the royal messenger permission to break the seal and read it out loud:

Dear Jewel,
I'm also extending a hand of friendship to you.
You know I'll never move to the Women's Quarter.
I am the lawful wife of the King.
Ahura Mazda's will was for me to be by His Majesty's side.
As a partner to him, we both decide on all the aspects

of the Persian Empire.
Therefore, for the King's sake, the people, and the
country,
step aside as a Queen.
In reality, our country needs only One capable Queen.
Let's work together to preserve the peace between the
Persian and Roman Empires.
Lady Thea

As soon as the last word left the messenger's mouth, the Queen lost the rein of her anger. She snatched the letter from him and threw it into the holy fire beside her. She was deaf and blind to the maids' being aghast for contaminating the divine fire. "Until there is no breath in me, I'll never let her win!" she howled.

THEA

CHAPTER 27

Tysfoon
2 BCE

T he King ... the ... the King ... His Majesty is ... the King isn't ..." The words that penetrated through the closed door were not clear. The men in boots running were alarmed.

I interrupted the breakfast with my son, the seven-year-old Prince Ardeshir, to step outside and discover what was happening. Instead, the guards in front of my chamber blocked my way, announcing, "No one is leaving!"

I pushed them, ignored their loud voices, and rushed to my husband's bedside. Unfortunately, a few others barred my way into his chamber. "No one is allowed to enter."

"Let me in," I demanded, "or I'll go through you."

They stepped aside when they read the anguish on my face. I still had to shove more guards aside to get to the muted crowd of advisors and Wisemen, including the medicine man, Behzad. He was the only one the King chose to look after His Majesty's well-being. The King put his trust in him without any questions. His stretched body, appearing still sleeping, gave me a cold sweat. Out of cover, his face carried a calm aura. My thumping heart was not ready to hear any dire news.

As soon as Behzad saw me nailed in place by the royal bed, he started to leave. Through my tears, I asked, "Please don't go."

He stopped.

In a shaky voice, I uttered, "His Majesty is still sleeping, isn't he?"

He calmly shook his head. "It looks like it." He walked toward me and whispered in my ear, "But he's not."

His words became real when His Majesty's hands and face were cold. I held my head on his chest and clung to his shoulder, calling, "Your Majesty! My King! Answer me!"

No response. Only some audience's sad eyes pierced me.

Full of tears, I raised my head to Behzad. "What happened? Last night, when I left His Majesty, he was fine. Later, he even kissed me and the Prince good night."

Behzad looked shaken. "Your Highness, his heart stopped while sleeping."

I implored, "Can you do anything for His Majesty?"

He shook his head and murmured, "Sometimes I can heal, but not to bring back a dead one ... even the King." He turned his face away from me and left.

While tracing my thoughts, a commotion behind

the door caught my interest. "What is it?"

A guard responded, "Lady Thea, the cupbearer. She insists on getting in."

"Let her in. It's all right," the words barely left my mouth.

Standing by the door, Gigi's voice filled the King's chamber. She addressed me, "Our Queen, our leader! How can I serve you!" She prostrated herself on the bare floor.

Isn't the prostrating act only reserved for the King? I was baffled.

As if her presence and words gave me strength, with a clear mind, I commanded King Farshad's butler, "For the time being, do not say a word to anyone. Go ahead and arrange for the funeral." His wide-open eyes grabbed me and compelled me to add, "We hope His Majesty might still wake up." Then, I left.

Zeus, or Ahura Mazda, must have heard my prayers to be the Persian Queen by taking Jewel out. But I had no idea I got my wish this way. To wrap my confused head around the King's death was more than I could handle.

"Your Majesty," Gigi mumbled while walking behind me, "I must see you privately."

I shook my head, "No time, Gigi."

"Please! Let me come now and talk with you about an important matter."

I let out a sigh. "All right. But be quick."

Her face in the chamber's light looked pale as a dead person. Then, in front of the maids, she prostrated again. "Your Majesty!"

After dismissing all the girls with a hand gesture, I

said, "Since when do you pay respect to your closest friend and treat her like royalty?"

"Your Majesty ..."

"Stop calling me that." I lost all my patience with her. "Remember! I'm always Thea for you."

She shook her head with teary eyes and muttered, "The King's death ..."

A knock on the door interrupted her. Ardeshir, with his nanny, walked in. They both had permission to come to me anytime and anywhere without asking through the gate between his chamber and mine. He ran toward me, kissed me, and sat on my lap. "Mommy, is daddy all right?"

I squeezed him tight to my chest. "Darling, I wish I could say yes."

In tears, his nanny suggested, "Lady Thea, why don't you command to increase the number of guards for the Prince?"

"Go ahead and arrange it." After caressing and kissing his head, I uttered, "Darling Ardeshir, it's time for your Latin lesson."

"For today, may I only see Sattar and ride him for a while?" he pleaded.

Sattar's name brought a smile to me. These days he was too old to give a "ride" to anyone, and Ardeshir loved to take him out for a walk. "Take the Prince," I told his nanny, "to have a fun time with Sattar as long as he likes."

"Hurray!" Ardeshir shouted while leaving.

Meanwhile, I had forgotten all about Gigi. I raised my head to let her know there was no time for conversation. Still standing by the door to my chamber, she said, "Your Majesty. Don't forget. Now, you're our Queen and the ruler of the Persian Empire."

Her words have a ring of truth. Or at least until the Crown Prince shows up. My son is also entitled to the crown.

Prince Ardalan had, however, returned to Rome right after my wedding. So, I summoned only the people in urgent need to know about the King's death. In their presence, I took the head of the table, which I had already changed the King's ornate chair to mine as an advisor. After formally giving the news of the King's death, I made them aware of the need to appoint me as the Regent in the absence of the Crown Prince.

They debated, argued, and punched a hole in my proposal. "Lady Thea." The oldest of the Wisemen looked at me. "It's unheard. To point a Westerner as our Regent!"

"Well, I'm the Prince's mother and the King's widow." In a firm voice, I continued, "All of you know I saved the King's life, brought the Crown Prince safely home, and served this nation. Because of my efforts, the peace between Rome and Persia is solid as ever."

After many hours of deliberation, they finally agreed to appoint me as the Regent until Prince Ardalan's return. Meanwhile, I had to actively look for him and smooth his path back to Persia.

Immediately, I sent several royal messengers to Greece and Rome to bring him back. After several tries, all the communications for locating Prince Ardalan failed. No one, not even Jewel, had any idea where he was. I even contacted Caesar Augustus directly. Our searches bore no fruit. As if he were a piece of meat and a wolf of the wilderness had swallowed him—no sign of Ardalan.

The Prince was not brave and strong enough to hurt any creature, so killing himself was out of the question. He believed he came into this world to have fun without any responsibilities. And the gods made him a prince in the Persian Court so as not to worry about making a living or bearing any of life's hardships. He even refused to get trained to become a future king. To some certainty, he wouldn't be back.

Next, I sent a guard to bring Jewel to my presence. Trailed by Kam, she showed up blinking in all her jewelry from head to toe. Her shimmering robe was an eye sore. As soon as she saw me sitting on the Throne, her shrieking covered the entire Palace, "You, the Roman Witch, killed the King to get your hands on the Throne!" She launched to grab my neck, but the guards intercepted. She stepped back and sent a stream of spit to my feet.

How did Cordelia's oil and green mixtures work on everyone except her? Nothing works to bring her back when the Ahriman consumes a person's soul.

I exclaimed, "Lady Jewel, you are no longer a Queen. Now, the Women's Quarter is under my purview ..."

With her index finger pointing at me, she interrupted me, screeching, "You! Witch of the West!" She sent me more spit my way.

A couple of guards went to remove her. But with a gesture of my hand, they let her be. I continued, "Right away, I break down the Women's Quarter door, and all the King's women, including you, are free. It's your choice to stay in the palace or go to your hometown."

The same repulsive look, similar to the one she had when the King summoned me to his chamber for the first time, burned in her eyes.

However, I turned a deaf ear and a blind eye to her and advised the royal announcer to declare: "Lady Thea has librated all wives, concubines, and slaves who live in Women's Quarter. In addition, all the eunuchs and enslaved persons presently serving those women are free too."

"Thank you, Lady Thea!" Kam's whisper did not miss my ear.

I looked Jewel square in the eyes and proclaimed, "From now on, we will do anything and everything to stop the murdering of innocent girls."

Jewel howled, "They do not have anyone or anywhere to go. All their lives, they were under the King's protection."

"I, too, as a ruler, shield them, whether they stay here or decide to go away."

With a paunch protruding under her royal robe, Jewel's piercing voice occupied the hall again, "Hey! A ruler is a man, not a woman. You do not have the authority to abolish the Women's Quarter."

"In the past," I pointed out, "Atossa and other Persian women walked away from being a king. Now it's time for Persia to have a woman as a *king*."

"Don't compare yourself with Queen Atossa," Jewel spat. "She was a Princess ..."

I prevented her from continuing, "Yes. King Cyrus's daughter."

I did my best not to let my dark seed take over when she mumbled, "Not like you, a slave girl!"

She turned her back to me and screamed, "Where is our Crown Prince to rescue us?" Wiping the foam off her mouth, she faced me. "Did you kill him too? Or *your* Caesar did?"

"Lady Jewel, stop all the nonsense at once." I paused and gestured to Kam to take her away.

With the help of other guards, Kam had to drag her out of my sight.

"Your Majesty, my condolences."

Jamshid's firm voice took me away, not to be wasted by vicious Jewel any longer. I looked into his eyes in a friendly voice and said, "Come, Jamshid. You have our ears now."

"Of course," Jamshid's smirk did not go unnoticed. "Now, it pleases the Caesar that his hand-picked woman occupies the Persian throne."

"It helped to keep the peace between the two Empires."

I gained tremendous confidence as a ruler when satraps from all over the Kingdom participated in the King's funeral. Their sign of alliance with me on the Throne gave me immense assurance not only that day but for a while afterward.

There was a considerable void in the chain of succession. As soon as Farshad's father died and he became the King, his suspicion took the better of him. He ordered the death of anyone who could uprise and become a king by poisoning them all—even his four uncles, two nephews, cousins, and Jewel's father. Then, he made a treaty with Jewel. He would keep her as the Queen for life as long as she did not divulge His Majesty's secret. But they forgot the walls have eyes and ears. And no secrets stayed uncovered for long.

These days, with Prince Ardalan being away, even if he were still alive, it would be at least several months until he returned to Tysfoon. And Ardeshir was too young to take over the crown. So, after six months, I asked for another meeting of the same circle of the Court, including Chief Commander Jamshid.

I explained to them my concern about the instability in the country and that we lived in limbo. Then, I asked them to appoint me as the Regent for an unknown time until the Crown Prince returned or Prince Ardeshir turned sixteen to take over the crown.

"As the protector of the Throne for the long term," I declared. "No one except me can shield the stability of the vast Persian Empire at this volatile time."

Only some people were pleased with my proposal. One of the Magi said, "Lady Thea, you show courage with your proposal. However, it is unprecedented."

He then asked me to step out and let them discuss the matter.

"If you choose another Regent," I said before leaving the room, "he will not protect the crown for Prince Ardalan or Ardeshir. But I do."

"We will make you aware of our decision as soon as we have one," an advisor said with a sour face.

Jamshid and Babak being quiet made me wonder.

While waiting, I went to visit Ardeshir. *If they reject me, I'll take Ardeshir and return to Rome as Mother Mithra departed from Babylon for Susa.*

It took them all day, even through the night. Finally, my appointment until the arrival of the Crown Prince was announced.

The next day, Jamshid came to see me. "Lady Thea, to witness how bravely you rescued the King and the Prince Ardalan, we welcome you as the Queen Mother and Regent to the Persian court."

It took many months until one of the royal messengers brought the news from the Crown Prince. Right away, I summoned the head of all the branches to the Court. After each confirmed the Prince's seal, I ordered the messenger to break it and read the contents.

To whom it may concern,
I do not wish to return to Persia as a Crown Prince or the King.
Being a king does not interest me.
Choose whomever you want to be, the King or Queen.
I am happy in this place and wish not to be disturbed anymore.
Accept this letter as my abdication from the Persian Throne.
-Ardalan

Once he finished reading, a heavy silence filled the hall. Everyone was aware that now my son rightfully was the King. However, he could not occupy the Throne until he turned sixteen. So, I stood by him to be appointed as the future King and me as his Regent.

Immediately, Ardeshir started training to be fit to be a king. Naturally, I watched him closely while attending to all my duties as a ruling Queen.

When Jewel and her confidant, Kam, moved away from Tysfoon and settled in the previous Parthian Capital, Mithridates, life became much smoother. And as a result, I had some time to revisit past events.

The King's death happened so conveniently that I wondered if he died of natural causes. He was old but strong, like an ox. He and I had such a harmonious life together.

In the Persian or Roman courts, poisoning a ruler was not unprecedented. Behzad, being so prudent in his practice, could quickly pinpoint the difference between natural death and death caused by poisoning. He flatly rejected the possibility of the King's death due to poisoning. Also, no one else was left to grab the crown. For sure, dark-hearted Jewel wouldn't cut the hand feeding her. She, like a cat, only chased and killed the innocent mice. So, I had to believe it was Haydes' job to take King Farshad to the underground.

Recently, I had peace of mind since Gigi volunteered to be my food taster and wine tester before I brought anything to my lips.

While I was fencing with Ardeshir, Gigi walked closer to me one day. She whispered, "May I have an audience in private with you?"

"Of course. Come tonight and have dinner with me, and we'll talk."

On her way rushing out, she shook her head and said, "I'll come to you after dinner."

Later that evening, while I was relaxing on the couch, Gigi entered the chamber. Her face looked yellow as turmeric. However, her large jet eyes were serene.

"Gigi, what's wrong?"

"Your Majesty. ..."

I rolled my eyes. "Again, you're calling me that. How many ..."

With a hand gesture, she showed me to stop. While looking down, she uttered, "Today, I'm talking with you as my Queen, and I need your ruling." She then told me about an older man in the bazaar who paid so much for her. And the two young Roman soldiers with blond hair who put her on my path in Sicily.

Caesar keeps a tab on me! And I thought I was traveling all by myself.

Gigi grew fonder and fonder of me throughout our journey, especially during our trip on the cargo ship. She stayed up for me, only pretending to be asleep, until I crawled into the cot beside her. Then, while caressing and kissing me, she was extra cautious not to wake me. When I parted from her at dawn in Tysfoon, she suffered it all quietly despite a wound in her heart. But she watched me through the delivery boys, guards, servants, and maids. And she heard of my progress in getting closer to King Farshad.

Suddenly, the guard's voice that day came to me: "Why don't you recommend Gigi as the King's cupbearer ..."

"Gigi," I had to ask, "Did you put the idea of being the King's cupbearer into the guard's head?"

"Your Highness, I had nothing to do with the guard's conversation with you." Gigi's sad voice brought me to her. "He came on and off to the tavern where I worked, and we talked a lot. He even mentioned something about many threats to the King's life." Gigi reached out and took my hand. "Thea, I couldn't help it. I was always in love with you. From the moment I met you.

I tried to bring you to see my love for you, but it never got anywhere. I don't think you ever had any passionate love toward anyone, whether a man or a woman. Your inside is as hollow as a cold cave, without a light of love."

"Did you cause the King's death?" I thought my heart was coming out of my throat while waiting for her answer.

She wiped her tears and nodded. "It was all for you, to make you happy."

"I never wanted him to get killed unless on the battleground, an honorable death." My voice sounded like wailing, which even surprised me. "How did you do it that even passed the royal Medicine man's eye?"

She swallowed hard, and after some sniffling, she owned up. Long ago, she heard about a scarce Indian bird as colorful as a rainbow. When someone drank its melted dung in wine, his death was inescapable. No medicine man could tell his death was caused by poison.

My voice echoed, "Whatever Gigi wants, Gigi gets! Is that right?" I was livid. You had no right to infringe on my life or the King's."

Gigi stopped wailing, and through tears, she said, "Now, Your Majesty, you know the fate of the King. His death was an act of treason punishable by death. It's clear. I never can taste the pleasure of having you as my lover. But I'm not afraid of dying either." She stood up and bowed.

Whatever Gigi said about me was true. I never felt a real passionate love toward anyone. Perhaps the dark seed always prevented me from tasting the joy of love. Even making love to the King was a task. I wanted a royal child, a mixture of East and West. However, my love for my son was completely different—so pure and innocent.

"I love you, Gigi, as a friend," I broke the silence. "I'm even ready to give my life to save yours. Why is it so difficult to take me as a brave, well-trained woman, not as wimpy as some other women, blinded by jewelry?"

Breathing became difficult, as if I was crawling to the top of the Mount Appendices again. Finally, through my teary eyes, I quietly instructed Gigi to leave the capital. "No one needs to know the truth. In the country, everyone lives peacefully. King Farshad is a mere memory."

After hugging her, I continued, "Sometimes, a harsh disappointment in life makes us do the unthinkable. I will always love you, my dearest friend, and I will take Behzad's diagnosis that the King died of natural causes."

The following day, I heard yet another dire news: the royal cupbearer, Gigi, had gone to bed after drinking the exact wine she served the King the night of his death. And like His Majesty, she never woke up from her sleep either.

I mourned the death of my dear friend, Gigi, when I realized the only thing I could do was hold on to her memories. Our voyage on the Mediterranean Sea, throughout the Silk Route, and in the Persian Empire left a sweet taste in my mouth.

CHAPTER 28

Rome
4 CE

I opened my eyes to the raindrops attacking the hut near Rome. I turned my face to make sure Ardeshir was still sleeping next to my cot. It was empty. His murmuring with other men from outside delighted me. However, ignoring a tangle hitting my chest was impossible.

The past covered me like a comforting blanket. But, as fast as the life labyrinth took me to the pinnacle, it dropped me to the bottom of its abyss. For my son's sake, I left the Persian throne behind. Saving my twelve-year-old Prince Ardeshir was the utmost task in my life.

I looked through the window. The thick heavy fog, like a lid, covered the entire land. My eyes gravitated to the muted robes on the table. Once, they were vibrant as the sky and the sun's rays. However, time chewed them and spitted them out as the discolored, torn silk robes—only the gold and silver threads barely kept them together. They were still soft at the touch, but their gems had fallen—only the naked bodies were left. They made me realize all the royalty was sucked out of me. No enthusiasm or patience to make any new ones, as if the Tigris River had washed out my talents of cutting and uniting any pieces.

I held mine close to my heart. So many happy memories were made while wearing it. The time I danced with the King. It appeared as if it was yesterday.

At first, he was shy and mumbled, "A Persian king never dances. The women entertain him."

"Your Majesty, now you dance to make yourself happy. You'll feel the joy you never felt before."

"Definitely, not in front of the musicians!"

After thinking for a while, a partition separated the orchestra from the King and me. At first, I started dancing alone. Then I wooed the King in. To take his hand and, with a gentle tug, brought him to my bosom. At that moment, he understood that if my strength was not more than his, it was equal to his. "Your Majesty, who can sit down and not move to the beat of drum and bugle?"

He smelled my hair and caressed it. "Thea, I love you!" After a kiss, he continued, "You're the first woman I felt love toward. You've been running inside of my head all day, every day."

I whispered in his ear, "I'm honored, Your Majesty. I love you too."

The happiest time of my life.

I had to forget my past. How could I? In my teary eyes, I started to dismember my robe, limb by limb, when a shiver took over my body. King Farshad, my son's father, was gone, and his eyes could never see me again— no reason to hold on to the past. With the shears' sharp point, I pulled the threads from the fabric, one at a time. Then, quickly the three parts fell apart.

I cut each piece into tiny slices but did not stop there, untwining the fabric until it became so little as the thread in the cocoon's body.

I picked up his robe and held it to my heart. The King's joyful face came to me. Each time he changed into this blue silk robe and fastened the yellow belt over it, it delighted me. While lacerating it, my past pounded my head.

As a ruler, one never knew who her friends or foes were. During my governing, the Silk Route merchants enjoyed the well-guarded roads to travel. They kept it hopping without a threat from either the East or West. A crossroad, Persia, bridged China to Rome. After some negotiations led by me, the Chinese agreed to deliver the cocoons to Persia at a lower price. We also sold it a little cheaper to Romans. Part of the profit went to building the roads, policing them, and ensuring the goods were delivered safely to each side. The merchants could then journey much faster than before. Also, slashing the exuberant cost of the royal expenses and his women added even more to the treasury. Everyone seemed happy in the Capital, especially since I stopped Jewel from butchering enslaved girls.

Two years after the death of the King, at the planning meeting for the anniversary celebration, I broke the idea to the Wisemen and Counselors, trumpeting the future King Ardeshir's well-being. "I will crown myself as the ruler of Persia before crowning my son, the Prince, as a Crown Prince."

Of course, it was only welcome news to a few. A counsel mumbled, "Prince Ardeshir is already the King. You're only the Regent."

"A formal crowning ceremony will never happen. Only an announcement," I offered.

"Your Highness!" In his stern voice, one of the Magi yelled in contradiction to the white cloak covering him, "But, you're not a Persian!"

"My marriage to the King, governing with him shoulder to shoulder, converting to your religion, and living here for many years ..." I paused. "Don't they make me more Persian than a Roman?" I did not allow any of the men to come back with another excuse. "Besides, I gave birth to the future King."

Another Magi responded, "He is the King. And there is only *one* King!"

"And you're doing a much better job than a king," Jamshid announced in his firm voice as if he had not heard the two other Magi.

His support surprised me. However, his words did not come across as genuine. A heavy and long silence covered the room when Jamshid uttered again, "Your Highness, it's a great idea. How about ordering the royal painter to draw a portrait of you wearing the kingship crown? It can be minted in gold or silver. Then, for years to come, everyone knows Persia has a woman as the ruler."

All the men looked at him with their mouths open as I said, "Great idea. Until the Crown prince becomes of age, people—domestic and foreign—must understand that our Empire stands as a strong and stable nation."

"How about ..." a counselor brought yet another idea, "instead of two faces of the Queen. One side hers, and another King Ardeshir's."

I agreed and worked out all the details afterward.

Everything went according to plan. While setting on my head the Diadem crown—only to be worn by a king—Mithra shared my delight with a smile and said, "I didn't know the woman I rescued would be our future Ruler."

At this moment, I wish King Cyrus the Great could see me as his daughter, Atossa, holding on to the Crown as the Persian Ruler—a moment of triumph for all the women in the East and West.

As nothing in life, whether good or bad, lasted forever, my reign, similar to Cyrus the Great or Alexander, did not last either. I kept hearing about some Magi who had pilgrimaged to Jewel's mansion in the former Capital. A supporter of mine, Jamshid, even visited her several times. Jewel would never rest until she got rid of me, especially after my crowning as the Ruler of this land.

In the beginning, I did not take her threats seriously. However, Jamshid ignored my messages to come and see me. Finally, I summoned him with an urgent message.

"Jamshid," I said, looking him square in the eyes, "I heard you visited Lady Jewel."

After barely paying respect, he claimed, "Yes, I did." A smirk crossed his face.

"I'm sure you have been aware of her vicious acts toward some girls."

"Your Majesty, she's very sick and wanted to see me."

"Everyone has lots of time on their hands since there has been no war between the Roman and Persian Empires."

While taping up his right palm with a short whip, he said, "I don't know what you're talking about. Persian forces are always ready to fight and protect the land and the Crown from domestic or foreign attacks."

His words pounded in my head. "We commend you for that."

After he left, he and Jewel's secret tapestry stretched before me. Initially, the Chief Commander, Jamshid, supported me and elevated me to a *female Ruler*. To uprise against me was more plausible. To their eyes, I was a Roman foreign adversary and was no one with the King's death. However, if I stayed as the Regent, he would have no course of action against Ardeshir. The legitimate son of King Farshad, Prince Ardeshir, had the right to the Persian Crown after his father and in his brother's absence.

The last straw came when the holy fire in my chamber quenched, and no one attended to it. After that, I had no confidence in anyone in the court except to call on Mithra, who accepted me as a human being, not a Roman girl from a foreign land.

"Your Majesty, you are in a tough position," she said after lighting the holy fire.

I asked anxiously, "What do you hear in the street?"

"Women are happy to have a woman as our ruler. However, interfering with the family unions, rewarding any man with only one wife," she swallowed, "and destroying the Women's Quarter caused them to revolt."

"Well," I pointed out, "I freed the enslaved women and eunuchs. I even stopped Jewel's torturing and murdering the girls."

"Your Highness," she argued softly, "we heard they didn't have any money or place to go."

The word on the street dumbfounded me, and I attested, "Not true ... I gave each plenty of money to learn a trade and start a new life."

"But, they're incapable of making a life independently," Mithra explained. "The king's women were always protected by him and considered him their benevolent protector when he cared for them lavishly."

"I hear you, Mithra. But, unfortunately, some women believe that only *men* with lots of money can protect them." I was delighted to control my thoughts and say nothing in anger in her presence. Instead, with a smirk, I uttered, "How many wives does your husband have?"

"Just me, Your Majesty. Our religion does not encourage polygamy."

"Then, I'm trumpeting the same tune. What's the difference?"

"But, there are always women like Jewel whose interest stops blossoming when a woman rules."

"Then, it's a war among women!"

"Yes, Your Majesty. I hate to admit it."

I claimed through my teeth, "Don't people know Jewel murdered many girls?"

"Your Majesty, I hate to say, but Ahriman has consumed Jewel." Mithra stepped closer to the throne and said, "Your Majesty, rest assured, I'll run for you at any sign of uprising."

I declared, "If people don't want me in power, so be it."

Then, on another occasion, Mithra made me aware that most of the opposition was for me being a Westerner.

"So," I proposed, "if I abdicate and give the crown to my son, would that solve the problem?"

She shook her head, came closer to me, and continued whispering, "Jewel has located one of King Farshad's illegitimate sons, Farhad, from an Armenian concubine, at age 20. So, she pushes for overthrowing you."

Not having anyone's support, including Jamshid's, I decided to leave quietly with Ardeshir not to endanger his life. I asked Mithra to plan for our escape.

Several days passed until one night; I heard Mithra's voice arguing with the guard behind my chamber. I got up and let her in.

"Your Majesty," she urged quietly, "here is a robe belonging to one of my members. You and the Prince must leave right away."

I banged on the door to Ardeshir's chamber in a rush and woke him up. "Dear Ardeshir," I murmured in his ear, "the time has come." I picked out the oldest pants and tunic, extending them before his face.

"Do we have to go now?" his sleepy voice reached me. "Why don't we wait until morning?"

"No can do!" Life in any court makes everyone lazy!

While Ardeshir was getting ready, I wore my silk robe under the garment Mithra gave me. I also folded the blue one over and over until it became a small piece and hid it in my bag. I gave it to her. Before stepping out, in a loud voice, she said, "Your Highness, see you later."

The Prince and I waited a few moments, then walked to the garden. In response to one of the guards who wanted to accompany us, I dismissed him with a hand gesture and answered, "We are just going for a stroll."

Ardeshir and I continued walking beyond the lush gardens of the court to the royal stable. He grabbed Sattar's reins, and we walked to the Tysfoon gate. Mithra was waiting for us; she handed me my bag and gave Ardeshir a prepared sack of fruit and dried nuts. Before leaving, my eyes fixed on the image on the gate.

They need to replace the image with a bull biting a lion.

On the way to Mithra's temple, Sattar's treading sounded like a funeral march. To say goodbye to him and leave him with Mithra at the temple was the most challenging task I ever faced. At this age, I would need extra help to take him. Even then, he would not survive the long trip back to Rome.

Persia is his home. Never easy to say goodbye to a friend.

Mithra was the only one I trusted Sattar with, and until his last breath, she would take good care of him. Ardeshir and I mounted the two stallions, all prepared for our departure. When we reached the extreme northwest of Tysfoon, Mithra turned around and left us in the magical land of the East, where my mother nudged me to go. At this time, however, it was filled with many hostile people against the two Westerners.

While riding along the Tigris River, I worked out our route map in my head. At Anatoli, we could cross the River and get to Greece, where Caesar controlled it, then to Athens to embark on a cargo ship to Alexandria. From there to Rome would be an easy voyage, as it was in my head.

The King's blue robe was still spread on the table. I reached, took, and smelled it. I recognized his preserved scent. I yearned to save it as a keepsake. But, I knew well. *It's impossible to repeat the past.*

I tore it up while wailing. After it became tattered pieces, I mixed them with the yellow shreds, gold, and silver threads. They turned to a pile of blue and yellow threads. With them, I yearned to revive all the silkworms as colorful butterflies.

But that isn't meant to be. Even Cordelia couldn't bring the dead to life.

When I raised my head and looked through the window, the fog had not let the sun come through. My first urgency was to burn the threads in the fireplace. *No. Fire is holy. We can't sully it.* I then gathered the mass, held it to my bosom, and entered the horrid cold. The gusty wind cooled down my feverish cheeks. I walked a long way until I reached a river. As I gave the heap to the water, I thought a large piece of my heart also went with it.

On my way back, I saw Ardeshir approaching me. He had Persian jet-black hair and unusual Roman green eyes—the perfect mixture of the East and West. I forced myself to smile when I heard him.

"Mama, would you like to play some music?"

"Darling, I didn't bring my lyre. It would be great if ..."

Without waiting for me to finish, he whispered, "I did." He brought his hand from his back and showed my beaten-up lyre. The one Cordelia had given me a long time ago.

As if I had seen a friend, I grabbed it and started caressing it. We sat by the fire in the room, and I played my lyre. The music took us to regal Persia and soothed my soul.

Come! Come and dream with me!

As much as I intended to forget Persia, Persia did not let go of me. I stared at the glowing fire all night and listened to its hissing and crackling. They sounded as if hearing the lamenting of all the women murdered by Jewel. I understood. *Thea! You didn't care for us. You left Jewel alive to continue her devilish acts. You're the chosen one to free us from her.*

CHAPTER 29

Tysfoon

4 CE

T he sky-high holly fire was the only light ahead of me to the Capital at dawn while I was galloping toward the temple in the heart of Tysfoon. In Rome, I could not sit quietly and let the despicable Jewel continue her devilish acts toward innocent people. It took much work for me, as a mother, to leave Ardeshir behind. He was safe; I made sure.

Before departing, I took him to the palace and asked Caesar Augustus to hold him under his protection. To my surprise, he agreed. However, he had difficulty understanding why I was determined to return to Persia, jeopardizing my life again. *I must answer my calling.*

To meet the honorable Reverend Mithra assured me. She would be instrumental in taking out Jewel, whose soul was consumed by Ahriman.

≫ ✲ ≪

In a vision, I saw myself as Mithra during Alexander's conquest of Persia three hundred years ago. Suddenly, my sister, Shirdokht, was side-by-side with me. Her gold necklace, a sign of being one of the Immortal soldiers, mesmerized me. She said, "Mithra, I'm so proud that I stood up to Alexander's forces and did not leave the All Nation Gate without a good fight."

"But, my dear," I countered, "you paid a hefty price for it."

"My life!" She smiled. "All of us must die. But at least I died with honor as a soldier. Not like our coward King Darius III. He ran away from the battle with Alexander and was then poisoned by his cousin."

"Yes, you're right. We can't possibly be a winner all the time."

"True, if it weren't for the weaklings around the royal family, Alexander never could've conquered Persia."

The day I learned about the death of our King, reading my husband, Kaveh's letter flashed before my eyes:

Alexander chases our King.
However, a satrap of a town in the north of the
Empire
invited Alexander to his house.
He revealed to our foe about the King's path.
When Alexander caught up to the King,
His Majesty was already poisoned by his cousin while
sleeping.

Alexander took the King's ring off his finger and put it on
his own,
and announced:
NOW I, ALEXANDER OF MACEDONIA, AM
THE RULER OF THE LARGEST EMPIRE IN
THE WORLD!
Then showing to the Persians
how benevolent he is,
he covers the King's body with his Greek cape and gives
an order
to carry it to Persepolis for the proper burial.

⇒ ✲ ⇐

That's how Alexander took over Persia ... without a good fight. I decided. King Cyrus, a hero, paid with his life to free the enslaved people, *so now I'm also ready, if necessary, to spend my life rescuing the enslaved people.*

"Thea, is that you?" Mithra's calm words were music to my ears. She stood by the holy fire under the dome. Through the four-opening walls, a speck of sun shined on her. She looked serene in her white robe and silvery hair.

I rushed to her and hugged her.

"So happy to see you." Her eyes resembled a frightened lamb waiting for the butcher knife to come down on her neck at any moment. "Don't you know Jewel put a hefty price on your head?"

I shrugged. "This time, I don't care whether it's her head or mine."

"Since you left, a lot has happened."

After my departure, Jewel returned to Tysfoon with the twenty-year-old King Farshad's son, Farhad. She made some Magi crown him as our King and successor to Farshad IV. Then, in an elaborate ceremony, she married him.

"Is she now Queen Jewel again?" I was baffled. "As if nothing changed."

In a sad voice, she uttered, "The young King is simply a pawn in Queen Jewel's hand."

Once again, Jewel created the Women's Quarter, but much more extravagant than during her first husband, King Farshad. "Also," Mithra continued, "most of the advisors at King Farshad and your court went away and refused to abide by the new King."

"Do you know where Babak went?" I sought to know.

"Based on what I've heard, he and his wife, Nur, live in Pasargad."

"The Capital during King Cyrus's rein."

She agreed. "Babak declined to obey King Farhad and Queen Jewel."

"Are you and your followers safe here?"

"So far…yes." Mithra raised her head, and her face had no happiness of the past. "Jewel's special forces left our faith alone." She pointed to the holy fire. "We're still allowed to gather here and pray before our holy fire."

Based on what Mithra knew, Queen Jewel eliminated all the Magi at the court. She served as the only advisor to King Farhad. The court became a swamp where Jewel governed as its only alligator. Even Kam, her faithful eunuch, escaped and hid secretly. Mithra had sworn not to reveal it to anyone, even me.

When I divulged my urgent mission to liberate all the enslaved people and dispose of Queen Jewel, she earnestly agreed to aid me in any way she could. But, as she knew, Jewel would never leave the Palace. And to take out this devilish queen bee, I had to go to her hive.

Mithra believed Kam could be a tremendous help if he and I could devise a plan. Right away, she bolted to go to Kam. To be safe, I stayed in the temple, out of sight of evil eyes.

The next day, by the first ray of sun, Mithra returned and gave me the good news. Kam would like to collaborate with me to end Jewel's devilish acts.

"Mithra, I always thought Kam loved Jewel as his daughter. So how come, now ..."

"Dear Thea," She interjected, "it's difficult for Kam to get rid of Jewel like a rotten tooth. However, ignoring the situation is also more harmful to so many innocent people."

"Yes," I agreed, "he knows Jewel's weak points like no one else."

"He welcomes you with open arms. He even permitted me to reveal where he's hiding out."

The same night, I bolted out of the city limits and found Kam in a cave near where I was bricked several years ago. His appearance shocked me to no end. His body reminded me of the skeletons Cordelia and I dug out of the ground. Every single bone was crooked and covered with wrinkled skin. He could barely stand on his feet. But his face filled with a huge smile. "Lady Thea, I'm so delighted to see you." He walked to me and bowed.

I took his arm and lifted him. "Oh, Kam, no need for it. You and I are humans, not one higher than the other." We then sat crossed-legged on the ground, and he offered me a goblet filled with wine.

"Lady Thea," he said in a shaky voice. "I'm so proud of you ... so accomplished and smart." He held my hand and said, "When I first met you, I wished you could've been my daughter. Damn, the rulers!" He swallowed hard.

"We're here now. You and I WILL take Queen Jewel out and liberate all the enslaved people."

"Amen!" His firm voice sounded like new blood had started flowing in him.

After disclosing my plan to him, he was anxious. "I'd be more than happy to help. But, according to Jewel, I betrayed her by leaving her side. So, there is a price on my head and yours."

"For a fact," I explained to him, "Jewel prefers to have me captured and delivered to her alive ..."

"So, she can destroy you based on her whims." With a smirk, he murmured, "Very clever, my Lady!"

I revealed the next step of my plan: "When you take me to her as a prisoner, she'll forget about punishing you."

With a huge smile, showing his toothless mouth, he exclaimed, "True, true! Jewel's only wish is to get her hands on you." He got up and put on his fancy cloak, which he used to wear in the Palace. "Whoever sees me in this will let me into Jewel without hesitation."

I raised my wine. "Hurray, Kam!" I drank to his honor.

The following night, in the temple, I took out my robe, and like the time in Sicily, as a fisherman, I covered my chest and waist with two pieces of dirty old cloth. Then, after cutting my long curly hair partly short as if it was pulled out of its roots and left some other parts long. I looked like a Roman slave girl. After covering my face and naked body parts with dirt, I repeatedly struck myself with a wooden stick until several crimson patches showed through my skin. Then I ordered one of the lads at the temple, who agreed to help Kam and me, to punch me.

"Lady Thea," he protested vociferously, "I can't possibly do that!"

"Yes, you can! I'm ordering you!" When he did not budge, I started smacking and hitting him on the head. At last, his anger took the better of him, and he lashed out with a vengeance. However, at first, his punches did not even hurt me. "Harder ... harder ..."

Suddenly, he stopped looking with horrified eyes at the dripping blood on my face and rushed out. "Forgive me. I can't do it any longer!"

It was time for Kam to deliver me to the Queen. He covered my fetus-shaped body with a blanket in the back of a wagon provided by Mithra. He and the chap drove us to the Palace. At the gate, the wagon stopped. Kam whispered something to the guard while slipping a small bag of gold coins into his hand. In no time, we had permission to ride our wagon through the Palace.

At the entrance to Jewel's chamber, Kam pushed away the guard, banged the door open while the young man dragged me inside like a rag, and threw me before the Queen's feet.

"Your Majesty!" Kam shouted. "I've brought you the prize you always seek!" He bowed.

Jewel was decorated with all the world's most priceless gems. She rushed and hid behind her colossal bed. Then, with squinting eyes, imitating a firm voice, she asked, "Who are you? Where are the guards?" She got louder and louder, screaming, "Guards! Guards!"

"Shush! Shush, Your Majesty!" Kam walked close and offered his hand to her. "Come on out, and look at what I've brought for you."

She rubbed her eyes. "Oh, you're Kam."

Her jaw could've landed on the ivory table if she had sat behind it. The Queen's voice jarred my ear, "We thought you were dead. And no one claimed his prize."

"As your faithful servant," Kam said with pride, "I knew what would make you the happiest queen."

"Don't tell me this creature is who I think she is," Jewel exclaimed as she sat on the plush sofa.

Kam walked to me and took the rag from my head.

Jewel shrieked, "Unbelievable! You brought me Thea, the Witch of the West! And she's alive! Except without her red hair!" Like a little girl, she jumped up and down.

Kam's voice filled her chamber, "Yes, Your Majesty." For confirmation, he grabbed a handful of my hair and pulled it away from my face. "Open your eyes, so Her Majesty can see your green eyes," he growled.

When I failed to obey, Kam even kicked me in the side. "Open your eyes, dirty slave!" He turned to the Queen. "I wanted you to have the pleasure of killing her yourself."

"Just like the other slaves!" Her laughing was so loud it shook the walls. "Kam, I thought you had turned against me. You left my side in the middle of the night."

She stared at Kam. A couple of teardrops wet her face. "I missed you and was outraged." Jewel sounded more like a two-year-old, not a mighty Queen.

"No, no! Your Majesty!" He shook his head. "I didn't want to verbalize my intention. But, as Your Highness is aware ..."

"Walls have eyes and ears," she mumbled. Jewel stepped toward me and screamed, "We understand!" Then, she kicked me. "Finally, you're mine. And your Caesar cannot do anything about it."

Kam said, "I doubt if he even cares what happens to her."

Jewel howled, "No slave is worth any ruler's attention." Her cackle pounded on my head. "No one even loses sleep over missing one or two." She rolled her eyes and shouted, "Now, YOU, THEA," she pinched my bare arm, "you are no longer the ruler of Persia. And your Caesar has no use for you. You are going to die, here and now!"

"Your Highness," Kam shot her a wicked smile, "for the sake of the old times, please give me the honor to take her to the dungeon and prepare her for you."

"Yes! Yes!" She giggled like a little girl, jumping up and down again. "I'll put on my boots and grab the thickest whip."

Minutes later, in the cell, my back to the door with my hands and legs tied up, I heard Kam say, "Your Majesty, why don't you use this scourging whip instead of the simple one you usually use?"

Jewel gasped, "Kam, I've never seen anything like this before ... a rope with huge metal balls and spikes."

"Yes, Your Majesty. This type of whip is used only in

Rome. It'll rip pieces of flesh from her body."

Jewel's loud laughs jarred my ears. "We'll have fun with this one. I can't wait to send chunks of her flesh as a gift to her Emperor."

The first few strikes felt more like swats. Jewel finally complained, "Kam, this is more difficult to handle." She drove another strike to my back.

"This is shorter than a regular whip," Kam said. "Get closer to the girl and use both hands."

The flogging resumed harder and harder. *Jewel doesn't know I used Cordelia's potion on my skin to prevent it from any significant harm.*

While she concentrated on hitting me harder and harder, I started wiggling my hands and loosened them from the poles. But soon, the jagged pain became like running my tongue over a broken tooth. When I felt Jewel's breath on my left cheek, with an agile move, I released my right hand from the rope and grabbed the head of the scourge. In shock, she froze like the lake on the top of Zagros Mountain. I was blind to the metal spikes poking my hand.

In another abrupt move, I turned my torso, grabbed Jewel's hair with my other hand, and forcefully pushed her down. She curled up on the ground in no time and started screeching, "Kam, where are you? Come! Come!" The Queen's voice only battered the dungeon walls.

"Queen Jewel!" It was my turn to shout in her ear. "Kam is no longer coming to your rescue."

Suddenly, as the spring sky changed instantly from cloudy to sunshine, she prostrated to the filthy, urine-smelling bare floor. I was baffled by her move. Instead of her head before me, her legs were in the front, and her torso was away. And, before I could comprehend her reaction, the slash of a thick whip landed on my legs. They were still tied to the polls. Jewel took the chance, pulled herself away, then stood up and lashed me repeatedly.

I lowered my head to protect my face while twisting and wriggling my feet. At this moment, she had no mercy in striking me. When I saw her drowned in the sea of hatred, I freed my legs, leaped over, and rammed her belly with my head. She had such a substantial girth, so it did not affect her. She kept striking me, but being close to her, she had difficulty using the whip effectively on my body. Finally, after reaching with my hands, I squeezed hers so hard that she had to let the whip go. To have control of her whip was my road to triumph over the evil Queen.

While I struck her, she whimpered, "Why are you doing this to me? No harm has come to you, dear Thea! Please! Stop hitting me! I can give you the crown back, you know!"

"Now! You're receiving as many strikes as you bequeathed the enslaved girls." More hits on her followed my words.

"No, No! You're mistaken!" she pleaded. "Kam did it ..." She swallowed. "I barely had the heart to watch any girls suffer."

"Then, as the Queen, why didn't you reprimand him as soon as you heard about *his* diabolical act?" The evil Jewel endangering Kam's life to rescue hers did not shock me. "Do you have proof that you didn't flog any of them?"

She looked befuddled for a moment, then exclaimed, "Go! Go, hurry up to catch him. He left ... he must be the guilty one."

"I'll deal with him later. Now, let's talk about YOU!"

"Nothing about me, dear Thea." She paused. To see the whip coming down, like a weasel, she hissed, "Dear, I'm just a sick, old lady, ready to die any time." She sighed.

"Who hit me in the back of my head before bricking me in the grave?" I demanded to know.

"I don't know!" she lied.

However, when the whipping started again, she said, "Wait a minute ..." She tried to reach up and grab the whip—a fruitless act. She looked afar and shrieked, "That was King Farshad's order! I'm innocent. You never liked me, for I was the Queen, and you weren't."

I scowled at her. "The King loved and cherished me not only as a woman but as a partner. So he'd never order anyone to murder me."

She laughed so loud that Kam walked in with a worried look. "Lady Thea, are you all right?"

I nodded. "Let's chain Queen Jewel to the ground as a prisoner."

Afterward, we walked outside. Kam claimed in a cheerful voice, "Let's arrest King Farhad and imprison him too."

"Is Jamshid still the Chief Commander?"

"No, My Lady. After the Queen forced him to uprise against you, his head was cut off from ear to ear while sleeping."

Horrified, I murmured. "Why?"

"Jewel knew that Jamshid as a king never would be a pawn in her hand."

"Who is the Commander-in-Chief now?"

"There's none appointed. The Queen announced that the King is the Commander-in-Chief." After a pause, he stepped closer to me and whispered, "Lady Thea, would you like to claim the throne?"

"No," I said with conviction. "I've already abdicated. However, I wish for the Persians to have an Aryan King, a direct offspring of King Cyrus."

With a broad smile, he said, "I know a man in Pasargad. He's the direct decedent of King Cyrus."

"Is he Babak? One of the Advisors to King Farshad?"

"Oh, you've heard of him," Kam said, surprised.

"Yes, he's the one who made it possible for me to meet King Farshad." I dried my forehead. "Where is he now?"

"He's waiting with some soldiers behind the Palace wall, ready for your order, whatever it might be."

"Wow, Kam!" I smiled. "You've thought of everything. We make a wonderful team to bring freedom back to the East and West."

"My Lady, I see a path very far in the distance."

After I refused to have my throne or save it for Ardeshir, Babak became the King, and his wife, Nur, became the Queen of Persia. The fate of King Farhad and Queen Jewel was in His Majesty's hands. He ordered the guards to carry their bodies and tied them to the poles outside the Palace wall. They had to wait for Hades to take them to the underground while vultures picked on their flesh.

I still had to fulfill my last calling in Persia. To travel to Pasargad and pay my respects to my hero, King Cyrus's tomb.

In Pasargad, at the sight of the monument, I believed it genuinely fitted His Majesty. After walking up its three broad steps to the central edifice of its rectangular stone chamber, on my way in, my eyes could not possibly miss the inscription on the wall:

O Man, whoever thou art, from wheresoever thou comest,
for I know you shall come,
I am Cyrus, who founded the Persian Empire.
Grudge me not, this little earth that covers my body.

I pushed my slim figure sideways through the tall, narrow entrance door. The stone coffin containing the King's body rested in the middle of the room. His Majesty's illumination, love, compassion, and courage were displayed everywhere.

On the right side of the casket stood a couch with gold feet. A Babylonian tapestry covered the table where the King's gold daggers, some gold pebbles, and jewelry were laid out.

My eyes couldn't possibly miss his handcrafted sword overshadowing the muteness of everything else. The canvased floor in washed-off purple rugs trumpeted the King's royalty, nobility, wisdom, and devotion.

≳ ✴ ≲

Then, I saw myself as Mithra, Princess Atossa's governess. The garments on the vast table looked familiar—a sleeveless cloak, Median trousers, and robes in blue were all testaments to his intelligence, loyalty, and honesty. The holy fire was still burning on the top of the stone coffin. *I was the fortunate one who could remember my past and live with this outstanding King. He fought only to liberate the enslaved people.*

When I exited on the high plateau, the sound of horns and drums suddenly took me back to the celebration of replacing his father as the King of Persia. Pasargad, where his Aryan ancestors arrived way before any kingdom was shaped, burst into happiness. Not only were people preparing for a celebration with music and food, but it also looked as though even nature was joyful. The blue sky was cloudless and seemingly endless in its vastness. The town was surrounded by low rolling hills covered in lush greenery. My eyes could not possibly miss the red and white poppies dancing in the gentle wind. The pomegranate trees burst with red and yellow flowers, displaying their joy.

Prince Cyrus, after mourning his father, King Cambys, for six months, decided to have his coronation on this plateau, the exact spot where his ancestors came to, and named it "Iran" after their Aryan race. At age thirty, he walked in accompanied by the court Wisemen and sat by the holy fire while wearing a dynastic heirloom— the cowhide, a long-sleeved coat once belonged to his grandfather, King Cyrus I. He ate a simple meal of sweet dates and pistachio nuts and drank a dish of thick, sour, fermented mare's milk—no sign of crowns ornamented with jewelry or a fancy throne to climb up.

Bravo, King Cyrus! Humanity was the hallmark of his crowning!

The sun hiding behind the hill in the West was all I saw. I shed tears of triumph while longing for the East and West one day to unite.

ACKNOWLEDGMENTS

Dear readers, thank you for being so supportive. I hope you enjoyed reading the depiction of Thea Mousa's life as much as it delighted me to research and write it while I was away from home. And without the support of friends and family, this work could not come to fruition.

My project started in Paris, attending Rohm Literary workshop headed by Wendy Goldman Rohm. I'm thankful to her for showing me a practical way to grasp all the emotions that Thea would feel during her odyssey.

Then, Thea took me to Rome. Upon my arrival, a stroke of sheer luck, I met a young Italian woman, fluent in English. Ana Maria Bianca Popa and her mother were imperative in coaching me to understand Italian culture. Despite several trips to Rome as a tourist, I never learned that Italians have their own pyramid, like Egyptians. Ana took me to the part of Rome where a miniature pyramid, a replica of the one in Egypt, was built during Julius Caesar's reign in honor of Queen Cleopatra. As if she were my daughter or a long-time friend, I am grateful for her spending lots of time and having many dialogues with me. In addition, Ana became a model for me as a Roman girl.

My four months journey away from home was not possible without the love and kindness of my friends and family. The support of Lauri Burke, my Soul-Sister, and her daughter, for giving me a fantastic vacation of my lifetime at the end of my writing and pampering me to the highest standard is unforgettable. Furthermore, my special friend, Loydene Lazich, by her phone calls and sending me one of her hand-made cards for my birthday, kept me grounded and not forgetting about the purpose of my journey. I am also thankful to my son and his family for sending love messages on my BE Day, and on weekends took me far from being homesick.

In Tucson, I'm grateful to my team, Rick Wamer, Dina Delaney, and Donn Poll, at A3D Impressions, who constructed an outstanding home for Thea. Their support and talents have been instrumental in having this book in your hands—my hats off to Donn Poll for creating and painting the exceptional cover of the book. He has captured the essence of Thea as a trailblazer woman in those years (20BCD—4CE). How many authors can dream of an original cover page for their books?

THANK YOU ALL
FOR MAKING YET ANOTHER
DREAM OF MINE
COME TRUE!

RESOURCES

Beckwith, Christoper. 2009. *Empires of the Silk Road: A History of Central Eurasia from the Bronze Age to the Present.* Princeton.

Brosius, Maria. 2010. Trojan's Parthian War and the Fourth-Century Perspective. *Journal of Roman Studies.* 80:115-126.

_____. 2010. *The Persians: An Introduction.* London.

Curtis, J. and Simpson, S. (eds). 2010. *The World of Achaemenid Persia.* London.

Frye, R.N. 1962. *The Heritage of Persia.* London.

_____. 1996. *The Golden Age of Persia.* New York.

Fuller, Margaret. 1999. *Woman in the Nineteenth Century. Dover Thrift Editions.* New York.

Gershevitch. I. 1985. *The Cambridge History of Iran. Vol.II:* "The Median and Achaemenian Periods." Cambridge, England.

Ghirshman, R. and herzfeld, E. 2000. *Persepolis: The Achaemenians' Capital.* Tehran.

Hopkirk, Peter. 1980. *Foreign Devils on the Silk Road: The Search for the Lost Cities and Treasures of Chinese Central Asia.* London.

Kurt, Amelia. 2013. *The Persian Empire: A Corpus of Sources from the Achaemenid Period.* Routledge.

Lightfoot, C.S. 1990. "Trojan's Parthian War and the Fourth-Century Perspective." *Journal of Roman Studies.* 80:115-126.

Llewellyn-Jones, Lloyd. 2013. *King and Court in Ancient Persia.* Edinburgh.

_____. 2022. Persians: *The Age of the Great Kings.* New York.

Paterson, J. 2007. "Friend in High Places: The Creation of the Court of the Roman Empire," in A. J. S. Spawforth (ed.), *The Court and Court Society in Ancient Monarchies.* Cambridge. 56-121.

Plutarch, 1968. *Lives.* Edited and translated by Bernadotte, Perrin. Cambridge, MA.

Rostovtzeff, M. 1943. "The Parthian Shot." *American Journal of Archaeology.* 47: 174-187.

Suetonius. 2007. *The Twelve Caesars.* Try by Robert Graves. London.

Surina-Mulford, Karen. 2001. *Trailblazers: Twenty Amazing Western Women.* U.S.A.

Thorley, J. 1971. "The Silk Trade Between China and the Roman Empire at its Heights." *Greece and Rome.* 18:71-80.

Wenke, Robert J. 1981. "Elymeans, Parthians, and the evolution of Empires in Southwestern Iran." *Journal of the American Oriental Society.* 101: 303-315.

Wilcox. Peter. 1986. *Rome's Enemies: Parthians and Sassanid Persians.* London.

Yeazell, R.B. 2000. *Harems of the Mind: Passages of Western Art and Literature.* New Haven and London.

Zhou, M. 2010. "The Cross-Cultural Comparison of the Tale of Genji and a Dream of Red Mansions: *Journal of Cambridge Studies.* 5 (2-3). 24-31.

Printed in the USA
CPSIA information can be obtained
at www.ICGtesting.com
LVHW051911010224
770404LV00001B/1